WHEELS DOWN

BETH BOLDEN

CHAPTER ONE

Ross Stanton was having an epically shitty day.

Really, it had been a shitty month.

To top off a pretty shitty year.

His ex-business partner had gone completely psycho, set Ash's food truck *on fire*—technically, Ross supposed, he had forced *Ash* to do it, not that the technicality had really made the situation any better—then after Aaron had been arrested, Ross had discovered that he'd been stealing money from the business.

All the money.

He'd asked Aaron more than once why, even though it seemed like they were always busy and in demand, they never had any savings, why they were always scraping by. Why they seemed to have less money, not more, as they gained popularity in the LA area.

Aaron had brushed him off with an excuse that Ross realized now that he should've seen through.

And now?

He was left with no partner, a busy food truck that he was essentially running by himself, and a whole shitload of problems that he didn't know how to fix.

Margo, his latest in a long string of temp help, eyed him suspiciously from her spot taking orders. Ross knew he wasn't good at reading people, but when even *he* knew that her days were numbered—like all the other temps who had quit in a huff recently—things were bad.

Not just bad. *Absolutely fucking terrible*, Ross inwardly moaned.

Margo had hardly been a fantastic employee, but she'd been an employee.

"Those fried heirloom tomatoes almost ready?" she demanded. "The customer's been waiting forever for them."

She hadn't seemed particularly impatient when she'd shown up two days ago, eager to work for one of the most popular food trucks in Los Angeles.

Ross thought the one thing he could count on, without fail, was making people hate him. Usually within a day or two. He was painfully reliable like that.

"One sec," he barked in her direction.

Probably why she hates you now, his brain unhelpfully supplied. *You're a terrible boss. Grumpy and mean and short-tempered. No wonder everyone leaves.*

Ross scooped the tomatoes out of the fryer with a pair of tongs, depositing them in a lettuce-lined paper boat, then reached down and grabbed a plastic tub of the homemade buttermilk dressing that accompanied each order. Realized that he only had a handful left, when the deep-fried heirloom tomatoes had been one of the more popular dishes today.

Shit.

"Here," he said brusquely, shoving the tomatoes at Margo. "I need more of the buttermilk dressing. You know, the one I showed you on your first day."

"I have to take orders," she said, and practically flounced back to the front of the truck.

"Shit," Ross said, this time out loud.

Things hadn't exactly been great the last few months with Aaron on board either—Ross had figured out pretty quickly that he was using again, which had really pissed him off, but he'd known better than to harass Aaron about it—but after he'd been arrested and Ross became fully aware of the situation he was in, things had gotten worse.

And today?

Basically, he was scraping the bottom of the barrel.

The flat-top grill was not working reliably. He needed to get a guy out to look at it, so he could go back to making multiple sandwiches at once. But he had no money to pay the bill, and the repair company wouldn't extend him any more credit. He'd been stuck making one at a time on a little dinky sandwich press.

And then his regular chicken delivery—organic and free range—hadn't shown up on time, and a call to the supplier right before the truck had opened for the lunch crowd had informed him that he was way behind on *that* bill too, and they were apparently under a rock and hadn't realized that Aaron wasn't working there anymore. They'd only had his number, and had been unsuccessfully trying to reach him.

"He's in jail," Ross had told them unceremoniously. "Don't think callin' him is gonna help."

They'd informed him that he wouldn't be getting any more chicken—his number one bestseller was the fried chicken plate—until the account was settled.

Which meant that Ross barely had enough chicken, already marinating in the big tubs of buttermilk and spices in the truck's fridge, to last him the next two days.

Then there was Margo, who was unlikely to last as long as the chicken supply.

The weekend was coming up, and it was the busiest time for Basket and the other food trucks at the lot.

"Two smoked turkey Reubens, a chef salad with extra deviled eggs, and another order of the tomatoes," Margo called out.

Ross' hands moved automatically, pulling out bread and slathering it with butter on one side, and then building the sand-wiches efficiently. First the spicy Russian dressing he'd developed himself, then slices of swiss, then the signature smoked turkey that he smoked himself, on his off hours, on the little smoker out back, behind the truck. One, and then the other, went on the sandwich press, as he began to assemble the salad.

Basket was as busy as ever, and it was a lot for one person to manage all the orders.

Ross, who'd been working in restaurants since he was a teenager, working in his grandmother's kitchen for longer than that, could even feel it at the end of the day, when sometimes he was too tired to even keep his eyes open.

Maybe if Margo—or any of the other temps—had been decent, he could've given over some of the more basic prep and assembly to her, but whether she was incapable or he was just a fucking terrible teacher, that had been impossible from the beginning.

When Ash had been working with him, it hadn't been so bad.

But then Ash had gone to start another food truck, and Ross hadn't felt like he could stop him, considering it was partly *his* fault that Ash's original truck had gone up in flames.

Salad finished, he arranged the deviled eggs on top, grabbed two sides of dressing, and dropped the already breaded tomatoes into the fryer next.

He was going to need a break to make more buttermilk ranch, but he didn't know when he'd get even a minute.

And that was when his day got even worse.

"Hey," a voice said. Ross, busy with slicing the sandwiches in half and depositing them onto plates, glanced over at the propped-open door. At one point, when things had been going really well, and they'd had money—before Aaron had stolen it all—he'd fantasized about putting a little portable air conditioner into the truck.

But these days, he was making do with a partially open back door and a dinky fan he'd stolen from his apartment.

He supposed that the visitor could've been someone he *really* didn't want to see. Like Tony. Or Tate. Or Alexis. Or another one of the food truck owners who made his insides feel like they were curdling with guilt.

It wasn't any of them; it was Shaw, who helped his brother, Jackson, run the Funky Cup, a bar that they all frequented, a few blocks away.

"You got a minute?" Shaw asked, tucking a strand of hair the color of the best grade of honey behind one ear.

"No," Ross said. He balanced the plates and took them to the front of the truck, calling out the name on the ticket Margo had tacked up, picking up three more.

"You look busy," Shaw said. He'd actually climbed into the truck now, even though he hadn't been invited, and even though Ross didn't *really* dislike him, he disliked people in his space, and the kitchen back here was absolutely, unequivocally *his* space.

"Yeah, what gave it away?" Ross grumbled.

"You should've told Ash to wait til you hired someone else," Shaw said.

"Yeah, no," Ross retorted.

Shaw was a frequent visitor to Ross' truck. In fact, since he'd joined the Food Truck Warriors lot a few months back, he'd guess that Shaw ate more meals at Basket than he did any other truck at the lot.

He was also a genuinely nice guy, one of the few around who would actually *talk* to Ross, not just tolerate his presence.

Ross was sure he was doing it *because* he was nice, not for any other reason—at least no other reason had ever materialized.

"I get it," Shaw said. Crazily enough, Ross *almost* believed that he might. But then, he'd taken pains to make sure nobody knew the constant gnawing guilt that he'd learned to live with. "I got in line," Shaw continued, "but your new temp looked frazzled, and I thought, better make sure Ross is okay."

"Ross is fine," he said. A terrible lie. He almost never lied, but he also had his pride to consider.

Nobody knew about the money problems, though he was sure they were passingly aware of his staffing issues, and Ross would rather die than beg for help.

"Ross doesn't *look* fine," Shaw pointed out.

Ross looked up from where he was prepping sandwiches for the little grill. "And? Is there a point to this exercise?"

"It's my day off, let me help you, at least for a little bit. I'm pretty familiar with the menu." Ross caught a brilliant lopsided smile when he glanced up. "I can do it."

"You're a bartender," Ross said brusquely. More roughly than he'd probably intended, because he was actually kind of tempted by Shaw's offer.

He didn't drink but he'd heard really good things about Shaw's unique libations. The man had an experimental touch that Ross could appreciate even though he'd never tried one of his drinks.

He'd probably be inexperienced and clumsy in the kitchen, but a voice in the back of his mind told him that he couldn't exactly be picky.

"Yeah, I am," Shaw said, leaning closer. He smelled like lemons and rosemary, and Ross resolutely pushed the thought away. If he kept telling himself that he wasn't attracted to Shaw, then he wouldn't be. Because after all this time, it was clear that Shaw wasn't attracted to him. And who would be? He was a grumpy workaholic with zero social skills.

"It's your day off, why do you even *want* to work on your day off?"

"Because a friend needs help?"

Ross looked up at that, surprised. "We're friends?"

He didn't have many, or *any*, probably because of how difficult social interaction was for him—and he was better at it now than he'd ever been. But Shaw didn't look mad or frustrated. Instead, he pulled his hair up and reached over and grabbed an apron, hanging on a hook in the corner. "Yeah," he said, with an actual smile, "we're friends, and friends help friends, especially when everything's going to shit around them."

Ross almost laughed. Shaw didn't even know how bad things were, and he *still* thought everything was going to shit.

"Fine," Ross said, giving in, because it had been inevitable, hadn't it? "There's a recipe posted on the fridge." He gestured with a hand. "For buttermilk dressing. Ingredients should be in the fridge. Make a double batch." Ross hesitated, and then tacked on an awkward, "Please?"

Shaw laughed. "You got it, boss."

Margo craned her head around the corner. "You still want your salad, Shaw?"

"I'll have it in a bit. I'm helpin' Ross out for a few."

"Sure thing," Margo said, bestowing a warm smile on him that Ross hadn't received in days.

Not since she'd gotten the job and discovered how terrible a boss he was.

"See," Shaw said, "things aren't so bad, after all."

Ross turned back to his sandwiches and tried not to glower at them.

They'd narrowly avoided the buttermilk dressing catastrophe, but there were half a dozen others, lurking in the back of his mind.

And he was pretty damn sure Shaw couldn't help with those.

The recipe for buttermilk dressing was written in a messy hand that Shaw realized must be Ross'. Ingredients and amounts were scribbled on the paper, some of them crossed out, a few of them adjusted two, three, even four times.

Shaw knew that Ross was a perfectionist when it came to his recipes, but he'd never realized that over time, Ross was continually changing and improving them. The paper was stained and crinkly with water damage, but he could tell that some of the changes had been made over time, with different pen ink, and even one set of changes in pencil.

He hadn't intended to work today—just to grab a quick bite and then head down to the beach for a relaxing afternoon *not* at the bar, but when he'd approached Ross' truck and seen the line, then observed the new temp's strained expression, he'd known things were bad.

As much as Ross tried to hide it, it was obvious to Shaw—if not anyone else—that he was struggling.

He'd tried saying something to Tony, when he'd come in for a drink a few nights ago, but Tony had brushed him off. "He's got more customers than the rest of us combined," Tony had said, "he's doing just fine."

Tony knew better than to believe that all you needed as a business owner was customers. Sometimes you could even have too many customers, overwhelming your capacity to serve them. The Funky Cup had been through one or two of those rough periods, before they'd managed to hire a few more good bartenders and waitstaff, and Shaw still remembered those times.

It wasn't that Tony didn't know, but it was more like he didn't care.

The rest of the food truck guys might have accepted Ross into their lot, but he wasn't their friend.

Shaw knew intimately how lonely a spot that could be, accepted but never included, and at first he'd started coming around to Basket to see if Ross needed a friend.

Ross did, unequivocally, even though he didn't seem to see it.

But more than just that, over the last few months, Shaw had fallen in love with Ross' food.

He was endlessly innovative and creative and never rested on his laurels. He was always trying to make the next new best thing on the menu.

The dressing was a simple enough recipe—mayo, sour cream, buttermilk, a bunch of herbs that Shaw chopped carefully and finely, knowing that Ross would freak and throw away a whole batch of dressing if it wasn't perfect—and he finished twenty minutes later.

When he turned to Ross to ask what he could do next, the man's dark eyes were focused on the sandwich press. And *that* made no sense, as there was an empty, clean expanse of flat-top grill right next to him. But maybe that was one of Ross' new innovations. Maybe things really tasted better on the press. It would be just like Ross to make that kind of change.

"Finally done?" Ross said, not raising his head.

Over the last few months, Shaw had discovered that the man's bark was always worse than his bite. Actually, he'd realized that he had *no* bite at all. He was terrible at making friends, and maybe even worse at keeping them, but he didn't have a nasty or cruel bone in his body. He usually meant well, Shaw had figured out after long observation, but he had no idea how to actually communicate that.

"Yeah," Shaw said.

Ross straightened and suddenly he was right there, in Shaw's space.

His dark t-shirt was old and threadbare, pulling tight across his biceps and his broad chest. The man was tall and broad, and Shaw didn't always remember just how big he was—actually, he *tried* not to remember, because it was clear that Ross lived for his work, and had never had a relationship that anyone could ever remember.

But Shaw, despite his best intentions, still sometimes felt that zing of undeniable attraction whenever Ross got close.

He pulled a spoon out and dipped it in the dressing, flicking his tongue out to taste it. Shaw swallowed hard.

"Needs more salt," Ross said, but before Shaw could grab it, Ross already reached across him, pressing one of those big, meaty arms against his own chest. Shaw felt heat and muscle and ground his teeth together in frustration.

He didn't want to be attracted to Ross.

Not only would it be totally unrequited, it would be a disaster.

Jackson, ever the overprotective older brother, was still feeling a boatload of resentment over what had happened to his boyfriend, Alexis' food truck because of Ross' ex-partner, and would probably never stop giving him shit for it.

"Better," Ross said. He looked at Shaw then, like he was seeing him for the first time. "I'm surprised."

Anyone else might be insulted, but Shaw wasn't. He got it. If someone showed up at his bar, without any training, and tried to make drinks, he'd be suspicious *at best.*

"Thanks," Shaw said. "What else can I do?"

"Slice and bread more tomatoes," Ross said brusquely.

Shaw resigned himself to not getting any lunch—and postponing his beach trip to next week.

Shaw cut a whole flat of tomatoes, and then breaded them in the station that Ross had instructed him how to set up.

Between the dressing and the tomatoes, Shaw felt like he was getting a good idea of the rhythm of the way Basket worked.

Then he made extra slaw, and whipped up a batch of honey butter. By the time they'd reached the end of the lunch rush, Shaw had a really good idea of why Ross looked grumpy all the time.

Ross was leaning against the grill, which he was able to do because it was cold and empty, drinking an entire bottle of water in one gulp.

"I know what's going on," Shaw said hesitantly. He hadn't been sure if he could bring it up—if he *should* bring it up—but by the time he'd made the honey butter, he'd known that he wouldn't be able to leave without at least trying to talk to Ross about it.

Ross crushed the plastic in one big hand. "What do you mean?"

"Why your grill's cold. Why there's bare spots in your fridge. Why three of the five big plastic containers you use to marinate chicken are clean and empty. Why you keep hiring cheap temps and not anyone who can actually help you."

Ross' dark eyes narrowed. "Oh?"

Shaw swallowed hard. He'd said they were friends, but he didn't know how far that friendship extended. If Ross would get angry with him for even suggesting it. But he knew enough about business, and about *this* business, to know that he couldn't keep quiet. Maybe he could help, somehow.

Not somehow. He knew how he could help.

The only question was if Ross would accept it.

"You're broke."

Ross looked away. "Think you've got it all figured out, huh?" The sentence might have normally come out in Ross' normal sneer, but today, it sounded quiet and defeated.

Things must have been even worse than Shaw realized.

How long had Ross been struggling like this?

Back before Aaron? Had Aaron caused it, along with all the other destruction he'd wrought on the food truck lot?

Had he tried to drag Ross down with him?

"I don't think I know anything." Shaw stepped closer. "I just know that you aren't using this grill, when it's way easier and more efficient than that little sandwich press. And then there's the chicken."

Shaw saw Ross' fingers tighten, the skin going white at the knuckles, around the crumpled water bottle. "What do you know about chicken? You've worked here . . ." Ross checked his watch. "An hour and a half?"

The more defensive Ross got, the more sure Shaw was that he'd hit on something important.

"You're right. I don't know exactly how much you need to stock to deal with the crowds, but it doesn't seem like you've got enough to last the week. You having an issue with your supplier?"

"Something like that," Ross muttered.

"And the grill?"

"Not working." Ross spit the words out from between his clenched teeth.

"For awhile now," Shaw guessed.

Ross didn't react. Didn't even blink. But Shaw knew he was right.

"You've got lines longer than anyone else, with way less help, you should at least be breaking even, if not making a decent living," Shaw said. Maybe it was stupid to prod the beast like this, but Shaw also knew if he didn't, nothing would change. Ross and his truck would go down as a cautionary tale, and then Shaw would have to find somewhere else to get his deviled egg and fried chicken fix. And worse than that, he'd feel guilty for letting the guy circle the drain without doing a thing to help him.

Jackson would tell him that Ross' problems weren't any of his business, but the way Shaw saw it, if he was in a position to help—and he thought he might be—then it was wrong for him to turn away and not say anything.

"*Should* be," was all Ross said. Cryptically.

And now, goddamn it, Shaw was curious too.

"Did Aaron do something?"

Ross looked up, finally meeting Shaw's eyes, and the emotion swirling in his gaze was like a gut punch. There was so much anger and hurt and frustration and helplessness there.

"What *didn't* Aaron do?" His tone was bitter.

How could Shaw see that, and *know* Ross was struggling and not do anything?

"Listen . . ."

"I'm not going to take your money," Ross interrupted him.

Shaw was surprised. "I wasn't going to give you any."

"Oh."

"I was going to say, Ash mentioned the other night that you've been trying to find a roommate, and I thought, that could be me."

"You?"

"Yeah, you could move in with me, above the bar. I don't pay rent, so other than helping with the utilities, rent would be free. That might . . . that might help you get back on your feet." And it wouldn't be such a difficult thing for Ross to accept. It wasn't like Shaw was going to write him a check. He'd have done it, if Ross would've taken it, but he already knew Ross' pride was going to make that impossible.

This was the best—and easiest way—to both help him out and make sure that he took the help.

"You want me to move in with you?" Ross sounded incredulous, and maybe it *was* a little crazy, but while he'd been cutting the tomatoes, it was the best idea that Shaw had come up with. Without paying rent, which in Los Angeles was fucking ridiculous, even on that shitty studio that Ash had mentioned he lived in, Ross should be able to at least begin to extricate himself from whatever terrible financial situation he'd found himself in.

"Yeah," Shaw said. "I've got a couch, it's pretty comfy, and it's free. And let's face it, neither of us is home much."

Ross drummed his fingers nervously on the stainless steel counter next to him.

"You don't know me," he finally said.

"I know you well enough," Shaw said cheerfully. "You're not going to murder me in my bed."

Ross raised an eyebrow. "You sure about that?"

"Your ex-partner was the psycho one. We already know that. And I'd guess that he's the one who left you in this situation, anyway."

Ross didn't say anything, which was confirmation enough, at least for Shaw.

Of course it had been Aaron. Maybe he'd stolen money. Maybe he'd just spent it. It didn't matter, because this would've normally been a financially healthy business, because costs were fairly low, and Shaw knew Tony kept the monthly rent reasonable. And also because Shaw was used to waiting in twenty- or thirty-minute lines on the regular to get his fried chicken fix.

The one thing Ross wasn't lacking was eager, dedicated customers.

"It doesn't matter how it happened." Ross' voice was hard. "Doesn't mean I can't figure it out on my own. I'm managing things."

"With temps and running out of stuff in the middle of the lunch rush and probably running out of your best-selling dish in the middle of the week? Yeah, no offense, but you're not."

"If I'm not," Ross said, "then that's *my* business, not yours. We're not even friends."

"Yeah, stupid assumption," Shaw said. He pulled off his apron and shoved it in Ross' direction. "'Cause friends wouldn't stop by on their day off to help out."

"But . . ." Ross started to say, but Shaw already knew he wasn't going to agree to the plan—the *very* smart plan—so he kept moving, heading towards the propped-open back door.

"See you around, Ross," Shaw said, hating that right now, he felt like he'd failed him, even though he'd given Ross every chance to come clean and to accept the help he needed.

CHAPTER TWO

"You're cleaning that glass very aggressively."

Shaw looked up from the glass in his hands at his brother's voice. Maybe he *had* been scrubbing it harder than it needed to be.

It had been two days since he'd helped Ross out and Ross had refused even the tiniest bit of additional help.

Shaw knew it was stupid to feel guilty. Stupid to feel bad.

He should be relieved that he wouldn't have to share his space with someone else. The apartment above the bar wasn't exactly huge.

But it would've been plenty big enough, that annoying voice in the back of his head reminded him.

"Just . . . thinkin' about something," Shaw said, with a casual shrug.

Jackson's eyes narrowed. "Since when do you let anything bother you? You shrug just about everything off. You still thinking about George?"

George was Shaw's ex. They'd broken up two years ago, so the idea he was still thinking about George was ridiculous and Jackson knew it. He was just trying to bait him.

Shaw shot his brother a look. "No, and you know I'm not."

Jackson leaned back on the barstool. He often did the books at the end of the night here, while Shaw did his final clean of the bar before closing.

There'd been a time when Jackson rarely emerged from the little office he kept, but these days, Jackson was better about not drowning himself in work. About actually *joining* in the community he'd helped to build.

"Well, what's got your panties in a twist, then?" Jackson asked. "You've been agitated, well, agitated for *you*, for days."

Shaw hadn't wanted to bring up Ross. The subject was still a sore one with his brother. Alexis, Jackson's boyfriend, had long forgiven and moved on, but that was Jackson for you. He practically enjoyed holding grudges.

The glass wiped out to his satisfaction, Shaw set it down on the shelf. "You been over to the food truck lot recently?"

Jackson rolled his eyes. "You know I have. You and Alexis are such mother hens. *Yes*, I've been eating regular meals."

"You been to Basket recently?" Shaw kept his voice deceptively casual.

"Oh, he's still in business?" Jackson said with a sniff. "What a surprise."

"You *know* he's still in business, because you're not blind or stupid," Shaw reminded him.

"I might've gotten a salad the other day," Jackson finally admitted. "And that's only because Ash was closed."

"No, it's because Ash doesn't sell your favorite salad."

Shaw loved his brother, but he could be so deliberately obtuse sometimes that Shaw wanted to smack him.

"Fine," Jackson grumbled, "Basket sells my favorite salad. Anyway, yeah, I was there earlier in the week. What's going on?"

"I think . . ." Shaw took a deep breath. "I *know* Ross is struggling."

"How is that possible? I waited at least twenty minutes. They had the biggest line at the lot." Jackson reached for his iced tea and took a long drink. "If anyone should be financially healthy, it's him."

"That's what I told him, and he wouldn't really explain, but my guess is that Aaron left him in a shitty situation."

"Ah." Jackson's expression spoke volumes.

"And," Shaw continued, because if he was in for a penny, he might as well be in for a pound, "I suggested that he move in with me, to try to help him get back on his feet."

"What?" Jackson nearly screeched. "You did *what?* And you didn't ask me first?"

"It was kind of a spur-of-the-moment thing, and besides, we own this bar *together*. If I want to invite a hundred guys to sleep on my couch, it's my business."

"Yeah, but . . ."

"Don't worry," Shaw said dryly, "he said no."

Jackson was quiet for a moment, clearly thinking.

"How do you know he's struggling?"

"I showed up to grab some fried chicken two days ago and he's got that new temp, who is nice but couldn't find her way out of a paper bag. And she's just the latest in a long line of temps since Ash left. If he could, I think he'd hire someone more permanent. A *few* permanent employees, at least. And that big flat-top grill he has? Not working. He's making sandwiches on a dinky little press that it looks like he stole from your kitchen. And worse, he barely has enough chicken to last the week in that fridge of his. He wouldn't tell me, but I'm guessing his supplier's cut him off."

Jackson tapped a pen on the bar. "Yeah," he admitted, "it does sound like he's in trouble."

He'd known Jackson would understand all the signs, because he was a brilliant businessman, great with numbers, and juggling all the various financial issues that cropped up was something he was fantastic at.

Shaw had also known that the easiest way to get Jackson to ignore his resentment over what Ross' ex-partner had done was to engage that particular part of his brain.

The part that liked to solve problems and was really fucking good at it.

"Ash mentioned the other day he'd unsuccessfully been trying to find a roommate," Shaw said, "so suggesting he move in with me, it made sense."

"No rent, I'm assuming," Jackson said. "To help him get back on his feet."

"Yeah, I think it'd help. Maybe it wouldn't fix everything, but it would . . . well, it would be something I could do."

"And why do you need to do anything for Ross?" Jackson's gaze narrowed. "Is there something you aren't telling me? You like him?"

"No, not like you're saying," Shaw said. It was none of his brother's business if he *was* attracted to Ross. Besides, it wasn't like anything was going to happen between them anyway, even if Ross ended up sleeping on his couch.

Ross clearly didn't do relationships, and Shaw definitely didn't think he was like Ren, who worked the Balls and Buns truck, who was renowned for his one-night stands.

"Okay, well, you can't blame me for asking," Jackson said, a hint of a smile on his face. "This kinda came out of the blue, you bein' all worried about Ross."

"Not really," Shaw said. "We're friends."

Ross kept saying they weren't, but Shaw knew better.

Jackson looked skeptical at this piece of information. "Really? He doesn't really come by here much."

"I don't think he drinks," Shaw said. Ash had mentioned it, and also some other stuff about addiction. He didn't really feel comfortable sharing any of that with his brother, because it was Ross' private business, but it had never hurt his feelings that Ross didn't come around the Funky Cup much.

He didn't drink, and it wasn't like the rest of the food truck group had ever really made him feel welcomed. Why would he come and hang out with them after hours?

"Well, I guess if you asked him, you must be friends," Jackson said. "Your apartment isn't that big."

"It's big enough. Besides," Shaw added, "he said no, remember?"

"He might change his mind," Jackson said.

"I doubt it," Shaw said. He tossed the last dirty towel onto the pile. "I'm gonna throw these in the laundry," he said. "You just about done with your number wizardry?"

"Yeah," Jackson said. "Pour yourself a beer when you get back, I wanna discuss something with you."

Shaw groaned as he ducked his head into the back, confirming the kitchen was clean and empty, and then tossed the dirty towel in the huge hamper that the commercial laundry service came to pick up every other day.

When he came back to the bar, Jackson had turned most of the lights down or off, and he'd come behind the bar himself, pouring himself a shot of vodka, and adding a splash of soda water and a sliver of lime from the freshly stocked bins.

"I could've gotten that for you," Shaw said, pulling one of his clean pint glasses from the stack and pouring himself one of his favorite drafts from a small local brewery.

"Yeah, well, you don't make it like I like it."

Shaw found that hard to believe; he was a damn good bartender. The truth was, Jackson liked doing things for himself. He always had. Shaw? He was much more lackadaisical. At least about everything but the drinks he served at his bar.

"So what's this thing you wanted to talk about?" Shaw said, pushing up the pass-through and settling down in the barstool next to Jackson's. "I told you, you don't have to get everything you want to do approved by me. I trust you to take care of stuff the way we'd both like it done."

"Yeah, not this," Jackson said and there was both excitement and apprehension in his voice.

And suddenly, the only thing on Shaw's mind wasn't whether Ross would change his mind (he wouldn't, Shaw would bet money on it), but what the heck was going on with Jackson and how *long* had it been going on. Had he been so preoccupied with Ross' issues that he'd somehow missed a problem at the bar?

"Remember that developer I told you called me last week?"

Shaw did, vaguely. Had also dismissed it completely because Jackson had made it clear he wasn't interested.

"Yeah . . ." Shaw said uneasily.

"I called him back," Jackson said. "I wasn't going to, I thought I wasn't interested, but I don't know, I couldn't stop thinking about it. Finally I decided, what's the harm in looking at what he's got?"

"You don't really want to add a second location?" Shaw said, somewhat in disbelief.

"Want to?" Jackson sipped his drink. "Not particularly, no, but then I thought, why can't we build the same thing over there that we built here? A safe place, a friendly place, for everyone? That's meaningful."

"It's meaningful enough we did it once," Shaw said, suddenly grumpy.

"But we could do it again. The space is great. We've got the money. It would be a good investment."

"A risky investment," Shaw corrected. "We don't know if it'd pay off, and it feels, well, it feels good to have that money in the bank, in case of a rainy day."

Jackson raised an eyebrow. "Or in case I go psycho and decide to make you burn down the bar?"

"I am not comparing our situation to Ross'," Shaw argued. "I just . . . it *is* a risk."

"Sometimes you've got to take some risks. We've done that, over the years," Jackson argued.

He wasn't wrong. They'd taken some risks. Putting in the back patio with its firepits hadn't been cheap, and for six months, money had been tight and Shaw hadn't forgotten the dark circles that had lived, semi-permanently, under Jackson's eyes.

But it *had* paid off, in the end.

Expanding the kitchen had gone the same way. In a few months, they were making enough money off the new menu—and off drinks to wash it down with—that in retrospect, it had looked like a really brilliant idea.

Shaw just wasn't sure if this one would be the same.

Sure, Jackson would run a dozen different financial scenarios, and he'd consult with their staff, and it would get discussed to death, like every other big decision they'd made.

But this was different.

"It's a great location," Jackson continued. "Needs work. A *lot* of work, and because of the location, rent is . . . high."

"Rent?" They owned this building free and clear—mostly because their dad had been good with numbers, like Jackson, and he'd scrimped and saved, paying off the loan just before he'd died.

It meant that Shaw hadn't ever had to pay rent, and could save the bulk of his salary.

It meant that whenever they'd needed to make changes, they could, with the bar's savings account.

"Yeah, *rent.*" Jackson sounded edgy and nervous about it. "That'd be new for us. We'd be operating at a loss, probably for at least a year. But after that? It'd be worth it. Think about it. A legacy for both of us. You could manage the new bar, like I do here."

Shaw lifted his beer to his mouth and took a long gulp. "What if I don't want to manage a new bar?"

"Well, then I'll take the new one, and you can have this one," Jackson said. "I don't care. But you're meant for more than just pouring drinks and chatting up the regulars."

Shaw should've seen it coming. Should have realized why Jackson hadn't been able to leave this idea alone.

"You think I'm bored?"

Jackson waved a hand. "Not *bored*, necessarily, but in a rut? Yeah. You can do more. You *should* do more. I know you don't like change . . ."

"An understatement," Shaw muttered under his breath.

"But," Jackson stressed, "that doesn't mean change is bad."

"Dad left us both this bar, I don't think he intended for us to end up in two different spots," Shaw argued.

"Dad didn't intend a lot of things, but they happened anyway," Jackson said. "The truth is, we've made enough money here that it's stupid to not consider expanding."

"What about that idea you had about opening a little bar at the food truck lot?"

"I looked into it," Jackson said, "and it's just too complicated with the permits. And there's not really the room, not if I do it the way I'd want to. Plus, it's only a few blocks away from here. We need *new* customers, not the same ones we already have."

"I don't like it," Shaw said, even though it was probably crystal fucking clear to his brother that he didn't. "I don't think we should do it."

"I knew you'd say that." Jackson sounded frustrated. "Just think about it, okay? I'm going to run some models. It's a good idea, you just don't want anything to be different."

"Why would I?" Shaw demanded. "I like things just like they are. They're great right now. You shouldn't try to fuck that up."

He loved his brother, but sometimes Jackson made him crazy.

Wasn't it enough that they'd built this? Why did they have to keep going? Why couldn't they just be satisfied with what they already had? Why did they need to go out and grab for more?

"Just . . ." Jackson sighed heavily. "Just think about it, okay? That's all I want. For you to not dismiss it out of hand."

"You aren't going to let this go, are you?" Shaw asked, even though he already knew the answer.

He knew Jackson had always felt stupidly guilty that their father had left him fifty-one percent of the bar, and Shaw forty-nine. He'd explained, before he'd died of the lung cancer that had taken him way too early, that it was because he'd wanted them to both have a stake in the bar, but that it would be too hard on their relationship if they owned a straight fifty-fifty split. Someone, he'd said, needed to be able to override the other and make decisions.

And for six years, that hadn't been a problem.

They'd agreed, ultimately, on everything.

But if Jackson wanted to go off and do this other crazy bar thing, he *could*.

And maybe he would, just because he was trying to make up for the fact that Shaw didn't really own anything. He already knew if the new bar succeeded, Jackson would try to give it to him—or the other way around.

"Fine," Shaw grumbled after finishing his beer, "I'll think about it, but I don't see my mind changing."

"You always say that," Jackson said, patting him on the shoulder, "but sometimes it does."

Shaw already knew he wasn't going to be changing his mind about this.

Ross' day was going marginally better—he'd convinced his poultry supplier to extend him some additional credit, though he was going to have to figure out how to start paying back the balance, at some point—at least until mid-afternoon when Margo marched back into the kitchen area of the truck with a determined stride, carrying her apron in her hands.

"What's going on?" Ross asked, even though he was pretty sure he already knew. She'd been stewing for at least a day, after he'd barked at her one too many times, and he supposed he should be grateful that she'd waited until the lunch rush was over to quit.

"I thought working here would be different," she said.

I thought working for you *would be different,* was what she really meant.

"I told you that it'd be hard work," Ross said, trying to be patient, even though he was terrible at it. He was *trying*. Aaron had always handled all their employees, though when they'd moved here, to Food Truck Warriors, they'd let all their part-time guys go. At the time, Aaron had said it was good to run lean for a few months, to recoup their losses.

At the time, Ross hadn't realized that their losses weren't because they'd expanded and hired people, it was because Aaron was recklessly draining their accounts.

He hadn't realized until it was too late.

And now, no matter how hard he worked to drag himself out of the hole, it just kept getting deeper and wider.

Shaw wanted to help you, and you threw it back in his face.

"It's not that it's hard," Margo said, "it's that it's too hard for what you're paying."

Which was minimum wage. It was all he could afford.

Thus, the series of temps that never lasted.

But Ross couldn't run the truck by himself, and he couldn't afford to pay more.

It was a wretched conundrum.

"I'd stay," she continued, "if you gave me a raise."

"Can you do more prep? Come earlier? Stay later?" It was stupid to even ask, because he already *knew* he couldn't afford more. Especially if Margo worked more hours.

"I already told you I can't. I teach yoga in the morning and in the evenings," Margo said. "This is just to supplement my income, and I can do a lot easier jobs for the same money."

"Then go," Ross said. He wasn't going to stand here and waste precious time by arguing with her, when she'd already made her decision.

"Fine," she said, shoving the apron into his middle. "You can mail my final check."

Then she was gone, the back door slamming behind her, and for a second, Ross felt the blow of it like she'd hit *him* and not the door.

He couldn't open tomorrow, not without any help, and he couldn't face calling up the temp agency again and begging for someone new. He'd already done it too many times, and the last time he'd called, they had sounded suspicious.

Like they couldn't figure out why he kept going through temps at such an astounding pace.

It's because I'm an asshole. Mean and too hard on them because *they don't really want to work. They just say they do.*

As shitty a partner as Aaron had turned out to be, at least he'd worked hard. Just as hard as Ross.

He could close early, tonight. He could use the money, but he didn't want to experience a dinner rush without help.

The good news was that there wasn't any live music tonight, so things could've been worse. Tony would probably get on his case if he found out he'd closed early, but there wouldn't be anything he could do about it, because it wasn't like Ross *ever* closed normally, not even for the allowed one day a week.

He would figure something out.

Surely there was someone he could call. A favor he could cash in.

But Ross already knew there was nobody. That was the problem with not making friends easily—he didn't *have* any.

Aaron had been the friendly, jovial, social side of their partnership. He'd made connections and created opportunities, and smoothed their way.

Ross knew he could never be that.

He'd tried, for years, and all it had gotten him was a breaking-down food truck, and no help whatsoever.

He was absolutely fucking alone.

And of course, with that horrible thought still echoing in his head, that was when he heard a knock on the back door.

He pushed himself off the counter, and telling himself to stop feeling so goddamned sorry for himself, went to open the door.

The woman standing at the base of the short stairs was familiar.

He'd seen her around the food truck lot for the last few months, working at various trucks. Sometimes with Tate and Rachel at Say Cheese, and occasionally with Alexis at his Greek food truck.

She was dressed in a t-shirt with Alexis' blue and white flag logo on it now.

"Hey," she said, "I just saw your latest temp go stomping off."

Great, exactly what he needed. Someone else who wanted to tell him just how fucked he was.

"Yeah," Ross said. "She left."

"I'm not surprised," the woman said. Ross was sure he'd been told her name at some point, but he couldn't place it right now.

He really did not need this shit right now, no matter what her name was.

"Yeah, I suck, I get it. Trust me."

"That's not what I meant." There was a glimmer of a smile on her face. "I think that you've been hiring the wrong kind of people. Who don't have the right experience." She shifted from one foot to the other. "Can I come in?"

"Why?" Ross wondered. He had no fucking clue where this was going, but it wouldn't be the first or the last time that he missed an important social cue.

"I'd like to work for you," she said.

"I'm not hiring," Ross said, even though that was a big fat lie.

"Yeah, yeah, you really are," she retorted, giving back as good as he'd given her. Which . . . that got his attention. "You've got the longest lines of any truck on this lot, and yet you're making do with crappy temps who can barely take orders. You need someone who can take orders *and* help you prep *and* help you if you get slammed in the kitchen." She paused. "So can I come up or not?"

She was not wrong, and it galled that she'd recognized the shortcomings in his plan so easily. *Just like Shaw did*, that annoying voice in the back of his head told him.

"Fine," Ross said, and gestured, pushing the door open further.

She took in the kitchen, including the cold, flawlessly clean flat-top grill with a slow observant spin. "Broken?" she asked, tapping her finger on the edge of the grill.

"Yeah," Ross said. "The heating element is working inconsistently. I need . . ." *I need so many fucking things.* "I need to get it fixed."

She shot him a look. "Yeah, I bet you do.

"I've been working at this lot for a year now," she continued, "I know the routine. I work hard. I'm quick, I'm efficient."

"So why do you want to work here?"

"I'm tired of working part-time places, I want to do something more permanent, more full-time," she said. "And that's what you need too, so I figured, why not ask."

"Why not," Ross muttered.

He knew that Tate spoke highly of her. Alexis was a notorious perfectionist and he wouldn't have let her near his truck unless she was everything she said she was. So why was he hesitating?

Oh yeah, that fucking money problem.

He had no money to even pay a part-time temp minimum wage; he definitely didn't have any money to pay someone full-time who deserved more.

There was only one way he could see where he could make it work, and it would mean swallowing his pride.

Something he'd never been good at.

"I'll give you fifty hours a week," she said, "at fourteen an hour."

It was exactly what he needed . . .

Ross swallowed hard. He'd hated Aaron plenty of times over the last few months, but never as much as he did now.

He could pay her, if he moved out of his studio and took Shaw's offer. The money he was spending every month for rent would cover her salary and it would give him a little extra, to start paying back his debts. Maybe even get the grill fixed.

It was the solution to all his problems, if he could just stomach it.

Shaw wasn't so bad, that wasn't the problem. The *charity* was the problem.

But there was nothing else to do but accept it, because Ross wasn't stupid. He knew he was out of options, and if he let this woman, with her experience and her self-starter attitude, walk out the door, he'd regret it forever.

"Done," Ross said, reaching out to shake her hand briefly. "You're hired . . ." Only too late did he realize that he *still* didn't remember her name.

She rolled her eyes, but there was not a speck of offense in them. Maybe they'd get along okay, after all. "Harmony," she said. "I'm Harmony."

"Great. Harmony." He paused. "How long are you working for Alexis today?"

She didn't even look surprised by his request.

Ross wondered how much everyone else knew about his endlessly shitty situation.

"I'm yours at seven tomorrow morning," she said.

"Okay," Ross said. He'd close early, anyway. Besides, it would give him time to . . . time to what? Go grovel at the Funky Cup and hope that Shaw hadn't rescinded his offer?

Yeah, something like that.

CHAPTER THREE

Ross closed the truck, put up a temporary sign, saying they'd be opened back up the next day, and went home.

He showered, and after he got dressed, he took a quick glance around the apartment. He wouldn't even need to rent a storage unit for all his shit, because well, frankly he didn't have much.

Anything that was actually worth anything he'd already sold. He could probably unload the IKEA couch, a few years old and definitely looking worn in spots, for fifty bucks, and the rest of it? Well, there weren't really many big pieces of furniture left. The lumpy stained mattress in the bedroom, where it was currently living on the floor in the corner? Well, that could go straight to the dump.

Otherwise, he could begin to pack up, when he got back from begging Shaw to take him in. The chance of it taking more than an evening, when he'd already ended up migrating whatever kitchen equipment he had to the truck, seemed unlikely.

He had some clothes, a few things left in the kitchen, a handful of books, his laptop, and that was just about it.

It was sad; he'd been living in LA for years now, and that was all he had to show for his time.

But then, he'd never really lived in this apartment. He'd lived at the food truck. That was where he'd spent all of his time. This had only been a place he'd slept, when he actually got to sleep.

All he was doing was changing up where he slept.

His food truck was still *home*.

It was that thought that helped him get up off the couch and head towards the bar.

It was early evening now, and people were milling around the outside of the bar, some of them smoking, and others meeting up with friends as Ross pushed open the door.

He hadn't spent much time in the Funky Cup, even after he'd joined the food truck lot down the street.

Aaron had liked to go—mostly, Ross thought, to rub Tony's face in his own dislike—but even when Ross had accompanied him, he hadn't really enjoyed it.

Even though, he thought as he walked in, the warm wood and smell of beer enveloping him, it was actually a very enjoyable place.

He'd always admired what Jackson and Shaw had built here, from the rudimentary skeleton of their father's dive bar. Now it was warm and cozy, with natural finished wood walls, and that gorgeous back patio, with all its lush landscaping.

It felt like you weren't in the concrete jungle of Los Angeles at all, but someplace else. Someplace *better*.

Shaw was behind the bar, his honey blond hair pulled back in a low ponytail, mixing drinks with a quick and easy efficiency, never failing to smile at a customer, or to crack a joke, or to make them feel welcome.

It was a whole range of skills that Ross had never had, no matter how much he'd practiced, and would likely *never* have.

He'd come to terms with it, but it still stung a bit to watch. And *not*, he told himself, because it was other people and not him. Ross told himself that it didn't matter if Shaw turned that charm on for the whole goddamn bar. They weren't even friends. Acquaintances, more like. And now, Ross thought, likely to be roommates.

There was an empty stool at the bar, and he slid into it, before anyone else could. He'd heard a group talking, a few months back, about how prized these seats were, and it wasn't because of the great customer service—though a spot here would guarantee it—but because the bartender was so great. Funny and relaxing and yeah, *charming*.

He flirted with everyone. Shaw had even flirted with him, as casually as he did anything else, Ross thought as he put his elbows onto the shining wood. Which really said it all, didn't it?

Shaw finished up pouring two beers, and mixing what looked to be a margarita, and turned to Ross, a surprised and pleased smile emerging on his handsome face.

"Hey, man, it's great to see you," he said, sounding like he genuinely meant it.

That was part of Shaw's natural charm, Ross decided, he'd learned how to always *mean* it.

"Hey," Ross said.

"What can I get you to drink?" Shaw was mixing another drink now, with muddled rosemary and lime, whiskey and a splash of cherry juice. It was inventive, but then most of the drinks here were.

That was Shaw's personal touch.

"Uh." Ross hesitated. He rarely drank, because he didn't always trust himself. Once an addict, always an addict, even though he'd kicked his addiction to the uppers ages ago. "A water is fine."

"Water? How about something sweet instead?"

"I don't . . ."

"Yeah, I know," Shaw said, shooting him another one of those quicksilver smiles. "You don't drink. It won't have booze in it, I promise. But I think you'll like it."

"How did you know? That I have a sweet tooth?" It wasn't like Ross' addiction to sugary shit was a state secret, but he didn't go around telling people out of the blue, either. He was pretty sure he'd never told Shaw about it.

"Been behind you a couple of times at the coffee shop down the street," Shaw said, filling a glass with ice. "You always get something real sweet there."

Shaw was right, he usually did. It was one of his only vices and so he'd always refused to feel guilty about it. But how had he missed Shaw? The coffee shop wasn't very big. He'd have noticed the man, if only because he was so easy to notice.

But then, Ross realized, he'd been living and working and nearly breathing in a fog the last few months. Stress and anxiety and guilt swirling inside of him, making a rather toxic combination. He'd barely noticed *himself* recently.

Shaw poured something bright red into the bottom of the glass, squeezed in half a lime with an expert motion, and then filled it with some clear effervescent liquid from the beverage gun.

"Here you go," he said, setting the pink swirled drink onto a coaster in front of him. "Enjoy, and let me know what you think."

Shaw had even managed to slip, almost without Ross realizing it, a lime wedge and a cherry onto the sharp end of a little pink umbrella, and it balanced just perfectly on the edge of the glass.

Ross leaned over and gave the liquid in the glass a quick stir with the black straw. "Thanks," he said. "What do I owe you?"

Shaw waved a hand. "It's on the house. Don't worry about it."

Ross didn't like that. He was already here to tell Shaw he'd changed his mind about the couch, and now he was going to accept more charity. He opened his mouth, but before he could protest, Shaw just shook his head. "We never charge for non-alcoholic drinks here."

Ross thought back, and realized that the handful of times he'd come here with Aaron, he'd always offered to get whatever he'd drunk that day—Coke or iced tea, usually—and Ross realized that he'd never even had to pay for it. His partner had gone out of his way to try to look generous, when in reality, he'd been in the middle of stealing every dime they'd ever earned together.

"You look surprised," Shaw said.

"I just . . ." Ross didn't want to talk about Aaron, but it was like word vomit. He couldn't stop it. "Aaron just always tried to pretend he was doing me a favor by picking up the tab. And now I find out that he never paid for my drinks anyway. He just wanted to make himself look good—while he was stealing all our money."

Shaw's gaze softened. He leaned over the bar, even though Ross could see that there were customers waiting further down. "That was real shitty of him, no joke."

"Yeah," Ross said shortly. He picked up the glass and took a drink. It was sweet, but a little sour, and it was really refreshing. "This is good," he said, hearing the surprise in his own voice. "What is it?"

Shaw smiled again. "A Shirley Temple," he said, but before Ross could say a word, he was gone, already heading down the bar towards the people who'd been waiting.

He hadn't had a chance to ask Shaw yet about the offer, and if it was still good, but he didn't mind waiting until there was a lull. He didn't have anything else to do tonight, except potentially start packing.

His lease was good til the end of the month, but it was a month-to-month commitment, so in two weeks, he'd have to be out. Hopefully it wouldn't take nearly that long to move out completely.

But next month? He'd be free and clear on rent, just having to cover utilities, and there'd be money enough to not only pay Harmony, but to hopefully start catching up on his debts.

The drink was tart and refreshing, and he found himself drinking almost all of it down in several long gulps.

He'd heard of Shirley Temples, of course, but he'd never had one, because he'd always assumed they were a kids' drink.

"Good, huh?"

Ross looked up and Shaw was standing in front of him, an amused expression on his face.

"Isn't this what they normally give kids?" he asked, pointing to the nearly empty glass.

Shaw nodded, and before Ross could say anything else, his hands were already working, making a fresh one.

Maybe if he had him here, right now, held hostage while he prepared his drink, he could bring up the thing he'd come here to discuss.

"That offer you made the other day," Ross said, his mouth suddenly dry.

"Yeah?" Shaw barely glanced up.

"You were serious about it."

"I was," Shaw responded immediately. "But *you* didn't seem to be."

"You . . ." Ross cleared his throat. "You caught me off guard, that's all. I appreciate it a lot. You figured out pretty easily I was struggling, and well, I hadn't wanted anyone to know."

"I don't think it's a huge mystery that Aaron fucked you over, along with everyone else," Shaw said, squeezing a lime into the glass.

"No, but the extent is what I was hoping to keep under wraps," Ross admitted. "It's hard . . . it's hard to say you need help."

"Especially to people who don't like you much," Shaw guessed, and it was impossible that he could know exactly how Ross felt but he kept hitting the nail on the head.

"Yeah, the other food truck guys? We're never going to be best friends," Ross agreed.

Shaw set a fresh glass in front of him and quickly disposed of the old. "You came here because you changed your mind."

"How do you *do* that?" Ross wanted to know.

But Shaw just shrugged. "Practice, I guess, and habit. Jackson thinks it's a natural skill, but I spend all day with people. I just watch, and it's not so hard to figure out what they're not saying."

"Well, you were right, I was wrong," Ross said bluntly. "If the offer's still on the table . . ."

"It is," Shaw said.

Ross was humbled. Shaw's answer had been *so* quick, he couldn't have even thought about it before he responded.

"Really?"

Shaw smiled. "You want me to change *my* mind?"

"No, no, I'm just . . . well, I'm surprised, I guess. Surprised you offered it in the first place, and surprised that you'd be so willing to go along with it now. I wasn't as nice before as I could've been."

"Hey, man, you need some help. And I'm in a spot to give it. That's all it is."

But Ross had a feeling it was more than just that, even if he couldn't figure out what it was. Shaw might be good at reading people, but Ross was terrible at it.

"I'm hoping to move out sooner rather than later . . ."

"Anytime," Shaw said firmly. "I've got a spare key, but it's upstairs. I can go grab it on my break and show you around, if you're cool with that?"

"Sure." Ross nodded. "I don't . . . well, I don't have much stuff. I can probably bring everything I've got by tomorrow night."

"Works for me." Shaw tilted his head to a group of guys waiting for drinks at the end of the bar. "I'll catch you at my break. In about an hour?"

Ross opened his mouth to agree, but Shaw was already down the bar, taking orders and giving out smiles like they were free.

Maybe for Shaw they were.

Ross took another sip of his drink. It was *really* good. No wonder kids always liked these.

Glancing around, he took in the various groups clustered around the seating area, and the bar, and he realized he didn't know anyone that was here.

Of course, it was still early; the food trucks hadn't closed yet, and even if they had, and the regulars had walked over, Ross wasn't sure he'd have approached them.

So what was he going to do for the next hour, while he waited for Shaw?

He could always head home and start packing up his meager belongings. But he really didn't have much, and there'd be plenty of time for that later.

Ross tapped his fingers against the bar. The TV was playing ESPN, some special feature about the Riptide's summer camp, and how much better the defense was looking with Spencer Evans on board. But Ross didn't usually follow sports, even the Riptide, despite Tate's boyfriend being a player on the team and his friends and teammates always coming around the food truck lot, so he got bored quickly.

He did send a quick email to his landlord, letting him know, officially, that he'd be moving out, and this month would be his last.

He still wasn't great with the online payroll program that Aaron had always used, but he'd figured out enough that he was able to send Harmony a link to set herself up. Also, while he was in it, he sent Margo her final check, verifying in his bank account first that he had the funds to pay her.

Then he flipped over to his notes app, and began making a list of things that he'd need to go over with Harmony the next morning.

The list was long, and he was almost afraid that he'd overwhelm her—like he tended to overwhelm the temps—but then he reminded himself that she'd asked to be hired. She knew what he was like, and she'd still approached him. She'd also claimed to be a quick learner, and it was better, Ross decided, to learn right away if she could handle what he threw at her.

He'd been taking it easy on the temps, taking on more and more himself, and it was impossible to miss the bone-deep mental and physical exhaustion that seemed to be more and more of a close friend these days.

Shaw, annoyingly, had been right. He couldn't keep going like this forever.

The next time Shaw checked his watch, it was an hour and a half later, and he was sure when he finally walked over to Ross and let him know he was ready, Ross was going to be grumpy about it.

Mostly because Ross, unlike the rest of the food truck guys, had never been comfortable just hanging out at the Funky Cup. He'd rarely come in, but when he did, it was usually for a reason. Like his ex-partner had dragged him. Or there'd been a meeting Tony was holding.

But to his surprise, Ross was still sitting right where Shaw had left him, typing something on his phone, his gaze intent on the screen.

"Hey," Shaw said as he approached. "You ready to go?"

Ross glanced up and their gazes caught. Shaw felt that frisson of *something*, that undefinable attraction that he kept hoping would fade.

It's not gonna now, you idiot, he realized, *he's gonna be in your space and you're gonna feel it more, not less.*

But maybe the opposite was actually true. Maybe he'd end up spending more time with Ross and discover that he didn't like the guy at all.

Except, that annoying voice added, *he's that kind of guy who doesn't make a good first impression but then grows on you later.*

It was true, much as Shaw didn't want to admit to it.

Maybe he shouldn't have suggested Ross move in at all, and not because of how annoyed Jackson was about it.

More because it was going to be tough to keep his thoughts—and his hands—off.

But then Ross smiled, and the sheer relief on his face, so clear now that Shaw had helped him find a way out of his shitty situation, made it crystal clear that he'd done the right thing in offering.

Even if it was hard, pretending like he wasn't attracted to the man, it would be worth it, to give him some peace of mind.

"Yeah, I'm ready," Ross said, sliding off the barstool. "Great drinks, by the way. That flavor combo isn't new, not really, lime and cherry? But sometimes a classic is a classic for a reason."

Good, Shaw thought as Ross followed him out of the bar, they could talk about flavor combinations all day. Keep it business. Keep it professional. And God knows, he'd heard that Ross was obsessed with flavors, so that would keep *him* occupied, and hopefully not noticing how Shaw felt about him.

"Yeah, I think it adds something with the fresh lime juice," Shaw said as he led him around the side of the bar, to the staircase that led to the upstairs apartment.

"Yeah, the tart balances out all that sweet," Ross agreed. Shaw could feel his eyes on his back as they climbed the stairs. "You ever have a problem with people coming up here?"

"Well, there's a lock for a reason," Shaw said, as he put his own key in and unlocked it, "but there's also a code," he typed that in next, "just in case. Once in awhile, we've gotta kick some crazy drunk person off the stairs, because they think it's their bed, but"—Shaw glanced back at Ross, at his big, wide chest, and those huge hands—"I don't think that's gonna be a problem for you."

"Oh." Ross looked momentarily confused. "It won't?"

Shaw rolled his eyes. "It won't. You're gonna be fine. And it doesn't happen all that often."

"Good." Ross hesitated. "What's the code?"

"I'll text it to you," Shaw said. "Jackson programmed a few of them in the system, it's actually connected to the rest of the security system he had installed at the bar."

"Okay."

Shaw pushed the door open and hoped that he hadn't left any of his dirty laundry lying around and that he'd stuck any of his dishes in the dishwasher and not left them in the sink.

Not that he did much cooking, but occasionally he'd fry up an egg in the morning, and yeah, *shit*, that pan was still on the stove.

Hopefully Ross wouldn't think he was a slob.

Shaw flipped the light in the corner on, and watched Ross take in the small apartment. It was mostly an open floor plan, with the living room and its couch, and the kitchen on the other side. There was a small counter with three barstools against it, and on the other side were two doors: one to the bathroom and the other to Shaw's bedroom.

"It's roomier than I thought it'd be," Ross said slowly, those dark eyes taking in every inch of the place.

Shaw fought the instinct to run over and stick the egg pan in some water.

"The couch is actually pretty comfortable," he said instead. "I've fallen asleep on it loads of times. Way more times than I should actually admit to, probably."

Ross didn't say anything, but just kept looking.

"There's also a pretty roomy storage closet," Shaw said, pointing it out, on the other end of the galley kitchen. "I don't think there's actually much in there, but I can make sure to clean it out before you move in."

"Oh, I don't have much," Ross said.

"Well, you're welcome to it," Shaw insisted. "You gotta have a place to put your clothes."

Ross just shrugged. Like he hadn't even *thought* about his clothes.

Shaw pretended that he wasn't noticing how threadbare his dark gray t-shirt was—or how well it hugged his body, after all the washings it had been through.

"And there's laundry, right there," Shaw added, pointing to the folding door next to the storage closet. "The machines aren't big but they're better than having to go out for laundry."

"Oh yeah," Ross said, and there was another smile. For *laundry*. "I don't have a machine in my building now, so this is great." He paused, turning towards Shaw. "I really, really appreciate this. I know I'm . . . well, I'm not good at saying it, but you're helping me out of a tough spot, so I want to make sure I say it right."

Shaw felt a sudden urge to reach over and pull Ross closer, hug him tightly. He'd been through hell, and everyone had ignored that, because deep down, maybe they actually blamed Ross for what had happened, even though it hadn't been his fault.

But he wasn't a bad guy.

Maybe not very good at expressing his "not bad guy" thoughts, but they still existed.

Shaw could see them in his face.

And not just because he wanted to rub his own face against that soft-looking dark scruff growing along Ross' jaw.

Down, boy, Shaw told himself firmly. *You are not going there.*

"It's not a big deal," Shaw said. "I could help, so I thought I'd offer."

He held out the key. "I'll have Jackson text you your entry code tonight. Before I forget. Feel free to move in whenever. I'm flexible."

"I'll probably bring my stuff over tomorrow night, if that's alright," Ross said, hesitating a bit as he took the key. Like he still felt like he needed to ask permission.

"Works for me," Shaw said, giving the man his friendliest, most open smile. Hoping to communicate, since words didn't always work with Ross, that he was fine. That he didn't have to worry—at least about this.

"Alright," Ross said, and he began to turn, like he was going to leave.

"Let me show you the bathroom real quick," Shaw said, suddenly not sure he wanted to let Ross out of his sight.

"Okay . . ." Ross said uncertainly, but he did follow Shaw as he pushed the door open and flipped the light on.

When Jackson had remodeled this apartment for Shaw, he'd done the bathroom in various shades of blue tile. The floor was deep cerulean, the walls were baby blue, nearly white, and the shower was done in turquoise. It was actually a really pretty effect, and as a result, Shaw had always tried hard to keep it clean.

It was at least cleaner than the kitchen was.

"It looks nice," Ross said. Uncomfortably. Like he wasn't used to complimenting anyone on their decor. Shaw was pretty sure that must be the case; also, he didn't know where Ross had been living, but there were several shithole apartment complexes around here, and he'd guess in one of those.

"I'll clear out a shelf for you," Shaw said, gesturing to the organizer in the corner.

"Great," Ross said, and then they were leaving the bathroom.

"And this?" Ross asked, gesturing to the other door, next to the bathroom.

"Uh, my bedroom," Shaw said. *The less we say about that, the better.*

Ross looked uncomfortable. Not an unusual occurrence, but Shaw noticed it anyway. Told himself as they exited the apartment, climbing down the stairs, that it didn't mean anything. That he wasn't supposed to assume about people's sexuality.

But he wouldn't exactly be shocked if Ross turned out to be ace or demi.

The man didn't get involved with anyone.

It helped, Shaw realized, to think of him as completely not interested. It meant that he wouldn't be angsting about what everything he said and did meant. He'd just assume Ross wasn't into romantic or sexual relationships, and stop worrying.

That would make it all better.

CHAPTER FOUR

"THAT'S A PRETTY COOL payroll system that you're using."

Ross was prepping, side by side at the long stainless steel counter that ran almost the full length of the truck, with Harmony.

It was halfway through her first day, and so far she hadn't proved to be much of a chatterer, which was a huge point in her favor. Ross had never been good with small talk; he worked much better in silence.

But this had come out of nowhere.

Ross' fingers didn't stop dipping the egg-covered heirloom tomato slices into the panko breading, but he didn't answer right away. Wondered if it was a trick question—or a trick statement.

"Uh, yeah," he finally said. "It's got a lot of functionality."

She shot him a warm smile. "That you're not using."

Ah, so this was what she was trying to get at.

"I'm not the one who set it up," Ross explained. "That was Aaron."

"Right, I assumed," Harmony said.

He'd mentioned, on the rundown he'd given her earlier this morning, that Aaron had managed a lot of the business, while Ross had been in charge of the kitchen.

It had been his way of trying to explain that if something didn't happen right—like he forgot to approve payroll or he completely missed giving her the breaks she earned during the day—it was because he wasn't *good* at that sort of thing. Trying to be better, Ross supposed, but he wasn't ever going to be on top of things like Aaron was.

At least Ross had assumed he was. It had turned out that things were a lot messier than he'd thought they were.

"I could help with that," Harmony continued as she efficiently filled a thousand small plastic cups with the buttermilk ranch dipping sauce for the tomatoes. "If you wanted."

"The payroll system?" Ross might not be good at the business part of the truck, but he wasn't stupid.

Harmony flushed. "Not necessarily that, but figuring out all that other stuff. I actually have an accounting degree."

"And you're working here?"

"After I graduated," she said, tucking a loose strand of blue-and-pink-streaked hair behind her ear, "I realized that if I spent the next few decades locked up in an office, behind a desk, I'd die early. So I got a job I really wanted, at a bakery. Then I moved on to the food trucks. I like those even better."

"I worked in a brick-and-mortar place for awhile, and that was almost as bad. Not like . . . an office and a desk." Ross couldn't even imagine *ever* wanting to do something like that. It never would've even occurred to him. But even though the similar routine at the restaurant had appealed to him, at least at first, the chaos had ultimately taken its toll on him.

Of course it could've also been his horribly shitty boss.

But he'd started the truck with Aaron because they'd agreed, from the beginning, that they could do whatever they wanted. Ross had found the idea of controlling the situation around him more and more appealing. It was harder to do that in an actual restaurant. But in a food truck? He could. Easily.

Ross hadn't even wanted to park semi-permanently at Food Truck Warriors, but Aaron had persuaded him that they could use the stability to their income.

Naturally, he hadn't realized at that point, it wasn't because their income *wasn't* stable, but because Aaron kept stealing all of it.

When he'd realized the truth, after Aaron's arrest, he hadn't tried to wiggle out of the contract with Tony because it had seemed easier to stay, especially when everything else was changing so rapidly.

And now? He'd come to realize that having the customers come to *you* was actually pretty freaking cool and Ross had no intention of giving that benefit up.

Harmony shot him a conspiratorial look. "What I'm saying," she said, "is that if you need any help untangling the mess that

Aaron probably made, I'm happy to help. I've got the degree, and someone might as well get some use out of it."

"Uh." Ross hesitated, not sure what to say. It was a convenient offer. *Too* convenient? Yeah, Harmony had been working at several food trucks at the lot, almost since it had opened over a year ago, but what did anyone know about her? He'd trusted Aaron too. He'd been a friend and a partner.

And he'd betrayed him, just as easy as blinking.

There wasn't much left to steal, but Ross wasn't sure he could take the risk.

"You don't have to decide now," Harmony said, seemingly unconcerned by his hesitation. "I just thought . . . I wanted to work here because you need more than just a temp or a part-time employee. You're missing a partner in this business. And maybe I could help with that."

It wasn't even that presumptuous of an idea; he *did* need a new partner.

But under normal circumstances, before he'd been betrayed, he'd been slow to trust. And now? Ross wasn't sure he'd trust anyone, ever again.

He just didn't have it in him.

"I'll think about it," Ross said. He dusted the last tomato with the breadcrumbs and set it on the pan to cool and firm up.

Harmony's smile was bright, like she actually believed he would. "Great," she said.

It had been a weird day. Harmony had actually been everything she'd promised, and instead of relaxing him, it had set him on edge. And it was about to get even weirder.

Packing up his apartment had taken almost no time at all. He'd sold the couch early this morning, before he'd met Harmony at the truck, and the two guys who'd jumped at a free mattress had just finished hauling it away.

Balancing the last box on his arm, he locked the door, and as his old landlord had instructed, slid the key under it.

The rest of his crap was packed into a handful of boxes, crammed into his old, run-down hatchback. He rarely drove anymore, because the food truck lot had been so close to this building, and now he was moving even closer.

He found a spot on the street by the bar, and parked.

What he should do was take his stuff and go upstairs and well, for better or worse, make himself feel at home.

But it was Shaw's home, not his.

Moving in was always going to feel a little weird, and inevitably make him uncomfortable, he'd known that when he'd agreed to the plan. But it felt even worse to do it while Shaw wasn't even there.

He was still working at the bar, and would be for hours yet.

Ross knew it was a chance to settle in without Shaw looking over his shoulder, and he *should* take advantage of it. But instead, he took two quick trips up the stairs, typed in his code that Shaw had texted him earlier in the day, deposited the handful of boxes in the living room, and then went downstairs.

The bar was pretty quiet, Shaw cutting up lemons on a little plastic board, his knife slicing through them as confidently and quickly as he did everything else.

"Hey," Ross said as he approached. Shaw glanced up and smiled brightly at his appearance.

"Hey, roomie," Shaw said. "Everything okay?"

Nothing had really been okay for months, and despite the slight improvement of the situation, it still wasn't.

But Shaw didn't want to hear that.

"Yeah," Ross said, taking a seat at the barstool opposite him. "Everything's fine. Code worked. Got my stuff in."

"Good. I was worried when I saw you."

"Maybe I wanted to . . ." Wanted to *what?* Ross felt stupid. He never came into the bar. He especially never came in alone, and now this was the second night that he was spending here.

It seemed . . . but no. He did not enjoy Shaw's company. And if he did, it was only because he was one of the few people he knew who didn't seem to judge him either openly or deep down for what had happened with his ex-partner.

"You want a drink?" Shaw asked.

Ross hated the itchy uncomfortable feeling that was still residing between his shoulder blades. Like he'd encroached on Shaw's territory, despite the invitation.

"I'll have a beer," Ross said.

Shaw raised an eyebrow.

"I know I don't usually . . ." Ross started to say, hating that the awkwardness seemed to be expanding, exponentially. This was why he didn't *do* this. Why he lived alone. Why he didn't try to make friends. He always fucked it up, made it worse.

"You don't have to explain yourself, not to me," Shaw said. "I know I pour drinks for a living, but nobody *has* to drink. Not if they don't want to. And it's fine if they do. Whichever."

Maybe that was why Ross had agreed to do this at all. If he could figure out a way to trust it, Shaw's lack of judgment was refreshing, and he felt like he could *almost* relax in his presence.

Shaw rested his elbows on his side of the bar. "Well," he said, "what kind of beer do you like?"

"Something, I don't know, light and wheaty. Citrus notes, maybe."

Nodding in agreement, Shaw grabbed a glass and turned towards the taps, filling it with a few expert motions.

He set it in front of him. "You eat dinner?" Shaw asked. "I know you were moving and packing. That's hungry work. We've got a good special tonight, you might enjoy it."

Ross had never eaten anything from the Funky Cup's kitchen, though he knew that most of the guys from the lot thought the food was actually pretty good.

"Sure," Ross said, his stomach grumbling on cue, like it had just been waiting for someone to mention food. He realized the late lunch he'd scarfed down had been hours and hours ago, and Shaw was right. Moving *was* hungry work.

"Don't even want to know what it is?" Shaw wondered.

Ross took a sip of his beer. It was good. Perfect and crisp, with just a hint of citrus, exactly what he'd asked Shaw for.

Maybe living with someone who knew just what he liked, who looked like human fucking sunshine, who smiled at Ross all the time, even when he definitely didn't deserve it, might not be so bad after all.

"Naw," Ross said, "I'm not picky."

Shaw shot him a faux glare. "That's not what I hear."

"I . . ." Ross realized as the first word came out of his mouth that he'd begun to say *I trust you*, but he knew that wasn't true. *Couldn't* be true.

How could he trust Shaw? He barely even knew him.

"I hear you have a good kitchen," he said instead. "Even Tony thinks so."

Shaw practically fucking twinkled, his blue eyes sparkling in that handsome face. Though Ross didn't usually notice—or *care*—about that kind of thing, it was hard to miss.

He was focused; he wasn't *blind*.

"Trusting Tony now, huh?" Shaw teased. He'd gone over to the touchscreen and punched in a few buttons. "I bet he'd be surprised to hear that."

"Tony knows his shit," Ross acknowledged. That much *was* true.

Done putting in the order, Shaw leaned against the bar. "Two nights, and you're even eating here. I think you might have finally succumbed to the lure of the Funky Cup."

Ross had succumbed to the lure of something.

Or maybe even *someone*.

Not that he would ever admit that.

Shaw was brilliant and gorgeous and funny and charming and every single fucking thing that Ross wasn't and couldn't ever be. The only reason he'd even invited him to live with him for awhile was because he was way too fucking nice. That was all.

Ross reminded himself that he'd only come here because it had felt way too weird to climb up those stairs and hang out in *Shaw's* empty apartment. Because there was no way he could think of it as his.

"It's a great place." A place he'd never felt particularly comfortable, but then he and Shaw hadn't been what they were now, back then.

Shaw kept saying they were friends.

Maybe, since Ross typically didn't *have* friends, and the one true friend he'd thought he'd had ended up stealing everything from their business and then forcing Ash to set fire to his own food truck, he should trust Shaw on this one.

"Jackson wants to do it again," Shaw said.

"Do what again?"

Shaw gestured around the bar. "Do *this* again. Build another bar."

"Really?" Ross supposed he wasn't so surprised to hear it. Jackson was ambitious, and his business was clearly very successful. Why wouldn't he want to duplicate it?

"Yeah, I'm not a fan of the idea," Shaw said, sighing. "Why can't we just . . . I don't know . . . enjoy what we've got?"

"So it's Jackson's idea." Again, not much of a surprise there. Maybe Ross should tell Harmony that she'd be better off working here, even though she preferred food trucks.

Even though Ross clearly needed her way more than Jackson did.

"He used to be okay with that too, you know. The just *being* part."

This was what friends did, Ross was sure of it. The whole sharing thing. He just hoped that Shaw didn't expect him to share in return, because he was utter shit at it.

"What changed?" Ross asked. It wasn't hard to talk to Shaw because he made it so easy. Ross didn't have to wonder what he should ask, because it was clear that Shaw *wanted* him to.

"He met Alexis?" Shaw made a face. "No, no, that's not true. Alexis has actually *helped*, in some ways, because his existence reminds Jackson that he can't work twenty-four seven. But Alexis did get a second truck, and hire some more people, and all *that's* done is give Jackson ideas."

"Ideas?" Ross raised an eyebrow. He had ideas, too, but they were always of the "would this taste good with this?" or "what if I turned this into this?" variety. Never "what if we expanded our business" ideas.

"I think he..." Shaw hesitated, and then leaned closer. So much closer, right across the bar, until Ross could see the turquoise and baby blue and cerulean in his eyes. His fingers tightened around his glass. The booze wasn't numbing him or relaxing him the way he'd thought it might. Instead . . . well, Shaw seemed to be doing both at the same time. Relaxing him *and* impossibly making his heart race.

"I think he wants me to have something of my own," Shaw said softly, "and before he starts down that road, I wish he'd *ask* me first."

"I thought you owned this with your brother?" That was something he'd overheard Tony say, because it wasn't like Ross was actually close enough to the other guys to indulge in all the friendly gossip he knew floated around the lot. Frankly, he was a lot more likely to be the *subject* of the aforementioned gossip.

"We do own it together." Shaw straightened. "He owns fifty-one percent, our dad designed it that way so someone would actually be able to get shit done. He was afraid we'd argue all the time."

"But you don't." Ross didn't know either of them well enough to say for sure, but he'd never heard even a hint of disagreement between the brothers, and they both spent enough time around the food truck lot that even Ross would've picked up on it.

"No," Shaw admitted. "Never. Not really about anything important, anyway. Until this. But I think he wants me to have something of my own. So like, he'd keep this bar, and then I'd take the new one, or the other way around."

"You don't want to do that?"

Shaw shrugged. "I'm happy here. I'm happy bartending. I get a lot out of my job. And that's what it's supposed to be, right? We're supposed to be *happy* at our jobs? Would I like my job so much if I was the boss and I had to make all the decisions, and I wasn't behind the bar anymore, but telling everyone what to do? I don't know."

Ross realized that Shaw might not know, but *he* knew.

He knew exactly what that felt like, because Aaron's imprisonment had dumped all the things he hated about their business suddenly onto his own lap.

And it *sucked*.

"I haven't exactly been having a great time," Ross said.

Shaw looked surprised. Like he hadn't expected Ross to share. And that made sense, because Ross knew he wasn't exactly the sharing type.

"I didn't get a choice," Ross continued, before he could lose his nerve and shut up, "but if you have a choice, you should do what you love. That's . . . that's more than most people get. We're lucky."

"But what if I don't hate it? I don't know if I will or not. It seems . . . I don't know . . . kind of silly not to try."

"Listen," Ross said, finishing his beer in one long gulp. "If I could give it all back, I would. It doesn't make me any stronger or braver, or more accomplished or whatever. It just makes me want to throw something."

Shaw laughed, unexpectedly, his eyes brightening.

You did that, and you can do it all the time. Because *you live together now.*

Ross suddenly didn't know if that was a really great thing or the worst thing in the world.

"I'll have to remember to duck next time I come around," Shaw said. "Another beer? I'm gonna go grab your food."

"No, just a water, thanks," Ross said. In the end, what he felt wasn't the artificial chill of the booze in his veins but . . . something else. Something he could probably lay at Shaw's door.

Shaw removed his glass, replaced it with a full cup of water and ice, and then a moment later he was back, with a plate full of delicious-smelling food.

"Steak and mushroom hoagie, with horseradish aioli," Shaw said, depositing it in front of him, "and our famous sweet potato fries."

"They're famous?" Ross wondered, even as he realized he *had* heard people talking about them.

"According to our Yelp reviews," Shaw said. "Can I grab you anything else?"

Ross was about to ask for napkins, because the sandwich looked absolutely delicious but also *messy*, but then one appeared next to him, like Shaw had known he'd need it.

"I think I'm good, thanks," Ross said, and picked up the sandwich. It had a surprising heft to it, and he had to give Jackson and Shaw credit—they'd revamped the kitchen and the work they'd put in showed. When he took a bite, he was even more impressed, half a dozen flavors exploding across his tongue as he chewed spiced sliced steak working in perfect complement to the earthiness of the mushrooms. He tasted soy and ginger and garlic, and then the horseradish in the aioli. He was impressed. It wasn't the most unique flavor combo in the world, but the execution of it was pretty flawless.

"You're nodding over there," Shaw said, his voice teasing. "Is that a good or a bad thing?"

Ross finished chewing and swallowed. "Really good," he said. "I'm impressed."

"Wow," Shaw said, looking surprised. Too surprised.

"Am I really that notorious?" Ross asked, before he thought better of it. He ate a handful of sweet potato fries and they were really good too. "That picky?"

He didn't really want to hear the answer; he really didn't want to hear *Shaw's* answer.

"Not exactly notorious," Shaw said, returning to slicing his lemons.

"Then what exactly?"

Shaw sighed and put down the knife. It wasn't the standard kind of cheap knife that Ross had used to see in bars, when he'd actually *gone* to bars, but a nice Japanese blade, clearly very sharp.

"You're gonna get me in trouble," Shaw said with resignation.

"I am?"

Ross almost told him to forget it. After all, hearing the truth was probably not going to be all that enlightening and might actually make the next few months of living together uncomfortable.

Shaw smiled then, and it wasn't the same smile he gave to all the random guys at the bar. It was softer, sweeter, more genuine somehow. Ross had never seen it before, and it hit him somewhere deep, a place where he hadn't felt much of anything in years.

Maybe the last time had been when his grandmother had smiled at him, over pots and pans and pie dishes.

"You gotta know that you've got the best food at that whole lot," Shaw said. "Objectively. The other food there is *good*, don't get me wrong, but those guys? You know why they keep you at arm's length? They're all terrified of you, though they'd rather die than admit it. You're brilliant. You should be working in the best, the fanciest, the most expensive restaurants, and instead you've got this food truck and it's just amazing. Every time I go to Basket, I'm blown away."

Ross had gotten lots of compliments over the years. Most people who came to his food truck loved the food. He knew it was good. Knew because he worked so hard to make sure it was. He wouldn't ever dedicate something to his beloved grandmother, and then not make it the very best it could be.

"And," Shaw continued, leaning over, his blue eyes twinkling again, and Ross' breath caught in his throat, "you're gonna get me in trouble, because Jackson would have my ass for not thinking Alexis serves the best food on the lot."

Ross felt speechless. He was never good at responding to praise, but this felt like more than praise.

"Uh . . . sorry?" Ross stammered. Sure that after Shaw's effusive words, he'd be hurt and frustrated that Ross hadn't known how to respond.

But Shaw's smile didn't waver. "You should be," he said.

"Really, though." Ross cleared his throat. He didn't usually try, not anymore, not when it never seemed to work out the way he hoped it would, but it felt wrong not to try now. "Really, that's . . . well, I'm glad you enjoy the food."

"Even shit I think I'm not going to like, I love," Shaw said, shaking his head. "It's kinda annoying, you know?"

"You're teasing me," Ross said, finally figuring it out after he took another bite and swallowed.

Shaw's grin widened. "Yeah, yeah, I am." He hesitated. "Is that okay?"

"Nobody ever teases me," Ross said.

"I know. It's a damn shame. You get so serious, and you could use some shaking up sometimes."

"And you're gonna do it?" Ross had never liked being teased. It had always felt like he was the butt of a joke he didn't quite get. But with Shaw, it felt different. Like this time, he was *inside* the joke. A joke they shared together.

Maybe . . . maybe Shaw had been right after all, and they *were* kinda friends.

"Oh, I am," Shaw said. "I figure we're friends, right?"

It was like Shaw had been reading his mind.

"Yeah," Ross said. "Yeah, we are."

To Shaw's surprise, Ross didn't just stop by, he *stayed*.

It was a pretty quiet night at the bar. During midweek they usually closed by midnight, but tonight, Jackson emerged from his office around ten, and when he walked over to the bar, Shaw held his breath.

Was he going to say something to Ross, who was still sitting right there?

They'd been chatting on and off since he'd arrived at eight, whenever Shaw wasn't busy or serving.

"Hey," Jackson said, leaning against the bar, right next to where Ross sat. He turned towards Ross. "You get settled in okay?"

"Yeah," Ross said. Looking apprehensive. Shaw couldn't blame him. Aaron had done terrible things to Alexis' truck, and even though Alexis hadn't been all that bothered, Jackson had been furious.

That was love for you.

"I . . . I really appreciate you letting me stay for awhile," Ross said. Probably nobody else knew how much that cost the man, except maybe Shaw.

Jackson shrugged. "It was Shaw's call. It's his apartment."

"Still . . . this is your building, technically."

Jackson shot Shaw a look. Clearly he'd figured out that he'd been talking to Ross about their percentage arrangement—after all, not many people knew that they didn't split the business right down the middle.

"Well, you've been through a tough time. We're happy to help out."

It was the first time Jackson had actually acknowledged that. Shaw loved his brother; knew he had a really good heart buried underneath all the stubbornness. Was glad to finally see it in action.

"Yeah, well, it means a lot." Ross looked uncomfortable now. Like he did whenever anyone directly or even indirectly brought up Aaron or what he'd done to the food truck lot.

Jackson turned to Shaw. "You ready to close up?"

Shaw was surprised. "Really?"

"Yeah, you haven't had a customer in here in at least half an hour . . ." Jackson shot him a look that spoke volumes. Specifically, that he'd been so busy chatting away with Ross that he hadn't even noticed the lack of customers. "And the back patio just cleared out. Let's close up."

"Sounds good," Shaw said. He rarely got an evening off, even though it was past ten. This was even better, because he could help Ross get properly settled in.

The bar was already basically clean, but he did his last few closing tasks, and then he and Ross took off, Jackson telling them he'd lock up behind them, and went up the stairs to the apartment.

Ross pulled out his keys, opened the lock and then typed in his code.

There were some boxes piled in the corner.

"Haven't unpacked yet," Ross muttered under his breath. "Sorry about that."

"It's fine," Shaw said. He didn't mind a few boxes. "I'm actually gonna go take a shower, if that's alright."

"Sure." Ross looked uncomfortable, suddenly, and Shaw wondered what had happened to the disarming, relaxed guy he'd spent the last few hours with.

He reminded himself that this was awkward—maybe they were friends now, but it was still new, and all of a sudden, they were in each other's space. That wasn't easy, for anyone, and harder for Ross than most.

Hopefully, when he got out of a nice, long shower, Ross would've relaxed again.

Shaw watched as Ross bent down, his worn jeans clinging to a beautifully curved ass, and wished that he didn't find the man quite so delectable. It would've made everything a lot easier.

He didn't normally bother even closing the bathroom door—or bothering to wait to strip down until it was closed. But tonight, Shaw waited until the door was fully closed behind him before pulling his shirt off. He'd have to be a lot more careful about remembering that now someone, and someone he was attracted to, could be hanging around the apartment.

That would be a surefire way to make Ross even more uncomfortable.

Shaw flipped the shower on hot, and pulled his hair tie out, shaking out his hair. Jackson kept making fun of him for it, but he'd discovered that he liked growing it out, even though it was summer and it was definitely hotter to have it long than it was to wear it short.

He took his time showering, washing and conditioning his hair, only to remember too late, after he was already drying off, that he hadn't grabbed a change of clothes to bring into the bathroom.

He'd had roommates before, and they'd walked around in a towel, with nobody giving a shit. Surely he could do that now, just to duck into his own room and grab something to wear?

Shaw made sure the towel was wrapped securely around his waist, and shaking out his wet hair, opened the door.

Ross was sitting on the couch, watching something on his laptop, which . . . Shaw *had* told him he could use the TV, right? Maybe he hadn't said it explicitly but he'd made it clear that Ross was welcome.

He was just going to have to be a lot more direct.

"Hey," Shaw said, walking over to where Ross was sitting. "You can always play that on the TV if you want."

Ross glanced up and that was when Shaw remembered—way too late—that he'd only intended to take the few steps to his room, and put some clothes on.

Of the two brothers, Shaw had always felt like Jackson had gotten all the looks, but from the way Ross was looking at him, maybe that wasn't entirely true.

Shaw hadn't even thought Ross *could* look at someone like that.

But he was doing it now, his gaze glued to Shaw's bare chest, still a little damp from the shower, and then traveled lower, and then lower still, to where Shaw's hand was clamped around the edge of the towel.

"Uh," Ross said.

What had Shaw even come over here to say? His brain felt sluggish. Slow. Suddenly very, very stupid.

Maybe this idea, that had seemed like the perfect solution to everyone's problems, wasn't very perfect after all.

Especially if Ross was feeling even a fraction of what Shaw was.

"The TV," Shaw said, suddenly remembering. "You can watch it, if you want. I have one in my bedroom, or I can even um . . . put some clothes on and watch whatever you're watching?"

He was rarely at a loss for words, but Ross was still staring at him like he was the hottest thing he'd ever seen and it was drying up every intelligent thought he'd ever possessed.

Shaw looked at the laptop.

He didn't know what he'd expected to be on the screen.

Maybe some kind of food show. That seemed on brand for Ross.

Maybe an esoteric documentary.

But no, it was *Home Town* with the Napiers, and Erin was in the middle of trying to convince a couple that they really wanted to buy and remodel this one particular house.

It was a white cottage, with a proliferation of honeysuckle and hydrangea in the front beds. Shaw hadn't seen the other options, but he was with Erin on this one.

"You watch *Home Town*?" Shaw asked before he could come up with something a little less ridiculous to say.

"Yeah." Ross sounded defensive. "It's . . . it's good."

"Yeah, it is," Shaw said. "I'm gonna . . . well . . . go put something on. And maybe we could watch it on the TV together?"

Ross nodded wordlessly, already leaning forward to close his laptop but that brought him in a lot closer proximity to Shaw's bare stomach.

Shaw swore he could feel Ross' hair brush his skin and he swallowed reflexively.

Don't get hard, he told himself firmly, *don't you dare get hard.*

Ross straightened and their eyes met.

"I'll be . . . well, I'll be right back," Shaw said.

He prided himself on *not* walking any faster to his room but mostly that was because he was afraid the towel would shift lower and make things even more awkward.

Closing the door behind him, he took a deep breath.

That had been close, and Ross had been living with him for approximately an hour. He was just going to have to be a hell of a lot more careful in the future.

Or . . . Shaw thought, remembering the way Ross' expression had gone hungry in an instant . . . maybe a little less careful.

Maybe Ross was less asexual than he'd guessed.

Maybe he was just picky, like he was about his food.

Shaw threw on an old Riptide t-shirt, and a pair of thicker sweatpants than he usually wore in the summer. Hoping that maybe if Ross got that look in his eyes again, he'd have a bit more coverage than just a light towel.

When he emerged back into the living room, Ross had figured out how to flip on the TV and he was signing in to his Discovery Plus account.

"It's my guilty pleasure," Ross said apologetically.

"You don't have to explain yourself to me," Shaw said. He wasn't quite sure where to sit. There was a chair kitty-corner to the couch, but he'd never actually sat in it before. But the couch? That was technically Ross' *bed* now, and it felt rude to invite himself to share it, even though that was where he always sat.

"You like it too?" Ross wondered, settling back on the couch, as he clicked down to his list, and there, along with a handful of the not-surprising food shows, was *Home Town*.

"Yeah," Shaw said. "It's good, like you said, and well, they're damn cute together." He finally sat down in the chair. It was just as uncomfortable as it looked and he was realizing now why Jackson had been so eager to give it up.

"Couple goals," Ross said dryly.

Shaw smiled. "Did you just . . . no, I can't believe it. Ross, I think you just made a joke."

Ross rolled his eyes and glanced over at the cushion next to the one he was currently on. "Get your ass over here. That chair looks awful."

"It actually is," Shaw said. "I'm going to have to give Jackson crap for it."

"Jackson gave it to you?" Ross asked.

Shaw nodded and moved over, settling down on the couch. Leaving a careful foot or two of room between them. "You just tell me when you're ready to go to sleep," he said. He wouldn't have been so scrupulously careful about anyone else, but Ross was different. Maybe other people might think in a bad way, but Shaw liked him. He never made assumptions, and Shaw knew when Ross said something, he meant it.

"I will," Ross said. "Early prep day tomorrow. But we can watch an episode first. It . . . it relaxes me."

"You gonna tell me why you changed your mind?" Shaw asked, suddenly realizing that he'd never asked.

"I hired someone, someone who can really help this time," Ross said. "Her name's Harmony. We're meeting early tomorrow. I'm teaching her how to use the smoker."

Before Shaw could overthink it, he reached over and patted Ross on the knee. "Glad you got yourself some decent help," he said.

Ross didn't look over, just hit play on the episode. "Couldn't have done it without you," he said quietly. Meaningfully.

Shaw dug his fingers into his sweatpant-clad thigh and told himself not to do something terribly stupid like reach over and pull the guy into a hug.

Ross wasn't exactly the hugging type.

But maybe he was wrong, Shaw realized. He'd never asked him.

Maybe Ross was different, deep down, than anyone had realized.

CHAPTER FIVE

Ross felt like there was something itching at him, just under his skin—but no matter what he did, he couldn't seem to scratch it.

And even worse, he couldn't figure out what was causing it.

In the last week, the truck was doing better than ever with Harmony. She hadn't brought up her suggestion again that she could help with the business side of things, which Ross was relieved about, and she'd proven to be just as good as she'd promised. She was quick and efficient and an excellent cook—and even more reassuringly, she was freaking great with customers. Way better than he was, and possibly even better than Aaron had been.

He was beyond relieved that he'd hired her. Sales were strong, and in the last week, he'd actually begun to pay down some of the debt he owed to his vendors.

As for his living situation . . . well, it was different than he'd expected.

Maybe the itch, right between his shoulder blades, had something to do with that.

Shaw and his quick smiles and his sweet eyes and all that stupid hair.

His willingness to hang out, even though he was clearly tired from working.

Their evenings watching an episode or two of *Home Town* had become the norm. Now Shaw took his shower and flopped down on the couch without an invitation.

Nothing usually relaxed him the way watching Erin and Ben bicker back and forth over tile and exposed brick did, but after they watched an episode and Shaw retreated to his bedroom, Ross would often just lie there on the couch and wonder why he couldn't fall asleep.

Why was he still so goddamned tense?

"I'm just about finished cleaning up," Harmony said as she approached him. He was supposed to be cleaning out the smoker, after it had run most of the day, but instead he'd been thinking, staring off into space.

Something completely unlike him.

He waved her off. "Go ahead and clock out when you're done," he said. "I've got a bit more on this." *A bit more?* He'd barely started the necessary cleaning job, but he didn't want to admit that. Especially because she'd probably ask him why, and then want him to talk about it.

He didn't know what to say if she asked, and even if he could figure it out, he knew he *definitely* didn't want to talk about it, so instead he said nothing.

"You sure?" Harmony looked critically at the smoker. He'd taught her only three days ago how to assemble, dissemble, and clean the thing, which had seen better days, and clearly she'd remembered how much work went into it.

"Yeah," Ross said with a nod. "I'll be fine."

"If you're sure," Harmony said, not looking like she wanted to leave him with all that work to do.

"I'm sure," Ross said. "The music's good. Hang out for a bit."

"Rach said it was," Harmony said, referring to her girl-friend—who also happened to be Tate's sister. "I'll see you to-morrow."

He watched her go, and returned his attention to the smoker.

He'd just begun to scrape off some of the caked-on smoke and fat from the inside cover when another voice interrupted him.

"That thing looks about a use and a half away from implod-ing," Tony said as he wandered over.

Ross shot him a glare. He knew he was here, *still*, out of Tony's good graces, and they'd mostly put the antagonism of the past behind them, but then he came over and said something like that.

Like Ross could ever fucking forget that four months ago, his partner and friend had forced Ash to blow up his own food truck.

That wasn't something a person was likely to forget.

"Oh," Tony said, coming to a stop right next to the smoker. He actually sounded contrite, unusually so for Tony. "That was probably too soon, wasn't it?"

"And here I thought I was the only one who was shit at reading the room," Ross muttered.

"No, I'm . . . well, I'm a real dumbass," Tony said apologetically. "Sorry. I just meant, wow I can't believe that thing is still going. You must be the smoker whisperer."

"Still going and still cranking out really tasty pork and turkey," Ross said, trying to temper the anger—and the hurt—in his words. Tony clearly hadn't meant to upset him. The problem was, Aaron's ghost still seemed to follow him around, no matter what he did to try to banish it.

Tony wasn't the only one who'd said something. It felt like not even a day went by that someone didn't mention the incident in passing.

It *had* been wild. Ash was lucky he hadn't been hurt or killed.

Ross knew Ash had hoped that by working with him while he was waiting for his new truck to be built that people might accept that everything was good between them. That Ash didn't blame Ross at all for what had happened.

It had helped, Ross was sure of it, but it hadn't solved everything.

"I heard you hired Harmony full-time," Tony said, leaning against the side of Ross' truck. "How's that workin' out for you?"

Ross already knew that although Tony acted like he'd just been walking by and stopped to chat, he'd actually come here with a purpose.

To ask about Harmony? Maybe. Possibly because he'd heard about the change in Ross' living situation, and since he was the biggest gossip on the lot, to confirm it.

"She's great," Ross said, "but you already know that."

"Yeah," Tony said, chuckling ruefully under his breath. "I tried to hire her for our truck, but she said she wasn't interested in just any job. Guess yours was the one she wanted."

"It was a good call. We work well together."

He'd discovered how smart and perceptive she was. Even though they'd only worked together for a week now, she often knew just what he needed, before he had to ask.

And he'd come to realize, over the last week, that she *had* thought about this ahead of time. She'd done her research. Found the truck that probably best suited her. Even the rumors swirling around Ross hadn't stopped her from approaching him.

It made him like her even more.

"And," Tony said, and here it came, Ross thought darkly, "I heard another rumor."

"Did you?" Ross retorted dryly. "I can't imagine what it might be."

"I heard you moved in with Shaw, above the bar."

"Yeah." Ross hesitated, scraping along the side of the smoker, where the deposits were the worst. He cleaned off the metal paint scraper he used, and then went back again. "And?"

"You what . . . hookin' up with Shaw now?"

Ross rolled his eyes. "Everything about sex to you, Tony?"

"No," Tony squawked. "No, no, I just . . . I didn't even realize you two knew each other. I was just surprised."

"He's a friend," Ross said, without even the slightest hesitation. If he hadn't believed it before this week, the last few days had cemented it.

"Well, you're not the only one who keeps your shit locked down tight," Tony said.

"You're just disappointed you didn't hear about it first," Ross said.

Tony laughed. "Yeah, that's probably true."

"Imagine how good your tacos could be if you spent half that energy working on improving them," Ross said.

"Hey, now," Tony said, still laughing. "Peace, okay, brother?"

Ross shot him a look. "Yeah, yeah, *pax*."

"I just wandered over 'cause I wanted to know if you were up for a drink later with Lucas and me. Seeing as you're headed that direction, anyway."

Ross hadn't been back to the Funky Cup itself since the first night he'd moved in. He hadn't wanted to seem like he was imposing on Shaw or his time while he was working, and if he wanted to see the man or talk to him, he could always do it when he walked in the door to the apartment.

But . . . he was still all itchy. He could use a drink, maybe. One of those Shirley Temples Shaw had made him, except with a shot of something stronger.

He needed to figure out how to fucking relax, and while he usually liked to do it without alcohol, maybe it was time to resort to it.

Sleep—blissful, thoughtless sleep. That was what he needed.

He was even willing to share a drink with Tony to get it.

"Hey, you coming?" Lucas, dressed in cutoff shorts and a loose tank, in deference to the heat, approached.

"Yeah," Tony said, "I just wanted to invite Ross here. Thought he could use some company."

"And a drink," Ross added.

Lucas looked surprised. "I haven't seen you much down at the Funky Cup," he said.

Despite Ross' feelings about Tony, he'd always liked Tony's boyfriend, Lucas. He was chill and down to earth, and at least if he did gossip, he gossiped less than Tony did.

Not that that was saying much.

"Yeah, I've been a little busy," Ross muttered.

"No kidding," Lucas said. "But I heard you've hired Harmony. She's gonna make your life a hell of a lot easier."

"Already has," Ross said. He finished scraping out the inside of the smoker. Did his spray down with the bottle of lemon juice-based cleaner—completely safe and completely biodegradable. He'd come up with the recipe himself, because he hadn't felt safe cleaning the smoker with anything commercial, and he hadn't felt safe *not* cleaning it either.

"That's great," Lucas said, sounding like he truly meant it.

"Actually," Ross said, "I kinda think she hired *me*."

Lucas grinned and gave him a friendly pat on the shoulder. "Hey, she might have. She's that smart."

"Let me just finish this up real quick, and I'll meet you down there," Ross said.

"Need help with anything?" Tony asked.

"Nope, just got to lock up," Ross said. "You'll only have a few minutes' head start."

"Sounds good. See ya down there," Lucas said, patting him again.

He and Tony wandered off together, Lucas reaching and taking Tony's hand.

Lots of people considered them the cutest couple they knew, but while he found their solid relationship good for the lot, as their two trucks were the foundation on which it was built, he wasn't sure he really envied them the way so many others did.

Maybe it wouldn't be so bad, finding himself in a relationship, Ross supposed as he dug through the storage bin of spare clothes he kept in the truck. He threw on a new shirt to replace his old, smelly one. Nobody ever wanted to be around him when he'd been cleaning the smoker—and Ross wasn't sure he blamed them. He could've changed at the apartment, but he had spares here, for exactly this reason, and he might as well take advantage.

But a relationship like Lucas and Tony's? It required the right ingredients. The right marinating and the right cooking time. It didn't just *happen*. And Ross had never found himself in a position with the kind of person he'd even remotely be interested in exploring any of that with.

It wasn't that he was *against* relationships—despite all the gossip to the contrary—but bad ones were time- and energy-consuming and he wasn't willing to give up either of those. They were precious resources, and now that Aaron was gone, he had even fewer of each.

He walked to the bar at a brisk pace, checking his phone as he walked, making sure that Harmony had clocked in and out properly. Not that he ever had to worry about that. So far, a week in, and he had yet to find a real fault with her, if he didn't count how pushy she'd been about helping him with the other aspects of the business. Satisfied, he shoved his phone into his pocket, and pushed the door to the Funky Cup open.

Shaw was at the bar, just as he'd expected, and even though he was busy with a big group, hands moving with that expected quick efficiency, he glanced up at the sound of the door opening and their eyes met.

For a second, it was like the whole bar faded away, the noises, the people, the clink of the glasses. Even Shaw's hands froze, wrapped around a bottle of rum.

Suddenly, that damn itch was back, right between his shoulder blades.

He turned away, breaking the moment, and he hoped, pushing it from his mind, but it was hard to deny. That feeling, the one he hadn't quite been able to kick, it must have something to do with Shaw.

He should've headed right to the bar, to order a drink, but something stopped him.

That itch?

Ross wasn't quite sure, but whatever that uncertain feeling was, it carried him away from the bar, and across the room, out the back door, to the patio and its firepits, where he knew Tony and Lucas liked to hang out.

They were already there, with beers in their hands.

"You said you wanted a drink," Lucas teased softly, as he sat down with them. "But you're empty-handed."

"Uh," Ross said. He hadn't anticipated the question.

"It's all good," Tony said, raising a hand and Chelle, who often waitressed outside, walked over.

"What can I get you guys?" she asked.

"Order of sweet potato fries, extra chipotle mayo, and whatever Ross here wants," Tony said. He turned to Ross. "A beer? I'm actually not sure what you like to drink."

Ross unstuck his tongue. "One of those . . . um . . ." Ordering this particular drink in front of Tony felt weird, but he hoped, despite Tony's general *Tonyness*, that he wouldn't make it any weirder. "Shirley Temples," he said, "but with a shot of vodka. Shaw, he'll know what I like."

"Sure thing," she said with a smile.

"Shaw knows what you like, huh?" Tony teased as soon as Chelle took down the order and walked away.

It wasn't optimal; Ross almost wished that he'd asked about the Shirley Temple, instead of the rest of the order.

"We do live together now," Ross retorted. Hoping—no, *praying*—that would be the end of it.

"Right, right," Tony mused. "I'd forgotten."

Lucas nudged him. "I doubt that."

"Hey!" Tony exclaimed in outrage. "I am not *that* bad. Ross here said they were friends, and I believe him."

"Shaw's a good guy," Ross said. "I needed the help . . . and well, he wouldn't let me say no."

"You could've asked us," Lucas said seriously.

He could have. It would have been easier to go to Lucas than to deal with Tony.

"Honestly, it never occurred to me to ask *anyone*," Ross said wryly. "I didn't ask Shaw, he approached me."

"He is pretty observant. Bartending skill, I guess," Tony admitted.

"I'm not sure his brother's very happy with him," Ross said. He hadn't really *meant* to say it, to even vaguely allude to the incident with Aaron.

Usually he got annoyed if anyone else did, and here he was, bringing it up on his own.

It was that goddamn itch, Ross decided, it was making him crazy.

Making him do insane shit that he never would otherwise.

Including confessing all sorts of things to Tony and Lucas.

They're your friends too, a voice inside of him said. It sounded annoyingly like Shaw's. *Even though you'd try to deny it.*

"Jackson will get over himself," Lucas said. "He's annoyingly overprotective. If Alexis hears even a hint of it, he's gonna be pissed."

"Alexis has every reason to be pissed at me, too," Ross said.

Tony looked shocked. Lucas' eyes widened.

Yeah, okay, he didn't really talk about it. He *never* brought it up.

What was there to say? *Sorry? My partner went insane and decided to turn Ash's food truck into a raging inferno?*

It never did any good, so he didn't.

But before either of them could answer, Chelle was back with his drink, setting it down in front of him.

There were four cherries bobbing in it, and a single sliver of lime.

"I think Shaw *does* like you," Tony complained. "I never get any fucking cherries."

"You also don't order Shirley Temples," Lucas teased him.

"Truth," Tony conceded. "But I think that might be changing."

"Honestly," Lucas said gently, turning towards Ross, "Alexis doesn't have any issues with you. And Jackson shouldn't either."

"Yeah, seriously," Tony echoed. "And if they *do*, you come and tell me. I'll straighten their asses out."

Ross shot him a look, picking up his drink and stirring it, before taking a sip. It was perfect, especially with the vodka addition.

Maybe Shaw did really know him well.

Better than he wanted to admit to, anyway. Especially to Tony, who was like a one-man gossip show.

"Ross is never going to come whining to you, Tony," Lucas pointed out. "You know that."

"No kidding," Ross said. He had his pride, didn't he? And Tony had been angry with him over Aaron's pilfered onion dip recipe.

Maybe . . . they'd buried the hatchet, likely under the burnt remains of Ash's food truck, but maybe he should tell him the truth of the onion dip recipe.

Someday, anyway.

He had enough shit on his plate right now, thank you very much.

"You need to work on that," Tony said.

"Work on what?"

The itch was still there.

Ross took another long drink. Could feel the vodka begin to settle into his system. But the itch hadn't gone away. In fact, it felt like it was even stronger than it had been before.

He felt like he was going out of his mind, and Tony was not fucking helping.

"This whole prickly and alone act," Tony said, gesturing.

"Yeah, no," Ross said.

Lots of people had assumed over the years that he was fixable. But Ross knew the truth. This was who he was. He couldn't change; at this point, he wasn't even sure he wanted to.

"Just . . . think about it, okay?" Lucas inserted. "I'm real glad Shaw helped you out, but we're here for you too."

It was easier to nod than to keep arguing. If his whole life hadn't been right on the brink of falling apart . . . if it had just been something minor and silly, like a busted appliance or a late delivery or running out of onions, he might've gone to Lucas. Or even to Tony.

Tony, as infuriating as he was, *could* be a professional. Ross wouldn't have ever agreed to join the food truck lot otherwise.

Chelle showed up then with the sweet potato fries, and for the next few minutes, Tony shifted into small talk—well, his version of small talk, peppered with little bits of gossip.

Ross wasn't particularly interested in gossip, so he half-listened as he chewed sweet potato fries dipped in the bar's famous chipotle aioli, and tried to figure out how they got the fries so crisp.

He'd experimented with sweet potato fries a few years back, and hadn't ever been able to make them anything but ultimately kind of soggy, and in Ross' opinion, unpleasant.

But the Funky Cup's were crisp and perfect, even the dregs at the bottom of the basket.

He asked Lucas what he thought—the man was obsessive about vegetables in a way that Ross admired—and Lucas just shrugged.

"Don't let him fool you," Tony said. "He's been trying to wheedle the secret out of Jose forever."

"Who's Jose?"

"He runs the kitchen here," Lucas said. "He's a good friend. But no dice. He usually just laughs at me."

"Maybe you could ask Shaw," Tony wondered. "After all, you're living with him now. That makes you practically family."

"We're not family." Ross found that he was actually sort of outraged at that assumption. Yes, Shaw and Jackson ran the bar together and *they* were family, but Ross was just living above the bar, with Shaw. That didn't mean . . . they *definitely* were not related.

Ross was afraid he was beginning to understand exactly what this infernal itch was—and what it meant.

He downed the rest of his drink and stood.

"Where are you going?" Lucas asked. "It's still early."

"Work to do," Ross said. He never lied . . . but it wasn't like he could tell the truth now, could he?

Even if he was in a confessing kind of mood, the last person he'd tell was sitting right next to Lucas. Everyone would know then, and Ross would be humiliated.

"Really, you're gonna work? It's after ten." Tony sounded surprised.

"I don't have a brother or a partner anymore," Ross pointed out, a little more snarkily than Tony likely deserved. "Shit needs done." He pulled out his wallet to pay for his drink, but Tony shook his head.

"We've got it," Tony said.

"Thanks," Ross said, a little embarrassed and also annoyingly grateful.

Yes, Tony was a pain in the ass, but Ross had come to know him enough to believe his heart was in the right place.

Asking Tony to help his *Tonyness* would be like asking Ross to be friendly and sociable. It wasn't ever going to happen.

"Well, we'll see you around," Lucas said, and stood too, patting him again on the shoulder. Ross wasn't used to being touched so much, and he didn't think he'd like it.

Well, he didn't *hate* it.

He refused to think how he'd feel about it if it wasn't Lucas doing the touching. If it was . . . for example . . . someone who worked as a bartender. Who was just inside the bar . . . who, in a few hours, would climb the stairs up to their apartment and give Ross that sweet smile, a little tired around the edges.

"Yeah," Ross said.

"I'm gonna go grab us some more beers," Lucas said to Tony, who nodded.

Ross hesitated, just about to turn to leave.

"Hey," he said, "really, thanks for the drink."

"Of course, anytime," Tony said. "There's more to life than work, you know."

Ross had never found that sentiment to be particularly true, but he'd always wondered at people who could live like that. Balanced, and all that shit.

He supposed that to do it, he'd have to find someone he wanted to spend all that extra time with.

He sure as hell didn't want to spend it with his own miserable company.

But watching at the look Tony gave his boyfriend as he walked off towards the bar, it was undeniable that *they'd* found it.

Found it and nurtured it.

Ross wasn't envious, not exactly, but he was more than a little baffled by it.

It was just like the Funky Cup's sweet potato fries, he thought, as he went out through the patio's side door, he appreciated the way they tasted, and the crispness of them, and he wanted to know how that was done. Even if he didn't think he'd ever put them on his own menu.

He was curious anyway.

That was the itch, he realized as he climbed the stairs up to the apartment. It was curiosity.

Curiosity was easy enough to satisfy, you just had to indulge it a little. He knew that much.

Once he was inside, he shut the door behind him, and pulling out his wallet and his phone, he dropped them on the coffee table with his keys next to his laptop and headed straight for the bathroom.

Ross knew Shaw wouldn't be off for hours yet, but he wasn't stupid. He locked the door anyway, because he definitely didn't want to be interrupted.

Especially not by the man currently on his mind.

Flipping the shower on, he made sure it was hot. He knew the rudimentary elements, even if he didn't do this very often. Even when he'd lived by himself, he'd rarely indulged.

But clearly, he hadn't been doing enough of this lately, if suddenly he was all itchy and curious about Shaw Finley.

He stripped down, leaving his dirty clothes in a pile on the floor, and got into the shower.

It smelled like lemons, like the shampoo that he'd discovered Shaw used, and the soap in the dish had herbs in it, and as a result it smelled like Shaw did. He'd already squeezed his eyes shut, stepping under the hot spray, but the color of tiles, nearly a perfect match for Shaw's gaze, was already imprinted on his consciousness. It was easy to believe he was right here, staring at him.

See, Ross told himself, *this isn't that hard after all.*

When he reached down, wrapping his hand around his dick, he discovered that he was. Hard as a rock.

Well, he corrected wryly, *actually it is.*

It wasn't even that tough to let his mind, usually uncooperative about this kind of thing, sink right into the fantasy of it. He'd open his eyes and Shaw would be there, would've snuck into the shower without a noise. He could be quiet on his feet like that. Water would cascade down his bare chest, surprisingly tan for someone who spent so much time indoors, down his taut stomach, and then lower still, *yeah*, Ross thought, *he was hard, too.*

Ross' hand loosened its grip on his dick, the pleasure momentarily overwhelming him. It felt good. It felt too good. He often got overwhelmed by that maddening rush of pleasure, which was why he didn't do this that often.

But the looser grip, just barely sliding over the head and then down lower, and then back up again, in a slow careful motion, it helped. And Ross' mind, without any prompting whatsoever, continued with the fantasy.

Shaw was there, with those powerful forearms, tanned and corded with muscle, reaching out for him. He'd curl his fingers just right around his cock, like he knew too much pleasure scared Ross. Made him uneasy.

But the pleasure was coming hot and heavy now, rocketing through him, and Ross didn't even flinch, just wanted more of what Shaw was giving him.

Shaw came closer then, closer than even Lucas had been. Ross could see every color in those incredible eyes, wide and bright and so fucking kind, they usually felt like a balm but right now they were more like lighter fluid, setting him on fire.

He leaned forward just a bit, brushing his lips against Ross'. Carefully. Softly. Like he didn't want to spook him, even as he continued to slowly jerk him off. Like he really *knew* that all the sex that Ross had had in his life had been painfully impersonal. That usually that was how he liked it, when he wanted it at all.

But this was undeniably personal now, with the kissing, and Ross realized he liked it. Slid his hand up, around Shaw's neck, and tugged him closer, so they could kiss deeper. Shaw's tongue slid over his own, wicked and sexier than Ross could even imagine, and faintly, like it was an echo of the fantasy, Ross' cock twitched in his hand. He was getting close, he realized.

Usually it took two or three attempts to reach orgasm before he actually did. The climb overwhelmed him and it took a long time, usually, for him to actually get crazy horny enough to let go, and just enjoy it. Most guys, thinking they were in for a quick, dirty hookup, got annoyed with Ross, thus why he hadn't been with anyone in years.

But Shaw was patient and sweet and the way he was curling his fingers over the head of his cock, coaxing him along, had him riding that razor edge, almost before he realized he was.

Shaw pulled back, just a fraction, breaking the kiss, and the way he licked his lips, like he couldn't quite get enough, like Ross had set *him* on fire the same way he'd so effortlessly set Ross alight, that was it.

Ross came hard, sparks exploding through his mind, the pleasure overwhelming, his fingers coaxing out the last bits of his orgasm. All the evidence was gone in a second, washed down the drain.

He glanced down at his softening dick, still in his hand. Had that just happened? *How* had that just happened? He'd never jerked off in a way that he'd call "normal" in his whole fucking life.

And just the *thought* of Shaw had coaxed him right through.

The problem with this was that instead of satisfying that itch, all he felt was itchier as he finished showering and got out, drying off with one of Shaw's towels.

He dressed quickly, in shorts and a worn-out tank top, and lay back on the couch. He didn't want to watch *Home Town*. There was already too much noise in his brain.

He really didn't want to wait for Shaw to come home and watch an episode with him.

He wasn't sure he was going to even be able to look Shaw in the eye after this. He'd only done it because he'd been *so* fucking sure that doing it would get the man out of his system and calm the itch.

Except the opposite had happened.

He already knew that the moment Shaw walked in the front door, the itch would not only be back, but it'd be back in spades.

He'd *want* him.

Ross hated admitting it, but that was the truth, wasn't it? And he'd never let himself hide from the truth. He might hide it from the world, but he always faced things, inside.

"Shit," he said out loud.

It was absolutely the coward's way out, but he got up then and turned all the lights off, and then lay down on his makeshift bed, the couch, and prayed that maybe sleep might take him before Shaw came home and things got *really* awkward.

CHAPTER SIX

WHEN SHAW PUSHED THE front door open, it was just after one in the morning—not horrible for a Thursday night, but not great either—and he was nearly about to call out to Ross, to ask him to get the episode of *Home Town* cued up before he realized that it was dark.

Pitch black kind of dark. All-the-lights-off kind of dark.

And there was the shape of Ross on the couch. Sleeping.

It was the first time in a week that he'd come home and Ross hadn't wanted to hang out. Hadn't *assumed* it, in that quiet, hopeful way of his.

This is fine, he's probably exhausted from keeping your brand of crazy hours, Shaw told himself, and crept quietly towards the bathroom, wanting to shower the stink of the night's work off before falling into bed.

He kept telling himself as he showered that none of this meant anything. No doubt Ross was tired. That's all. But it felt pointed . . . and weird.

Not the same kind of weird that some of his interactions with Ross felt; this was different.

Ross had never deliberately avoided him, and as much as Shaw tried to convince himself that it wasn't avoidance, it was just life, and probably exhaustion catching up with him, he couldn't push the thought from his head.

He changed into a pair of loose sleep shorts—he'd learned to make *sure* he had a change of clothes, whenever he stripped in the bathroom—and decided that since Ross was asleep, it was overkill to throw on his shirt. After all, he was just going to take it off again to sleep.

He crept into the dark kitchen, trying to decide what he was craving. It was something sweet, probably, he thought, opening the fridge a crack. He was debating pouring himself a glass of the orange juice he kept around on the off chance he might cook himself breakfast one late morning, and then retreating to his room, when he heard a noise coming from the direction of the couch.

There was rustling, and breathing, and *oh*, now that he was really listening, it didn't sound like Ross was sleeping after all.

He was trying to *pretend* like he was sleeping.

Hurt speared through Shaw.

It had been a lot easier to ignore when he'd been trying to convince himself Ross was just tired.

His fingers tightened around the orange juice, yanking it out of the fridge with a lot more force than was really necessary, half-slamming it on the counter. He opened a cupboard for a glass and then let it close shut without dampening the noise, like he might have done if Ross was *actually* sleeping.

Ross sat up then, because he must have realized that Shaw knew he wasn't asleep.

"Hey," Shaw said shortly. "Want some orange juice?"

Ross shook his head. But instead of staying put, he got up, venturing into the kitchen, and when Shaw opened the fridge to return the orange juice, he reached in too and grabbed a bottle of water.

Shaw watched, his face barely visible, the night light in the bathroom illuminating it *just* enough to see, as Ross didn't really open the water, just twisted the cap back and forth.

"Everything okay?" Shaw asked.

He didn't think he'd done anything to bother Ross; how could he? They hadn't spoken today, and last night, when they'd gone to bed, everything had felt fine.

Ross didn't say anything, just kept twisting that cap off and on, his shape a dark blob against the counter.

It occurred to Shaw then, in the middle of that awkward, uncomfortable silence, that other people might be angry and not hurt, like he was.

Maybe Ross was bracing himself for that anger.

"Hey," Shaw said, reaching out and finding Ross' forearm in the dark. Squeezing it reassuringly. "Hey, you can talk to me, okay?"

Shaw swore he saw hesitation in Ross' face, nearly hidden in the dark shadows.

"Seriously," Shaw continued. "What's up? Talk to me, man."

"I . . . I feel weird," Ross finally said. "I . . . I think I fucked this up."

Ross' words shouldn't have surprised him, but they did.

"What? No? You didn't mess anything up. What's weird?"

Ross shot him a very clear and obvious look of exasperation, evident even in the dark. "You've been nice to me and I've . . . I'm . . ."

"You're what?"

Ross made a huff of frustration. "I'm . . . you're too nice, you know that?"

Shaw grinned. "Should I apologize for being too nice?"

"For being too nice and too charming and too . . ." Ross growled, practically.

Shaw shouldn't have found Ross' irritation so sexy, but if he kept making those noises . . . it was going to be impossible not to.

"Too?" Shaw wondered.

Ross turned, his face only partially in view now, though Shaw could barely see it at all, considering how dark it was. "How . . . well, you know you're attractive," Ross muttered. "That's not news."

It wasn't. But it was fucking news that *Ross* thought he was.

"Oh," Shaw said. A little speechless, like the word *attractive* had just punched right through Shaw's stomach.

"Yeah." Ross sounded depressed and angry. Like maybe that realization *had* ruined everything.

"Hey," Shaw said, reaching out for him again. Ross reared back, and the panic in his face had Shaw dropping his hand. "Hey," he repeated. "It's totally cool. We both . . . well, we're both in a small space together, and we're not used to having other people in it. I'm . . ." He hadn't ever intended to confess this, because he'd categorically believed that Ross couldn't be interested. But Ross had been honest about his own attraction. Whatever that meant. Maybe he should know Shaw felt the same way.

Shaw took a deep breath. "I think you're attractive, too."

If Ross had looked shocked before, he looked downright floored now.

"What?" he squawked.

"Yeah," Shaw repeated, nodding. "Yeah, but you know what? You're clearly . . . uncomfortable about it. So don't worry about it. We don't have to . . ." He cleared his throat. "Nothing has to happen. Nothing that you don't want. We can be friends. I like being your friend."

Ross still looked astounded. "You do?"

"Yeah, I do," Shaw said. This time when he reached out for Ross, he didn't shy away, he let Shaw pat his shoulder. And then this time Shaw was the shocked one, because Ross shifted his weight, and leaned in closer, and suddenly they were embracing. Quickly. Not for long. But for long enough that Shaw felt the indelible impression of Ross' big, strong body against his.

Why didn't you put a shirt on? Shaw wondered.

Because you didn't know that this was going to happen. This wasn't even on your freaking radar.

He was glad he'd at least put shorts on. Not if he got an erection that the loose, light material was going to do much to camouflage it.

The hug ended almost as soon as it had begun, Ross shuffling off a few feet, not really meeting Shaw's eyes.

Shaw watched as Ross swallowed hard, his Adam's apple bobbing. "Did you really mean that?"

"Mean what?" It had just been a hug, a bare fleeting thing, but the lack of blood in his brain was impressive. If things ever went further than this, Shaw was afraid of what he might be capable of.

"Mean that we can . . . that we can still be friends." Ross looked really concerned about this.

"If that's all that ever happens," Shaw said, meaning it, "I'm happy to be your friend, Ross."

Ross finally opened up the water bottle and took a quick, short drink. Like he needed something to do with his hands.

"Really? Why?"

It was impossible not to roll his eyes. "You've got a great sense of humor. You're fun to hang out with. You're honest about stuff. You came out and told me the truth tonight, even though I know it was probably hard for you."

"I couldn't lie." Ross' voice was paper dry. "I tried that and it . . . well, I'm shitty at lying."

"See? That's one of the things I like about you. I know you aren't going to bullshit me."

Ross didn't look completely convinced. "Trust me, that hasn't been my experience so far."

"That people don't like you being honest?" Shaw took a drink of his orange juice. "I can see that. Most people are terrified of hearing the truth."

"Yep." Ross sounded darkly amused. "But not you, apparently."

"It's better to know than to be lied to," Shaw said. "So yeah, I do like your honesty. And you're just a neat, chill, very talented guy. I'm glad we're friends."

"I'm . . ." Ross hesitated. "I'm glad too."

"Good." Shaw gave him another quick pat. Resisted the urge to pull him into another longer hug, because that might make Ross think that he was pressuring him for more. Wanting to turn their relationship romantic—or sexual.

And he definitely would not mind if that happened, but Ross was so edgy and uncomfortable about it—clearly he was not used to having those kind of relationships, or those kind of *thoughts*—that Shaw intended for any movement in that direction to be made by Ross himself.

He could be patient. It might give him some bluish balls, but it wouldn't kill him. And if he won Ross over in the end? Shaw couldn't help but think how amazing and satisfying that would feel.

Of course, if they stayed friends, that would still feel pretty dang amazing. Just wouldn't be quite as satisfying.

"I'm gonna . . ." Ross gestured to the couch. "Gonna actually sleep now, I think."

Shaw was gonna go take another shower, and *then* maybe he could sleep. Right now he felt keyed up, both in the best possible ways and also in the worst.

"Okay, well, goodnight," Shaw said. He finished his orange juice and rinsed the glass, sticking it in the sink.

Ross shot him a look and reached over, fingertips practically brushing Shaw's bare stomach, causing goose bumps to break across every inch of his skin. "How hard is it to put the glass in the dishwasher?" he asked, almost under his breath, like he was talking to himself and not to Shaw. "It's *right there.*"

Shaw threw back his head and laughed. Laughed like he would never stop. Couldn't ever stop.

"That right there," he said between gasps of laughter, "that's why we're friends."

Ross, putting the glass in the dishwasher, looked up afterwards, like he'd grown a second head. "What? Me lecturing you about glasses in the sink does it for you?"

Shaw shook his head, amused even though maybe he shouldn't be. Definitely charmed, despite everything. "Apparently."

"I hate to say this," Ross said, "because usually it's what people say about me, but that's weird, Shaw."

"Yeah, yeah, I know." Shaw couldn't help it. He chuckled again, under his breath.

And when he lay down in his bed, he was still smiling.

After Ross had broken down and been more honest with Shaw than he'd thought he *could* be, the itch hadn't gone away. But it was still more bearable than it had been before.

He hadn't been sure if, in the daylight, things would be awkward between him and Shaw now, but Ross hadn't been able to lie.

He'd always been shitty at lying, but lying to Shaw had felt even worse. Ross had been on the couch, squeezing his eyes shut as he'd heard Shaw's steps on the stairs up to the apartment, and then the door opened and his stomach had dropped out.

The sound of the shower turning on had been a mixture of humiliation and also the inevitable itch, back again, because just the thought of Shaw getting naked made him sweat.

He'd heard Shaw come back out again, the swish of cloth as he walked into the kitchen. Saw the sliver of light as Shaw opened the fridge. He'd turned over then, half-hard, and not sure if he was annoyed at himself, or at Shaw.

Before that moment, he'd been quiet, quiet enough like he really thought Ross was asleep.

But then the cupboard door had opened and then practically slammed shut, which wasn't even something Shaw *normally* did when he knew Ross was awake.

He'd known.

Ross had known he'd known.

At least it had been dark, so Shaw couldn't see his face as he'd confessed the truth.

Sure that he'd be asked to leave.

Sure that their blossoming friendship had been destroyed.

But instead, Ross was still amazed that Shaw not only felt it too, but that he *wanted* to be friends.

Not just because he felt sorry for Ross. But because he genuinely *liked* him.

"You look like you're daydreaming there."

Ross looked up and suddenly Shaw was there.

It shouldn't have been a surprise. After all, he was at the Funky Cup, which is where Shaw worked. But he'd deliberately gone in the side door, to the patio, because he hadn't been sure he was quite ready to face him in the light yet—and of course Tony had decided tonight was the perfect time for a staff meeting.

But here Shaw was anyway, and he was smiling.

The awkwardness that Ross had been certain he'd feel melted away under the sunny force of that smile. Instead, it wasn't awkward. It was . . . well, Ross didn't know what it was. Kind of like the itch from before, but *more*, somehow. Magnified, now that he knew it wasn't just *his* itch.

It was *their* itch.

"I was . . . uhhh . . . thinking," Ross said.

"I gathered," Shaw said. "Can I grab you anything?"

"I didn't realize you were waiting tables out here," Ross said.

"Chelle's on a break, and the bar's quiet so far," Shaw said.

"I . . . uh, a Shirley Temple?"

"With or without the shot?" The corner of Shaw's mouth quirked up, and Ross had a sudden visceral need to reach up and kiss it off him.

It would be easy to use booze as a crutch; there'd been a time when Ross had done that. It had made these kind of difficult (for him) social situations easier. But then he'd gotten dependent and even addicted, and that wasn't any good.

The alcohol dulled his senses, and that was a crime Ross couldn't stand for.

"Without," Ross said.

Shaw nodded and moved on to where Tony and Lucas were grouped together with Gabriel by the firepit.

Sean came and sat down next to him. "How's it going, man?" he asked.

"Uh, good?" Ross said. He never knew what to say to that question. Nobody ever really wanted to know the truth.

Even if he wanted to tell it.

"I hear you're working with Harmony," Sean said. "I really like her. She's great."

"She is," Ross said. That much was true. And he realized . . . all of a sudden . . . that things *were* going good.

He'd hired Harmony, who was honestly and truly working out great. He was paying off his debts, had gotten the flat-top grill fixed, and was slowly but surely figuring out most of what Aaron had let slip. And he hadn't ruined his friendship with Shaw. That felt like it loomed almost as large as all the other problems had.

Yeah, they might find each other attractive, but like Shaw said, that didn't mean anything had to change. Not unless he wanted it to.

Not unless he was *ready* for it to.

"And you're living with Shaw?" Sean's voice trailed off, inquiringly, but he was smiling, still.

"Tony is worse than my Southern grandmother was," Ross grumbled.

"That he is," Sean said. "But we love him anyway."

"Yeah, yeah, me and Shaw . . . we're living together above the bar," Ross said, finally. Figuring if he was clear up front, then this might stop being such a topic of intense interest. "We're roommates. He's just helping me out for a bit. And friends," he tacked on belatedly. "We're friends."

"Right." Sean didn't look amused at his expense or even incredulous that Shaw would want to be his friend.

He was really an underrated truck owner, as far as Ross was concerned.

He could take or leave Gabriel, who could be loud and forceful and thus, *annoying*, but Ross liked Sean, his boyfriend.

Kinda the same way he preferred Lucas to Tony.

A minute later, Shaw was back, distributing bottles of beer to everyone ringing the firepit, handing Alexis his short, squat glass of vodka over ice, and leaving Ross' drink for last, skirting behind the group as he reached out with it.

Shaw, who had the balance of someone who'd been slinging drinks and waiting tables for his whole adult life, still put a hand on Ross' back, the pressure and heat of it a fleeting thing, but making his heartbeat pick up anyway.

"Thanks," Ross said.

Shaw threw him a smile—one that *might* have been the same as the one he'd just given Tony or Gabe, but Ross saw the difference. It was a little quieter, a little more private. Might have even reflected the conversation they'd shared the night before.

They . . . well, Shaw hadn't gone as far as to say he *liked* Ross, but he was actually honest-to-God attracted to him. Ross could hardly believe it, even though he'd heard the truth in Shaw's voice.

This morning, too early, he'd stared in the mirror, trying to see what Shaw saw.

His scruff—heading halfway towards beard territory—outlining his jaw. A jaw he'd always seen as too harsh, too unforgiving. Dark eyes that never gave anything away. Dark hair, shaggy and a bit too long. Ross couldn't see it. But Shaw did, and maybe that was all that mattered.

"Yeah," Sean teased in a low voice, leaning in a bit closer, "yeah, you're *friends*."

"What's that supposed to mean?" Ross felt a momentary flash of panic. He'd just managed to quell everyone's questions about him and Shaw being roommates. He didn't know if anything with Shaw would ever happen; if he even *wanted* it to happen. He was still getting used to the idea. The last thing he needed was to dredge up even more speculation.

He hated being the center of gossip. The center of attention.

It was bad enough that everyone looked at him now and still thought about what Aaron had done.

"Just . . . you look like you're friends in the same way Gabe and I were enemies," Sean said softly. "He doesn't smile at many people like that, and you smiled back. I'm not sure I've ever seen you smile before, Ross."

"I smile," he argued. Even though Sean was probably right. He hadn't had many reasons to smile in the last few months, and it wasn't like he smiled frequently, before that.

"Not like that," Sean said. "But hey, it's okay. It's fine. I'm not going to go blabbing about it, not like Tony."

"Not like Tony what?"

"It's bad form to eavesdrop," Ross told Tony stiffly.

But Tony didn't look perturbed by his accusation.

"I hear my name, my ears perk up."

"We're just wondering what fresh bullshit you've decided to gift us with now," Sean said. "That's why you called this meeting, right?"

Ross shouldn't have been surprised that Sean didn't tell the truth. He'd promised to keep it to himself, after all, but Ross hadn't been quite sure he trusted him yet.

He supposed that he had to now.

"I'll have you know, I've got a *great* idea," Tony said. He looked around the rest of the group, circling one of the firepits. "A fantastic promotional opportunity." He motioned to Lucas, who ducked behind one of the trees and wheeled out a cart full of . . . smaller boxes. Ross couldn't quite make out the writing on them, but from the collective groan that went up, it seemed like this wasn't good news.

"August twenty-four is National Waffle Day," Tony continued, "and I thought, we shouldn't just celebrate it . . ."

"None of us even serve waffles," Ash interrupted.

"Well, about that . . ." Tony grinned. "You're gonna. Thus, the waffle makers. I'm even gifting you one. You're welcome."

"What?" Gabriel demanded.

"We're all going to have a special dish *just* for August twenty-fourth," Tony said. "And it's going to be a competition of sorts. Winner gets free rent for three months."

"How are you going to determine the winner?" Sean's gaze had narrowed.

"Number of social media tags," Tony said. "I'm ordering placards, and we'll do some flyers for the tables, explaining the rules. It'll be up to you to come up with the best possible waffle dish *using the general theme of your truck* and promote it."

"I hate this," Gabriel grumbled, "you're practically handing Ross this win on a silver platter."

Ross was surprised. Why did Gabriel think he would win?

"You don't have to look so shocked," Gabriel said to Ross, "I mean come on. You already make the best fried chicken on the lot. The *only* fried chicken. Chicken and waffles? Kinda a no-brainer."

"I don't know what I'm doing yet," Ross said awkwardly.

Had Tony designed this whole thing as a way to give him a few free months of rent?

After all, they'd just talked the other day, Tony learning that Ross had needed help and Shaw was the one who was giving it to him.

Was this just a way to get around Ross' reluctance to accept help?

"What do you mean . . . in the theme of our truck?" Sean asked. "I make wraps. How can I do a waffle wrap?"

"You'll figure something out," Tony said confidently. "I know you guys are all amazing cooks, you make fucking amazing food. This is an easy ask."

"What if we don't want to participate?" This question came from Alexis.

Tony shot him a look. "If you look in your contract," he pointed out, "you agreed to participate in group promotions, to be determined at a later date."

It was an excellent reminder that while Tony might be a meddling blowhard, he was also a fairly astute businessman.

"Fine," Alexis grumbled. "A freaking *Greek* waffle. Waffles aren't Greek!"

"You're gonna figure something great out," Tony said, patting him on the shoulder reassuringly. "I'd never give you guys something you couldn't do, you know that."

"Right. Of course not." Gabriel did not sound convinced.

"So you've got two weeks to figure out a dish, perfect it, and prep for it," Tony said. He was still smiling like he was in on the world's greatest practical joke. "And make sure to pick up your waffle maker on the way out."

"Freakin' waffles," Gabriel grumbled as he sat down heavily next to his boyfriend. He turned to Ross. "Can you believe this?"

Ross thought for a second. "Well, it's Tony," he said slowly, "so yeah, kinda."

"He's got a point," Sean said.

"Not you too," Gabe groaned.

"Gabe's right, this challenge is tailor-made for Ross to win," Ash said, coming to stand by them. Ross took a long drink of his Shirley Temple. Suddenly wishing that he'd asked Shaw to put something stronger in it.

"So, what? You're just going to phone it in?" Ross challenged.

"Hell no," Ash said with a grin. "I'm going to try to beat your ass."

"As if I would ever do chicken and waffles," Ross muttered under his breath. "*So* predictable."

"But predictably delicious," Sean pointed out.

"I don't need to be predictable to make something delicious," Ross said.

Gabe gestured with his beer bottle. "Yeah, yeah, we know. You're the culinary savant of the Food Truck Warriors."

"I don't know what that means," Ross said. Felt like he was under attack because he was the best—and wasn't that the way it always was?

Gabriel just shrugged but it was Ash who answered. "It means that you work harder than all of us put together, and that annoys Gabe because it makes him look bad."

"Hey!" Gabriel exclaimed.

"The truth hurts," Ash said succinctly.

"Yeah, it does," Gabe muttered.

"I'm not trying to make anyone look bad," Ross said slowly. He was just about done with his Shirley Temple, and it was a testament to how uncomfortable this situation was that he was ready to go back into the bar and see Shaw.

"We know you're not. It's just the way you are," Sean said, patting him on the back.

Ross stood. He knew the guys would often hang out for hours after Tony's "staff meetings." He just wasn't that social, and everyone's insistence that he was the best would have driven him away under normal circumstances.

But that itch was also back, and even if he wasn't going to have Shaw scratch it, he still thought seeing him and talking to him, even for a few minutes, might help calm it.

"Yeah, well, I can't help it," Ross muttered. "See you guys later."

"See you around," Ash said cheerfully.

He grabbed his waffle maker from the stack, the first guy to do so, and took off towards the bar itself.

It was cooler inside, and not nearly as crowded as it was outside. There was an open seat at the end of the bar, and Ross took it, setting the box next to him.

"What's that?" Shaw asked.

Ross had seen him make the drink he liked enough times now to know the way Shaw made it, and he was making another now, like Ross didn't even have to ask.

How had he known he wanted a second one?

Ross didn't know. Was afraid to ask.

"A waffle maker," Ross ground out. "One of Tony's 'grand ideas.'"

"You don't sound very happy about this one," Shaw said, dropping a cherry into the glass and setting it, delicately pink and fizzing, right in front of him.

"He likes meddling too much," Ross grumbled.

"I won't argue with that," Shaw said, leaning a hip against the bar, wiping his hands on a towel. "What's the grand idea this time?"

"A competition for National Waffle Day. Whoever gets the most social media votes for their dish gets three months of free lot rent."

Shaw understood without Ross even explaining why this was Tony meddling yet again. "You think he's trying to give you the rent without actually giving you the rent," he guessed.

"I didn't think so, didn't even consider it, because Tony's always coming up with weird-ass ideas, you know? But then Gabriel pointed out that chicken and waffles are a popular Southern dish."

"And you make the best fried chicken in LA," Shaw said with a grin. "I can see why he might think so. And why Tony picked waffles. Seems like an easy win to me."

"Yeah, I don't want an easy win."

Shaw's expression softened. And Ross realized that they *were* friends. Maybe they had more complicated feelings, because Shaw's face was handsome and his eyes were kind, and sometimes, Ross couldn't quite tear his gaze away from his tanned, muscled forearms. And those hands. So efficient. So quick. So brilliant.

What would those hands feel like on him?

Ross felt the hair on the back of his neck stand on end.

He knew you weren't supposed to think those things about your friends, but it hadn't seemed to bother Shaw to admit it last night. Maybe it wasn't a big deal.

"I get it," Shaw said. "You want to earn it."

Ross nodded. "Not with chicken and waffles, either."

"You would make a killer chicken and waffles," Shaw pointed out.

"Yeah," Ross said. His grandmother had made the best waffles in their small town. The best everything, to be honest, but her waffle recipe had been renowned across several counties. And he'd learned at her elbow, soaking in everything she'd ever said about food and the way it was prepared.

It had been so much easier to be with her than to be with his parents, who never knew what to do with him.

But Bethany Stanton, she had loved him. No matter how awkward he was. No matter how many weird things he said. It was why he still felt more comfortable in a kitchen than any place else.

The only one who ever made him feel the same . . . well, he was standing right in front of him.

And that decided Ross. He'd break in the waffle maker, next time it was Shaw's day off, and make him waffles and bring him chicken from the truck.

Ross could see the hunger in his eyes when he'd talked about it, and he wanted, more than he was comfortable with, to satisfy it.

"I was thinkin' like a totally different direction," Ross continued. "Like . . . who's gonna make a dessert?"

Shaw smiled. "You?"

"Yeah," Ross agreed. "Nobody is going to think of doing that. Maybe Alexis because he's creative. But I was thinking of something luscious and rich. Chocolate. Caramel, maybe. Pecans? A butter pecan ice cream? I can do a no-churn one. Freeze it in a hotel pan . . ." He was already thinking of the logistics. Of the ingredients. How he would serve it.

"You're going to make homemade ice cream?" Shaw turned back from pouring a series of pints. He raised an eyebrow. "You realize . . . it's not a crime to just take the win."

"Not if I haven't earned it," Ross said. Knew he was being stubborn, but he didn't know how to be any other way. It was in his blood and bones and his brain. *Earn your own way.*

"You could earn it without making homemade butter pecan ice cream," Shaw teased.

"Yeah," Ross agreed. "But it's a fun challenge."

Shaw shook his head, chuckling under his breath. "Anyone ever tell you that you're an overachiever?"

"My whole life," Ross said seriously.

"I'm going to be your taste tester, right?" Shaw asked.

"Of course." Ross said it automatically, without even thinking about it. "I wouldn't pick anyone else." *I couldn't.*

"You'd better not. I'm your guy." Shaw stopped in front of him, forearms braced on the bar, and he leaned in, and Ross couldn't help it, his breath caught in his lungs. He didn't know how to compartmentalize his attraction and separate it from the friend-ship. It felt like the two were bleeding into each other, mixing and combining until he felt dizzy with it.

He'd never had sex with someone he actually trusted before.

What would that feel like?

Ross didn't know. But he was beginning to think he might find out.

CHAPTER SEVEN

"So," Shaw said, from his spot next to Ross on the couch, "you finalize your recipe idea yet, for the waffle thing?" Shaw asked.

It was the night after the staff meeting, and two nights after their confession, and it seemed like everything had gone back to just about normal.

They were back on the couch, with an episode of *Home Town* playing in front of them, and it was like they'd never admitted that they were attracted to each other.

But that, Ross realized as he looked over at Shaw, wasn't quite true.

They couldn't shove the knowledge back into the box and close the lid. It was out now, and simmering between them, in the slightly elevated tension in the air.

He knew now that he could lean over and kiss Shaw and he wouldn't push him away. That he'd welcome it.

That he'd kiss him back.

Ross dragged his attention back to what Shaw was saying.

"No," Ross said. "I'm still playing with the idea in my head. I like the idea of a hot fudge brownie waffle. I like the ice cream idea.

Butter pecan maybe. Or sea salt caramel? Or maybe the caramel drizzled over the top?"

Shaw flashed him a smile, white teeth straight and even in his mouth. He was dazzling, just like this, on his couch, at twelve thirty in the morning, eyes sleepy, and in a pair of ratty pajama pants and an even rattier t-shirt.

"I love caramel," he said. "Did you know it's my favorite?"

He hadn't, but now he was more determined than ever to incorporate a caramel element into the dessert.

Ross shook his head. "But who could blame you? It's sugar, butter, and cream."

"Better than the sum of its parts, which are all pretty dang fantastic on their own," Shaw agreed.

They were quiet for a moment, watching on the screen as Erin teased Ben about something.

Ross couldn't help it; he wondered if he and Shaw would ever be comfortable like that in their affection.

He'd never imagined that he might have that with anyone, and it was still so early with Shaw that God knew if it would ever happen, but Ross had discovered that he hoped it would.

That maybe this completely impossible thing was actually possible after all.

"Do you know what anyone else is doing?" Shaw asked, breaking the comfortable silence.

"No," Ross said. "But I've already had three people get all worked up that I'm not doing chicken and waffles." He was trying not to be disgruntled about it, because he had to admit that it did make sense. He served great fried chicken. It wouldn't be very difficult to come up with a semi-unique waffle recipe. Maybe some kind of hot honey drizzle.

But if he'd ever been happy just doing what was expected of him and nothing more, he wouldn't be sitting here right now.

He probably never would have left the small town he grew up in, deep in North Carolina. Working for Stephan Atkinson would've been out of the question. And without that job, he never would have met Aaron, never would have started Basket with him. The one negative was that Aaron never would've betrayed him.

But while the knife in his back still hurt, and there were days when Ross wasn't sure he'd ever truly get over it, he was coming to terms more and more with the idea that *good* things had come out of it.

He was part of a group now, even if it didn't feel like they truly accepted him.

Tony clearly wanted him to succeed, if the waffle contest was any indication.

And he'd never have become friends with Shaw.

They never would've sat together like this. And that, Ross knew, would've been a damn shame.

"Can you blame them?" Shaw asked. "You're tailor-made for it. You know why Tony created the contest like he did."

"I can win without going the obvious route," Ross said stubbornly.

Shaw smiled. "I've said it before, and I'll say it again, you *scare* them."

"Yeah, no," Ross said. Tony was full of confidence—real or misplaced—and so were the other guys. They weren't *afraid* of him. They just didn't like him.

"We're gonna have to agree to disagree," Shaw said with a shrug. "Hey," he added, his expression brightening, "what if you *stuffed* the waffles with caramel? Like you think it's just a brownie waffle . . ." Shaw chuckled. "*Just* a brownie waffle, with your ice cream or whatever on top, and then you take a bite and you realize it's got gooey caramel inside."

Ross was intrigued. He only liked surprises when it came to his creations; probably why he served the food that his Southern grandmother had taught him to cook, but always with an unexpected gourmet twist.

"I . . . that could work," Ross mused. He'd been trying to find another angle for the dessert idea. Something more unique. Anyone could make a brownie sundae, even making the brownie into a waffle. But a brownie stuffed with caramel sundae, that was something a little off the beaten path.

"Officially, I am a genius," Shaw announced. "Probably more like I'm picking up on *your* genius."

"I'm not a genius, I just work hard," Ross argued.

Shaw didn't look convinced. "You not wanting to take the easy win and call it good? That's genius."

Ross considered that pure ridiculous stubbornness—not genius—but he'd discovered that he didn't like arguing with Shaw.

He changed the subject instead.

"You have tomorrow off, right?" Ross asked.

"Yeah, I'm looking forward to it." Shaw stretched out, his thigh falling closer to Ross' leg on the couch. It would be so easy to reach out and touch it. His fingers itched. "I'm gonna sleep in. Maybe head to the beach. Catch some rays."

Ross did a quick mental calculation. Based on when Shaw often stopped by the truck for lunch on his days off, he thought he could duck out for a quick break and have Harmony handle the orders.

They were usually quiet on mornings when there was music in the evenings—and tomorrow they had one of the more popular bands playing.

"Sounds like a plan," Ross said.

"What about you?" Shaw asked. "You ever take a day off?"

He hadn't been. Not in a few months. Sometimes he'd close the truck for the morning or the afternoon.

"Not really."

Shaw smiled, and patted him on the shoulder, his arm stretching out behind Ross, and to his surprise, he didn't move it. Just settled in, the tips of his fingers brushing Ross' shoulder.

Ross felt nervous and jumpy. Shaw had said that whatever happened would be his choice but . . . this was practically cuddling.

He's barely touching you, and you're freaking out.

Logically, he knew it wasn't really cuddling, but his brain was screaming.

Screaming . . . at how much he liked it.

Shit.

Ross shifted slightly, knowing he barely moved, but hoping that Shaw would understand. But even though he'd considered shifting away, instead he found himself shifting closer. Wanting to *be* closer.

There were only about ten minutes left in the episode, and Ross barely paid attention, even though they'd stopped chatting and were both supposedly watching the screen.

Instead he was thinking, almost nonstop, about the feel of Shaw's fingertips against his shoulder, and the pressure of his arm behind Ross' neck. Sometimes the briefest of touches overwhelmed him in the worst kind of ways, but he was pretty sure this was the best kind of way.

When the episode finished and Shaw reached over to grab the remote to turn the TV off, he moved his arm and Ross nearly reached out and snatched it back.

It had felt so warm and reassuring—and it had also electrified him, until it felt like he was sizzling, despite how tired he was.

Shaw yawned, stretching again, his shirt riding up and exposing a sliver of his stomach.

Ross remembered—because it had been so undeniably memorable—that first night, when Shaw had showered and had walked out in only a towel.

It had left him so itchy and surprisingly desperate to experience that kind of itch all over again.

"See you in the morning?" Shaw asked, as he stood and there was that hopeful note in his voice again. Ross could hear it.

"Uh," Ross said. If Shaw was sleeping in, then Ross normally *wouldn't* see him. He didn't want to say yes and give away the fact that he would, because he had every intention of surprising him with chicken and waffles when he woke up.

"Oh, that's right." Shaw smiled, sleepily. "I'm not waking up early tomorrow." He gave a weak little fist pump. "Yay!"

Ross fidgeted on the sofa. He wanted to get up and give Shaw another one of those hugs, but that wasn't something they normally did and he didn't know, even if he really wanted it, if he was ready for that yet. What if Shaw took that as an indication that he was ready for more?

"See you tomorrow," Ross said.

"Yeah," Shaw said, and then he was gone, walking towards his room.

Ross stood then, still antsy, and went and brushed his teeth. Changed into the t-shirt he wore with his boxer briefs to sleep, and then flipped the lights off, as he headed back towards the couch. He lay down and tried to will his brain to shut off, to fall asleep, but he was still keyed up.

Still wishing that he'd ignored his hesitation and had just gone for it.

Shaw woke up and smelled something *amazing*.

It was sweet, sugar and cinnamon and butter, and it was also spicy, the tang of cayenne in the air.

Opening his eyes, blinking away the sleep, he couldn't decide what it could be. The kitchen at the bar didn't start their prep this early, and nothing they'd ever made had smelled *sweet* like this. Maybe he'd slept longer? Maybe Jackson had suggested to Jose that they add some desserts and he was experimenting, before the kitchen officially opened for the day.

Shaw glanced over at the clock. It was just past eleven.

Unfortunately there was no way to know what that incredibly delicious, complex aroma was unless he got up out of bed. Stifling his groan, Shaw stretched and rubbed a hand over his face.

He'd had the dreams again, the ones that wouldn't stop plaguing him for the last few days, with Ross so close, just outside his bedroom door, and yet so far away.

Last night he'd dreamed that Ross had leaned in even closer to his touch, had turned his head, had known somehow that Shaw was dying to kiss him, and felt the same. They'd ended up making out on the couch, Shaw in Ross' lap, rubbing his hard cock against the bulge in Ross' shorts, and well, it was a miracle he hadn't made a mess.

He shouldn't have pushed Ross with that whole "oh so casual, hand over the back of the couch" maneuver. He'd made a promise—both to himself and to Ross—that he'd move at Ross' pace. But just when he'd thought he should apologize, that he'd gone too far over the friend-zone line, Ross had actually leaned into the touch.

Like he really enjoyed it.

That had definitely not helped Shaw's dreams any.

He'd get up, see what that delicious smell was, and maybe make himself some pancakes. He had a box of mix in the cupboard, and then he'd grab lunch on the way down to the beach.

Even if Ross' truck hadn't been his favorite on the lot, Shaw already knew he'd want to stop there just to wave hi and talk to him, if only for a minute.

He was officially pathetic. This crush had snuck up on him almost without him realizing it, and now he was in deep. It really hadn't helped that he'd learned, shockingly, that his feelings were at least a little mutual.

Shaw ran a hand through his hair and groaned as he got out of bed. All these long nights were getting tougher. Maybe Jackson was right and taking a more administrative role at the bar, or even God forbid, doing the same at a second bar, would make things easier as he got older.

Padding to the door, Shaw pushed it open, and to his shock, saw Ross standing in the kitchen. He was mumbling something under his breath as he leaned over the counter.

Not the counter, Shaw realized, as he took a few steps closer. The waffle maker he'd brought home from the bar the other night.

"You recipe testing?"

Ross looked up in surprise. "You're up."

"Yes," Shaw said. He headed towards the coffeemaker, his hip barely glancing off Ross'. He could've waited for Ross to move but the spark of awareness he felt was what he'd really been after.

"I woke up," Shaw continued as he popped a pod into the Keurig, "and I smelled something amazing. Should've guessed you'd be here. Harmony holding down the fort?"

"I'm not recipe testing," Ross said. "I'm here to make you brunch."

Shaw felt his shocked gaze hit Ross. "You're here to make me brunch?"

"You said you loved chicken and waffles," Ross said, his voice sounding undeniably self-conscious. "I wasn't going to make them for the dish, for the contest, but I thought I could make some for you this morning, on your day off. As kind of a . . ." Ross hesitated. "A thank-you for being so nice. For being a friend."

"Aw," Shaw said, "that's sweet. That's what I smell, then? The sweet and the chicken? That spicy scent?"

"You've got a good nose," Ross said with a nod. "I made some chicken at the truck and brought it over, it's staying warm in the oven."

"You used the oven?"

Ross shot him a look. "Someone should."

Shaw couldn't help the laugh that escaped out of him as his coffee started brewing. "Well, I'm flattered."

"Don't be flattered just yet," Ross said, returning to the waffle maker. "This thing is a piece of shit and I'm going to have to yell at Tony. It either burns my waffles or it undercooks them."

"It's not like Tony to buy shitty equipment," Shaw said, grabbing the half-and-half from the fridge. He poured in a generous amount and went to sit at one of the barstools.

"Yeah, well, even Tony makes mistakes sometimes," Ross grumbled. "If I can't even make a regular waffle, how am I ever going to make a brownie waffle stuffed with caramel?"

Shaw felt a frisson of excitement race through him. He knew how particular Ross was about his ideas. How much development went into his recipes, and the thought behind each one. The idea that Ross could be using one of *his* ideas was freaking awesome.

"You're going to do that?" He tried to pretend casual, but he was no good at it. Not with this guy.

"Yeah," Ross said with a nod. "I want to anyway."

The waffle maker beeped and Ross popped it open, groaning a little as he pulled, with his bare hands, a beautifully bronzed waffle onto a plate. He brushed it with melted butter and then sprinkled it with cinnamon sugar.

"This is going to have to do," he said, at complete odds to the way Shaw's stomach was grumbling. It smelled incredible, and it looked even better.

He barely even ogled Ross' ass as he bent over to grab the chicken from the oven. He settled two pieces of crispy thigh—Shaw didn't want to think about what that said about their relationship that Ross knew exactly which parts of the chicken he liked—and then drizzled the whole thing with what looked like syrup from a little pot on the stove.

He set the plate in front of Shaw with a flourish, like he was still working at a Michelin-starred restaurant. He grabbed a knife and fork from the silverware drawer and handed them over.

"Oh my God," Shaw said, exhaling slowly. "This looks fucking amazing."

"I hope you like it," Ross said modestly.

"I'm gonna love it," Shaw said. "It's almost too pretty to eat, and then I smell it and . . . well, my self-control just isn't that great."

The corner of Ross' mouth quirked up. "Maybe I don't want it to be."

Shaw didn't know if Ross was talking about eating the food or . . . well, something else. But he decided, for the sake of his stomach and for the sake of his sanity, he was going to believe it was the food.

The chicken, even though it had been in the oven for who knows how long, was still unbelievably crispy on the outside, the inside soft and juicy, perfectly cooked.

"Insane," Shaw said through a mouthful of chicken, the spice offset with the sugary waffle. "I'm in heaven."

"I should get going, after I clean up a bit," Ross said, turning away to load the few dishes into the dishwasher. He glared at the waffle maker. "I'm gonna have to talk to Tony about this piece of shit."

"It's not a piece of shit and you're a miracle worker," Shaw insisted as he kept eating. He couldn't really stop. It was too good. "And for the record, you'd win every award, hands down, if you put this on the menu."

"Yeah," Ross said.

Shaw wasn't surprised he'd agreed. Modesty wasn't really Ross' kind of thing. But when you were that good, should it be?

"But you get why I don't want to, right?" Ross asked, as he shut the dishwasher.

"I do," Shaw said through another bite of chicken and waffle. They were good on their own, individually, but together? They were something special.

Shaw had always imagined that was what the best kind of relationships were like—two parts coming together and making a better whole. That was definitely how his brother and Alexis were. And Tony and Lucas . . . well, Shaw wouldn't argue with that either. Sean had come out of his shell, and Gabriel? He'd gotten a lot less brash, more thoughtful.

"Good. I . . . well, I wouldn't want you to think I'm crazy." Ross shoved his hands in his pockets. Shifted his weight from foot to foot. He had that awkward look on his face again, the same one he'd had last night.

Shaw wondered, suddenly, if it was because he wanted more, and he didn't quite know how to reach out and take it.

If it was up to Shaw, he'd be touching Ross all the time.

"You're not crazy, not even a little. And don't talk about my friend that way," Shaw said.

The corner of Ross' mouth quirked up in a smile. "Alright," he said.

"And, one more thing," Shaw said. He slid off the barstool. "Come over here. I wanna give you a hug, if that's okay. This is the best surprise that anyone's had for me in ages."

"Really?" Ross' dark eyes brightened. "Okay."

He skirted around the counter and hesitated, standing in front of Shaw.

"Get over here," Shaw said, and reached out for Ross, pulling him in closer.

He'd only intended it to be a quick, grateful hug. A *friendly* hug, but the problem with that was that while they were friends, they weren't *only* friends.

Shaw had been having some decidedly not-just-platonic thoughts about Ross, and he was beginning to realize Ross was right there with him.

His head hit Ross' shoulder, that was how tall Ross was, and though his chest was wide and hard, he was actually surprisingly soft. Shaw forced himself not to nuzzle into the planes of his chest, not like he wanted to, and stopped himself just in time from digging his fingertips into those equally broad shoulders.

The shoulders that always seemed to take everything on and never let anything drop.

He knew just how difficult it was to win Ross' trust, and just how precious it was.

He'd intended to let Ross go after just a moment. A quick, friendly hug, that was all it was supposed to be, because he didn't want to push him for more than he was willing to give.

But Ross was right there, holding him close and tight, like he couldn't quite bear to let him go either.

And well, Shaw wasn't going to deny them something they clearly both wanted. So he didn't let go, just kept holding on, kept glorying in the feel of Ross so close, so big and strong and yet undeniably soft and vulnerable.

It did not help the growing situation downstairs, but Shaw couldn't believe just how well they fit together. Better than any of his fantasies. Better than any of his dreams.

Finally, Ross pulled back, but he didn't quite let go of Shaw, his hands still lingering around his waist.

"Thank you," Ross said seriously.

"I should be the one thanking you, that was the idea anyway," Shaw said.

"Not just for . . . for everything." A wrinkle appeared between Ross' dark brows. "I'm . . . I'm not good at saying it, but I appreciate it. More than you know."

Shaw felt a little guilty. He hadn't done it *entirely* out of the goodness of his heart. He'd been drawn to Ross from almost the first time he'd met him.

He'd been prepared to just be friends, but well . . . it was dawning on him that friendship wasn't the only thing they shared.

"You're welcome," Shaw said. "Anytime. And I mean, *anytime.*"

Ross smiled then. He didn't smile often, but when he did? It felt like the sun, breaking just over the edge of the world, the first rays warming everything they touched.

Shaw felt the loss of it when Ross dropped his hands from his waist. Wanted to grab them and put them back, even though he knew he shouldn't.

This was all supposed to be at Ross' pace, not his.

"You mean that?" Ross asked.

"Of course I mean it." Shaw returned to the food.

"So you wouldn't mind if I did some recipe testing here? It's just . . ." Ross' smile went a little bashful around the edges. "Tony and some of the other guys have been poking around the truck, and I want the dish to be a surprise."

"You are absolutely free to use this kitchen as often as you want," Shaw said, gesturing around with his fork. "In fact, if you don't, I'm gonna be disappointed."

"Why?"

"Because then I wouldn't get to try all your attempts," Shaw said with a teasing voice.

"How do you know they'll be good?" Ross sounded actually honest-to-God concerned about this.

"I know," Shaw said. "I just know."

"Okay, well . . ." Ross looked awkward again. "Thanks again."

"You're welcome. You're always welcome," Shaw said, and put a hand on his shoulder, squeezing lightly.

CHAPTER EIGHT

Ross hadn't expected to see Shaw again that day.

Told himself as he took his cleaning supplies out to the smoker that this was totally normal and perfectly understandable. Shaw had the day off, and would be doing his own stuff, and Ross had always planned on working later than he normally did, because they had one of the lot's favorite bands playing tonight.

Plus, it would give him some time to right his equilibrium after the hug.

It was just a hug.

That was what he kept reminding himself.

He'd wanted to do it, wanted to give Shaw something of himself, more than just the food, because what he'd done had been extraordinary in Ross' life.

He'd reminded him that he wasn't alone. That there were people out there who didn't judge him for Aaron's behavior. Who cared what happened to him.

Shaw had done it even when Ross had been resistant at first. Even when he'd tried to claim he didn't need the help, Shaw had still extended it, selflessly.

That was part of why he liked him so much, Ross thought as he scraped the fat and smoke residue off the lid of the smoker, but it was more than just that.

Shaw was funny and sweet and it was easy for Ross to be around him. Add to that how attractive Ross found him, and he was not only becoming more and more essential to Ross, he was becoming downright irresistible.

So much so that he wanted, when he finished cleaning the smoker, to head back to the apartment. Hoping that he'd see Shaw there.

It's just one night, you can live without him for just one night.

Except Ross was no longer quite sure that was true.

He didn't *want* it to be true.

"Hey."

Ross glanced up from his work on the smoker, and like he'd conjured him from thin air, there was Shaw.

"You look surprised to see me," Shaw said when Ross was indeed *speechless*. Was he actually here? Had his fantasies started to walk and talk, too?

He'd never thought of his imagination as that powerful, but maybe . . .

"It's your day off, what are you doing here?"

Ross knew he sounded gruffer. Way less pleased than he actually was.

But Shaw's smile didn't waver. Not even for a second. Like he *knew* what Ross was actually trying to say.

I'm glad you're here. I missed you, even though I shouldn't. I was hoping to see you, even though I knew I probably wouldn't.

"I wanted to hear the band, and Jackson said he and Alexis were hanging out here, plus some of the other guys. And . . ." Shaw shot him a lopsided smile. It was fucking adorable, and Ross felt the impact of it, right to the sternum. "And I thought I might have to drag you away from your truck. Guess I was right."

"We're still open, technically," Ross pointed out, as he sprayed down the interior of the smoker with his lemon cleanser.

Shaw glanced around. "How many orders have you gotten in the last . . . twenty minutes?"

Ross sighed. Knew he had a good point. "I'll close up, I just . . ."

Shaw didn't move, didn't take a single step towards him, but somehow Ross felt it anyway. Felt those arms coming up tightly around him, holding him close, reminding him that he was worthy and worthwhile.

Maybe all he was feeling was the look in Shaw's eyes.

That kind, steady reassurance.

"You're worried about hanging out with the other guys," Shaw guessed, following Ross as he turned to go put his cleaning tools away in the truck.

"I guess so," Ross admitted. He didn't guess so. He *knew* so. But it was hard to admit that to someone who everyone knew, and everyone liked.

"What if you came with me? What if I wanted you there?" Shaw asked, pausing on the side steps as Ross stowed the supplies in a cabinet. After he was done, he flipped the sign, closed the front window, and then locked it with the padlock.

"I'd say . . ." Ross hesitated. Was this like a date? No, it wouldn't be. Shaw had already said he wouldn't push him. Besides, hanging out with a group of Shaw's friends and his coworkers, that wasn't a date. Ross might not *go* on dates, but he knew what they looked like. At least what they were supposed to look like.

Dinner at some fancy restaurant. Candles. Roses. Wine. A kiss at the front steps of someone's house, at the end of the night.

This definitely wasn't that, so maybe Shaw just . . . well, maybe Shaw felt just like Ross did, and he'd missed him.

"Please," Shaw said. His voice was dark, and Ross could hear something in it, something he hadn't ever heard before.

"Okay," Ross said. How could he say anything else, after that?

"It'll be fun." Shaw's voice had grown lighter. "You'll have fun."

"Fun? What's that?" Ross teased darkly.

"I was just about to say that," Shaw agreed. "You could use some fun, every once in awhile."

Ross rummaged around in the extra clothes he kept, and grabbed a t-shirt. Plain. Blue. Not something you'd wear on a date, but that was okay, because this wasn't a date.

Without thinking, he stripped off the one he was wearing, with the Basket logo, and halfway to putting this one on, he froze.

Shaw was watching him.

Not just watching.

He was staring.

Like he was mesmerized by Ross' bare chest.

He didn't get it, but the heat in Shaw's gaze lit a fire inside him anyway.

Ross' first inclination was to pull on the shirt as quickly as possible. Hide whatever it was that had Shaw looking like that, but then he thought again, thought how much he liked it. Thought how he trusted Shaw not to push him.

And instead, he pulled it on slower. Deliberately flexing maybe just a tiny bit.

Aaron had always marveled at what great shape he was in, but then he worked his ass off, sometimes twelve hours a day, seven days a week.

He didn't have a gym body, all perfect abs and chiseled muscles, but he was strong and he knew he could get the job done.

Shaw definitely didn't look like he minded that Ross hadn't been to a gym in years.

Ross took a step closer and then another step, finally clothed again. He watched as Shaw swallowed hard.

"You ready to go?" he asked.

Ross nodded. He'd cleaned up and put most everything away, already, before he'd gone out to do the smoker. Had already come to the same conclusion that he wouldn't be getting many more customers tonight.

When he walked down the stairs, locking the door behind him, Shaw was still close.

As they walked towards the front of the lot, with its stage and the band on it, the lights above them twinkling, Ross couldn't help but think about the hug again.

And how much he wanted to do it again.

Maybe this time Shaw wouldn't have to voice it, he could do it without Shaw asking.

They approached a table full of guys. Ross recognized everyone.

Sean and Gabe were there, and of course Tony and Lucas. Lennox was standing next to the table, listening to something Ash was saying, and Jackson and Alexis were heading in this direction.

Even Ren was here, surprisingly, tilting his head up, listening to Ash too.

Or maybe he was watching the guy next to Lennox, the one that Lennox had said was his partner.

Ross couldn't remember his name, but he'd liked the guy. He was friendlier, more apt to smile than Lennox. Hadn't looked at him like he wanted to kick his ass.

Probably because Ross hadn't been the partner of the guy who'd tried to blow up his boyfriend. Ross didn't think the guy even *had* a boyfriend.

Definitely not, because Ren was still looking at him like he wanted to eat him for dinner.

Huh, that was interesting.

Ross didn't pretend to understand romantic relationships, but he was one hundred percent sure he did not understand Ren or how Ren conducted his business.

"Hey, guys," Shaw said, and all those heads swiveled in their direction.

Except Ren, who was still looking at that other guy. Who was now looking right back.

Ross was never going to understand how any of this worked.

He also wondered if he and Shaw looked at each other like that—like the whole world had faded away.

He hoped not. Mostly because then everyone would know, and he wasn't ready to tell anyone yet. He wasn't even ready to take the next step with Shaw, even though he trusted him, and deep down, he already knew he *wanted* to.

"Hey, Shaw," Tony said, then his gaze focused on Ross. "You guys comin' to hang out?"

"Yeah," Shaw said, answering for both of them. Ross took a seat next to him, at an empty spot at one of the tables they'd pushed together.

"You actually close at a decent hour?" Gabriel asked Ross.

"Everyone was listening to the music . . ." Ross said uncertainly. Not sure if Gabriel was poking fun or something worse. That was often the problem with the guys here; he didn't know if he should be taking them seriously or not.

"And," Shaw added with a grin, wrapping his arm around Ross' shoulders for a split second, just long enough for Ross' heart to start racing, "I told him he could use a little fun in his life."

Tony nodded encouragingly. "Yeah, yeah, he could. He works crazy hard. You need to learn how to relax, Ross."

"Seems unlikely," Ross said. He was the way he was now; he knew that. It would help if everyone else he knew could get on the same page.

Tony laughed. "Yeah, yeah, it kinda does. But at least Shaw's encouraging you to kick back, every once in awhile."

"I try," Shaw said, modestly. Because without him, Ross wouldn't be here at all.

He was here, and he was going to try to have a good time. He was actually going to try to relax. Despite his statement to Tony.

"Want a beer?" Shaw asked him, nudging him with his shoulder. "Or maybe something else?"

"A beer is fine," Ross said, watching as Shaw motioned to his brother, still walking over, and made some complicated hand signal.

"What was that?" Sean wanted to know. "Some supersecret bartender code language?"

"No," Shaw said with a laugh. "Not even close. He's probably going to show up with like two hard seltzers or something."

"What's a hard seltzer?" Ross asked, confused. He didn't want that. He wanted a beer, thank you very much.

Tony laughed.

That was why Ross liked Lucas better. Sometimes it felt like Tony was laughing *at* him, not *with* him, and the difference was . . . well, it meant something to Ross.

Maybe Tony didn't mean it, maybe they'd never understand each other or be best friends, but that didn't mean he shouldn't avoid being an asshole.

"You don't want to know," Lucas said, patting him on the shoulder.

But Shaw knew he wouldn't have asked for no reason, and he said, "It's like seltzer water, flavored, but with alcohol in it. Some of them aren't so bad, actually."

"Well, you're the expert," Tony grumbled.

"Yep," Shaw said cheerfully. "And oh look, he didn't bring seltzers. He got the beers I wanted."

Jackson approached the table, setting them down by Shaw, who flicked off their lids with an expert motion.

"Was I supposed to bring seltzers?" Jackson wondered as he and Alexis took a seat further down the table.

"Nope, you got what I wanted," Shaw said. "Thanks, by the way."

"You looked like a drunk flamingo coming in for a landing," Alexis added. "So thanks for the chuckle."

"You're welcome." Shaw seemed completely unperturbed by Alexis' joke, which was definitely at his expense.

Ross wished that he could be that easygoing. That he could just not care what people said about him.

"So, Ross, you decided what you're serving yet for Waffle Day?" Lucas asked.

"I'm playing with a few ideas," Ross said cautiously.

"What? No chicken and waffles?" Ren sounded disappointed. "I was actually looking forward to see what great twist you'd put on those."

"Truth is," Shaw said, "he didn't need one. He made me a plate this morning and I was glad he left while I was demolishing it, because he wasn't around to see me lick it clean after."

"You made Shaw chicken and waffles and you're not making them for Waffle Day?" Lucas sounded surprised.

"He likes them," Ross said, trying to keep his defensiveness to a minimum. "And I wanted to try out the waffle maker." He frowned. "Tony, I think you need to consider buying better equipment."

"They were absolutely fucking delicious," Shaw said, chuckling. "Bum waffle maker or no."

"So what *are* you doing?" Ren wanted to know. Demanded, more like it.

"A dessert," Ross said. "The rest is going to have to be a surprise."

"You know." Shaw nudged Ross with his shoulder again. Somehow they'd gotten even closer on the bench seat, until their thighs were touching. "You should really think about putting that on the menu, not for Waffle Day, but for real. You've already got the chicken. And now you've got the waffle maker."

Ross hadn't considered that. He hadn't wanted to *win* Waffle Day by doing something so expected, so pedestrian, but maybe . . . maybe Shaw wasn't wrong.

Okay, who're you kidding, Shaw has fucking fantastic instincts.

"Maybe I'll give it to Harmony, see what she can do with it," Ross said.

Shaw smiled, and even though he smiled all the freaking time, at practically everyone, there was something special about this one. Like they'd just shared a private joke, something only the two of them were meant to know.

No one else.

Frankly, Ross would put a hundred predictable dishes on the menu if it would get Shaw to smile like that at him every single day.

"She's great, isn't she?" Sean said enthusiastically. "When she told me she was going to work for you . . . I was thinking, *yeah, that makes sense.*"

"Really?" Alexis asked dubiously. "Because I was annoyed she was leaving me."

"Tate wasn't very pleased either," Sean agreed, "and it's not like I was *happy* about it. She was a great employee. But she deserves a place where she can really stretch her wings, be a strong number two, and I think Ross' truck is just the place for that."

Ross nodded in agreement. "When she came to me and said Basket was where she wanted to be, I wasn't going to argue with her."

"Wait," Tony said, "are we *really* not gonna talk about the elephant in the room?"

"What's the elephant?" Shaw wondered.

"That *Ross* made you food."

"Ross brings me food all the time."

He did, he was always leaving leftovers in the fridge. Things that he knew Shaw would like, because Shaw's busy schedule often meant he didn't have time to eat something healthy and filling before his long shifts at the bar.

Not just because he'd said he would, when he'd agreed to move in.

"Yeah, but he made this for you *special*," Tony said slyly.

Ross watched as Lucas elbowed his boyfriend, *hard*. "I told you to cut that out," Lucas said firmly. "This isn't our business."

"Fine, fine," Tony said raising his hands in mock surrender.

Ross was pleasantly surprised—both that Lucas would intervene and that Tony would give up so easily.

"Seriously though, guys," Shaw said, smiling and obviously trying to lighten the mood, "whenever chicken and waffles goes on the menu, be prepared to be amazed."

"I'm still trying to figure out how to make this gigantic waffle fry work," Alexis complained. "Ross isn't wrong. Your waffle maker sucks, Tony."

"It came highly recommended," Tony said stiffly.

"Yeah, highly recommended that everything you put in will stick," Gabriel complained.

"You put *cheese* in it and expected it not to stick," Sean said, shooting his boyfriend a glare that melted, almost as quickly as cheese on a hot waffle maker, into absolutely charmed goo. "Any idiot would know better."

"Yeah, but think of how good it might have been if it worked out! A waffle of *melted cheese.*"

"Besides, you don't think Tate's going to do that?" Sean asked.

"I have it on very good authority that Tate's thinking of making a macaroni and cheese waffle with a hot red pepper dipping sauce," Gabe said.

"Oh, yum," Jackson said. "Sign me up for that one."

"It's definitely the sticking," Alexis said. "But mine is also not getting hot enough. The potato is not getting crispy. Can we get a different waffle maker?"

Ross had already considered doing it. The one Tony had gotten them was fine for waffles on Saturday mornings at home—as long as you greased the fuck out of it so the waffles wouldn't stick—but he was thinking it might be a good idea to invest in something a little more suited to a commercial kitchen. Especially if he was going to put the chicken and waffles on the menu, after all.

Harmony would need something good and solid and dependable.

"No, no, no," Tony said, bursting his bubble—and Alexis' too. "You're using the one I gave you. No questions. No comments. No complaints."

"But it . . ." Alexis continued to argue, despite what Tony had just said.

"Nope," Tony interrupted. "The whole point isn't that you guys can't make great food. You can. You can do it in a little tiny kitchen on wheels. You do it every single day. But the idea was to give you something a *little* more challenging to work with."

"Really?" Gabe crossed his arms over his chest. "You gave us a shitty waffle maker *on purpose*?"

"Well, I didn't think it was shitty," Tony muttered. "I just thought, it was a cheap, easy-to-use waffle maker. I didn't think any of us would be using it past Waffle Day, anyway."

"You should know better," Alexis said. "You give us a mile, we're gonna take it."

"You should," Lucas teased. "Now come dance with me, before these guys bum you out and you sit here moping all night."

Tony nodded and took Lucas' hand, following him out to the front of the stage, that had been transformed into a temporary and very crowded dance floor.

Ross watched as Sean and Gabe left too, then Jackson and Alexis, and finally Ash and Lennox also left, leaving only Ren and Seth, eyeing each other, and him and Shaw.

Should he ask Shaw to dance? He was *not* a dancer, had never thought he was even really capable of it, but if Tony could wriggle his ass around to the beat, then Ross could too, right?

Still, just the thought made his palms sweat.

If he asked and Shaw said yes, everyone would be talking about it.

Even Lucas wouldn't be able to stop them.

Did that bother him? Ross wasn't sure. He knew at one time that it would have. But now? He was beginning to think all he'd feel was pride.

"Hey." Shaw leaned in, his breath brushing Ross' ear, making his insides jump and his heart rate spike. "You find this a little weird, right?" He glanced over in Ren and Seth's direction.

They were sitting opposite each other, not speaking, not looking particularly friendly, but also looking like they wanted to eat each other up.

It was like they were having some kind of staring contest, and the first one that broke . . . well, Ross wasn't sure he wanted to know what they'd punish each other with.

"Uh, yeah," Ross agreed. "Do they do this often?" He nudged Shaw back. Maybe they couldn't dance, but he could absolutely sit here like this, their bodies touching in half a dozen places, and love every second of it.

Shaw nodded.

"It's . . ." Ross didn't know what it was.

He wasn't even sure *they* knew.

"Sean and Gabe were bad enough, during the height of their name war," Shaw said under his breath, "but these two?"

"Lennox's friend isn't bad looking," Ross said, objectively. "You'd think Ren would make an offer."

Everyone knew that Ren made offers to everyone. He'd even made one to Ross, who hadn't understood what he'd meant, until Aaron had pointed out what he'd been trying to do.

In a dark corner of Ross' mind, he was actually a little envious of Ren. Sex was great, but he'd never been able to have it easily, like Ren did. If he could, well, he wasn't sure what he'd have done, but he didn't think he would have held back.

"He has," Shaw whispered. "He turned him down."

"Huh. Well, I guess I can see it. I did, though I wasn't sure what he was asking, actually."

Ross thought he could believe it. If, the night that they'd confessed their attraction to each other, Shaw had made a Ren-like overture, inviting Ross to his bed for the night, but just for the night, he'd have turned him down.

Not because he wouldn't have wanted to. Or he thought he wouldn't enjoy himself—he was beginning to think he would, more than he had with anyone else—but because he wouldn't want just one night.

He wouldn't even want only a casual sexual relationship.

He'd had one or two of those before, and while they'd satisfied him well enough, he hadn't wanted to spend any time with the person before or after.

Ross already knew that he wanted to spend more time with Shaw.

That he couldn't get enough of the guy's company.

He wanted to laugh with him, and watch TV with him, and talk about their days, and hear about what was going on at the bar. He even felt comfortable sharing a little about what he was doing at the truck. He'd never shared with anyone before. Even Aaron had forced him, on more than one occasion, to open up about their business.

But with Shaw, it felt like it came more naturally than it had with anyone else.

Probably because he trusted him. Respected him. Downright *liked* him.

"I didn't either," Shaw said matter-of-factly.

Ross was pretty sure he knew what he was saying but . . . maybe he should make sure he knew what Shaw was saying, *exactly*.

"You didn't . . . with Ren?" Ross wouldn't have blamed him if he had; Ren was attractive and available, and undoubtedly, it had been long before he and Shaw had even known each other.

He wasn't jealous; not really.

He was . . . well, he was something.

Itchy. He was fucking itchy.

Maybe he should have asked Shaw to dance after all.

"Nope," Shaw said. "Not really interested in that kind of thing, honestly. Even after my ex and I broke up, and everyone thought I would be. I was just . . . I was sad, and lonely, yeah, but not that kind of lonely."

"You were lonely for more than just a few hours," Ross said, because he got exactly how Shaw felt. That was often how he was lonely. He wanted someone who understood him. Someone's true companionship. Occasionally he'd had that with Aaron, if only because of their shared life experience, but he'd never felt it again, not with anyone else, before Shaw.

"Yeah, yeah, exactly," Shaw said, and shot him a smile that warmed him from the inside out.

When Ross looked over again, both Seth and Ren had disappeared. Where? Nobody knew. But it probably wasn't something anyone was going to want to accidentally see.

"Hey," Ross said, swallowing down his nerves, "you wanna . . ." He cleared his throat again. "You wanna dance?" He could not quite tack on the *with me* but he thought that Shaw, from the way his lips curved upwards with pleasure, understood what he meant.

"Yeah, that'd be nice. I'd like that a lot," Shaw said, standing up and putting his hand out. Ross hoped he wasn't gaping at it. Shaw wanted them to hold hands? *Oh my God, he'd never done that before, not with anyone. What if he did it wrong? What if he embarrassed himself?*

It's just holding hands, Ross told himself firmly as he stood up. *You are a semi-almost-successful business owner. You can fucking hold hands.*

And he did, reaching out for Shaw's hand and intertwining their fingers together.

Shaw squeezed his hand reassuringly, and together they walked towards the group of moving bodies.

To Ross' relief, Shaw didn't 1) take them too far into the crowd, because he must have known that Ross couldn't deal with all those people and 2) let go of his hand.

His own hand was a little sweaty and he was probably moving in a slightly robotic, likely terrifying way, but Shaw just kept smiling at him as they started to dance. Slowly at first, cautiously—at least on Ross' side. He could hear the music, hear the beat, and he tried to match it, tried to mirror Shaw's movements. Likely, he was doing a shit job of it, but Shaw didn't look embarrassed to be seen with him. Just kept smiling at him like Ross genuinely made him happy.

It gave Ross enough confidence to move a little closer, to grip Shaw's hand a little tighter. To reach up and put a hesitant hand on Shaw's waist, tugging him closer still.

"I like this."

Ross was pretty sure he'd heard Shaw correctly, but bent down so he could hear better. He realized his mistake a moment too late, because there was Shaw's mouth and it was *right there*.

"I said, *I like this*," Shaw said, the corner of his mouth curling up in amusement. And something else. Something else that made his stomach quake and his palms sweat.

You could kiss him, that annoying voice inside him tempted him, *it would be so easy. Just lean down and do it. Don't overthink it. He's just waiting for you; he said he was.*

It wasn't like Ross *hadn't* thought about kissing Shaw.

He had.

It was impossible to live together and *not* think about it.

But right now? With everyone undoubtedly watching? With no privacy?

"I like it too," Ross said, pulling back instead of dipping his mouth lower.

Was that a flash of disappointment in Shaw's eyes? Ross thought it might be. But he hadn't wanted their first kiss to be like this.

"You dancing and liking it?" Shaw grinned. "I think the earth might stop rotating."

Ross dug his fingertips into Shaw's waist in retaliation, and this time, he definitely didn't miss the flash of heat in Shaw's gaze.

Maybe Shaw was being patient. Maybe he was letting Ross take things at his own pace. But that didn't mean Shaw didn't want him.

That filled him with a particularly buoyant sort of joy. It was getting easier to slide from one song to the other. This one was slower, with a low sexy beat that made the itch almost unbearable.

"I *dance*," Ross teased. "Maybe I'm just more discerning than everyone else."

"Maybe," Shaw said speculatively. He looked pleased at Ross' suggestion.

Ross was just about to say, *no, I was wrong, I really* am *discerning and careful and you've crossed all my boundaries and I barely blinked.* Because *I wanted you there.*

But before he could lean down and confess the truth, the band played a last celebratory chord and instead of segueing into the next song, the singer announced that they were taking a twenty-minute break.

"Oh," Ross said instead. Shaw took a step back, and Ross dropped his hand, even though he didn't want to. Let go of his waist, even though he *really* didn't want to.

"I should . . ."

"We should . . ." Shaw said at the exact same time.

Ross hesitated. "What should we do?"

"What were you going to say?" Shaw asked, shaking his head.

"Uh, I was gonna say, I should probably head back to the apartment." Ross had been scrupulously careful *never* to refer to it as his home. It was Shaw's home. Not his. He was just staying for a little while.

"Really?" Shaw looked disappointed.

"I've got work tomorrow morning, and a late night tomorrow, testing for the new dish," Ross said.

He wasn't tired. He felt electrified. But he also didn't know how to tell Shaw that he wasn't quite ready yet—at least he wasn't ready to kiss him in front of God, AKA Tony—and everyone else.

Shaw wasn't stupid, not by a long shot, but what if he misunderstood? What if he thought Ross was saying he didn't want to, not ever?

"If you're sure," Shaw said. "I know you've got lots of balls in the air. Lots of things going."

He did. And he'd never been the kind of person okay with them dropping . . . but . . . Shaw made him want to not *drop* them exactly, but take a break from juggling.

"Maybe I finish up early tomorrow, we can watch another episode of *Home Town*," Ross said, hearing the hopefulness in his own voice.

"Yeah, yeah, I'd like that," Shaw said, patting him on the shoulder.

That wasn't enough.

Not anymore.

Maybe it had never been enough, and Ross was just beginning to realize that.

But he threw caution to the wind and reached out, pulling Shaw in for a quick, tight hug.

"See you tomorrow night," he murmured into his shoulder, before letting him go and turning to walk back to the apartment. Afraid if he didn't go now, he never would.

CHAPTER NINE

Recipe testing was one of Ross' favorite things to do.

He could get lost for hours, minutely adjusting one ingredient, then another, finalizing and perfecting a method, until he looked up and realized that the kitchen resembled a demilitarized zone and it was the middle of the night.

He'd started earlier tonight, hoping that wouldn't happen. Harmony had agreed to do the cleanup—she was learning quickly enough and just plain fucking good enough that Ross didn't even hesitate to leave her to the last few dinner stragglers and the cleanup after—and so he'd come back to the apartment just after seven after stopping at the grocery for supplies.

He'd made the caramel filling first, needing it to cool completely and then set, if he had a hope of getting it to not ooze out of the brownie waffle while it was halfway through cooking.

It was currently in the fridge, doing its final chill, before Ross planned on scooping it out and rolling it into flat pancakes, so he could fill the waffles.

So far, the biggest problem had been the lack of equipment in Shaw's kitchen. Ross almost regretted doing his testing here, because instead of a glass bowl he could rest inside a saucepot for a quick, makeshift double boiler to melt his chocolate in, Shaw not only didn't have a glass bowl, he didn't have a metal one either.

"Fucking plastic bowls," Ross muttered to himself as he watched the microwave like a hawk. Any longer than a few seconds at a time and the chocolate would burn instead of melt.

He yanked the door open after ten seconds, and gave the chopped chocolate an experimental stir with his spatula. Not quite ready yet. He set the timer for another ten seconds, and waited impatiently as the bowl rotated around inside the microwave.

His eggs were already out, and the dry ingredients measured and sifted, ready to add once he whisked the eggs into the melted chocolate.

Then, while the batter rested, he could mold his caramel inserts and finally preheat the waffle maker for the first trial run.

The microwave beeped.

Testing the chocolate with his spatula he decided some vigorous stirring would help it along until it was melted just enough.

The bowl was hot on its side. "Plastic," Ross said again, in disbelief, and set the bowl on the counter, hissing as it hit his bare torso.

While he was at home early, he'd decided to run a few loads of laundry, and figured he might as well throw in everything he was wearing, including the shirt he'd worn today. Shaw wasn't supposed to be home for hours, and Ross wouldn't bother showering until he'd finished his testing—so he'd thrown in his shirt, and not bothered to put a clean one on.

But he hadn't expected the plastic bowl problem either, or how it was holding the heat. He angled his body away from the bowl, stirring the chocolate briskly, making sure it was completely melted.

Trading the bowl of chocolate for the caramel in the fridge, he pulled out a spoon and began to roll the firmed-up mixture into balls. He flattened them, one at a time with a clean palm, making sure they weren't too thick—or too thin. Too thin and he wouldn't get the effect that he wanted. Too thick and the caramel wouldn't melt all the way through.

When he finished, Ross checked the chocolate. It had cooled enough, and he whisked in the eggs, beating the mixture for a few minutes, ignoring the burn in his arm as he manipulated the chocolate and the eggs. This part needed to be light and fluffy, before he folded in the dry ingredients.

"Well, Tony, let's see how shitty this waffle maker really is," Ross said to himself as he plugged it in, and cranked it up as high as it would go—which frankly wasn't high enough. But maybe it would work for his purposes.

He'd just have to find out.

Shaw had a rudimentary set of measuring cups, and as the waffle maker heated up, he grabbed the smallest one and was just giving the brownie batter one last whisk when unexpectedly the front door opened.

"Hey," Shaw said, walking in, a plastic to-go bag in one hand.

Ross didn't know who was more surprised; him to see Shaw, at only nine o'clock on a night he normally worked, or Shaw to see him making brownie waffles without a shirt on.

They stared at each other for a long moment, the food bag still dangling from Shaw's fingertips, his expression blank.

"You're here," he said, his wits and sanity the first to recover.

Ross considered grabbing a kitchen towel and draping it over his upper body, but that would be ridiculous. It was just a chest. With two nipples. And with hair, a little bit of it anyway, dark and leading to . . . well, *that* wasn't exposed, though it was definitely aware of what was going on between him and Shaw. A little too interested, if Ross had anything to say about it.

"Uh, yeah," Ross said, his voice low and rumbly. "Uh, I was doing some laundry and some brownies and uh . . ."

"You're fine." Shaw waved, like he came home early to Ross baking in his kitchen, half-naked, all the time.

Except he hadn't.

Not once.

This was definitely the first time. Ross would have remembered if it had happened before, because it was kinda unforgettable.

"What did you get?" Ross asked because food he could deal with.

The waffle maker beeped, signaling it was hot and ready to go.

Not the only thing in this kitchen that's hot and ready to go, Ross thought.

"Oh, Jose packed one of those subs I like for me, the one with the smoked turkey and the cheddar and the red pepper relish? And of course," Shaw said, whipping the plastic storage container out of the bag and opening it, "a generous helping of sweet potato fries."

Ross' stomach, just about as uncooperative as the rest of him, chose that moment to grumble.

Shaw just laughed. "I guess I'm not the only one who's hungry."

"You're . . ." Ross cleared his throat. Willing himself not to flush. Feeling it creep up his bare, completely exposed chest anyway. "You're off early."

"It was slow, and Jackson wanted to work with the new bartenders. Gave me the night off," Shaw said, munching on a handful of fries. "Thought you could use some help. I could always come around, feed you sweet potato fries as you make waffles."

Ross felt hot and cold all over at the thought of Shaw feeding him by hand.

"Uh, no, I'm good," Ross said weakly. "So good."

"Yeah, yeah, you are," Shaw said, and there was a sly edge to his voice. He was definitely looking at Ross' chest. Ross wasn't sure he'd *stopped* looking.

And hey, he got that. When Shaw had emerged wet and shirtless that first night, with just a towel wrapped around his waist, he'd nearly swallowed his tongue.

He felt itchy just thinking about it.

Or maybe that was how he felt with Shaw's undeniably hungry gaze on him now.

"So, tell me how it's going," Shaw continued, and he was walking around the countertop anyway, headed right for Ross and his brownie batter. Ross was still staring helplessly at him. He couldn't help it. He was supposed to be recipe testing, but all he wanted in this moment was to say *fuck Tony and fuck waffles* and pull Shaw tight against him, and kiss him, the way he'd been dying to last night.

"Uh, it's fine," Ross said stupidly. There wasn't much blood left in his brain, a situation that, any second now, Shaw was going to become aware of.

"This looks delicious," Shaw said, peering into the bowl with interest. "Can I have a little taste?"

Normal Ross would have told him no. Normal Ross wouldn't have even been very nice about it. But Normal Ross was not present. Itchy, Utterly Horny Ross was who was currently available, and he was ready to give Shaw just about anything he asked for.

Including, but not limited to, raw brownie batter.

"Sure," Ross said, and handed him the whisk. He didn't need it anymore, anyway, all he'd been planning to do with it was set it in the sink to rinse later. If Shaw licked it clean, then that would save him a step.

He should have realized what was going to happen *if Shaw licked it clean*, but again, he was lacking serious blood in his brain. Ross didn't realize his mistake until Shaw took the whisk eagerly and then his tongue flicked out, tasting just the tip of it, then curling around the wire loops, licking every single bit of chocolate off.

It was like . . . Ross' brain short-circuited.

It was like he was making out with the whisk.

Slowly. Deliberately. Enjoying every second of it.

Ross didn't think.

He was past thinking.

Thinking, he realized, was completely overrated.

"What are you doing?" he asked, his voice whisper-quiet.

Shaw glanced over at him. Looked. And then kept looking. "What?"

"You're . . ." Ross couldn't say the words. He just gestured, helplessly. "You're . . ."

Shaw set the whisk down in the sink. It made a deliberate click, metal on metal.

"Are you jealous?" he asked. "Of the whisk?"

Ross couldn't answer in words.

So he reached over, tugged Shaw against him, and told him in actions, instead.

Shaw melted against him, like the chocolate had, and his tongue was as sweet or *sweeter* than any sugary treat that Ross had ever craved. It curled around his own, the kiss ratcheting into even hotter territory, their mouths moving wetly together, just as their bodies did.

Shaw's fingers dug into Ross' shoulders, and then slipped down his back, and Ross realized dimly that he was tracing every muscle there, even as he pulled Shaw tighter against himself. Shaw's curious fingertips against his bare skin ratcheted his desire up even higher.

Yes, more, please, his greedy mind shouted, and he took even more, rubbing his hard cock against Shaw's. And it was definitely just as hard as his own. *Shaw wants this, he wants you, how did you ever get so fucking lucky?*

Ross didn't know, but he wasn't going to look a gift horse in the mouth. No, he was going to taste it and take it and eat it all up, until his craving ceased to aggravate every nerve ending in his body.

Until he wasn't so goddamned itchy anymore.

Shaw gasped, and yeah, that was probably because Ross' hands had found the pockets of his jeans and he was cupping and molding and just goddamn *feeling* Shaw's perfect ass. He hadn't even realized he was going to do it, or thought about it at all, he'd just done it. Like he couldn't get enough.

You can't. You already know you can't.

But then Shaw tore his mouth away, his breaths coming in deep, uneven pants. Like he'd just run a marathon.

Dimly, Ross could feel his own uneven breathing.

"That was . . . well, I guess you *were* jealous," Shaw joked weakly.

Ross didn't know where to look. Shaw's hands were still on his back, and everywhere he touched, his skin burned. Reluctantly he pulled his own hands away from Shaw's ass, allowing him to take another step back if he wanted.

To find reality.

To find *sanity*.

Shaw was such an even-keeled, kind, sweet sort of person.

Ross hadn't realized just how deep his feelings ran. Hadn't realized that he could be intense and sexual and needy, just like Ross was.

It was blowing his mind apart, and he didn't know how to start putting it back together again.

Another kiss would be a great place to start, his mind wheedled.

"You said that it was on my terms," Ross said quietly. "I wanted this. I wanted you."

The corner of Shaw's mouth quirked up. "*Wanted* or *want*?"

"Want. Definitely want."

Shaw's gaze softened. "I want you too. But I don't want to move too fast. Do something you'll regret. I know . . ." He hesitated and Ross could see the wheels turning in Shaw's brain. What was he thinking? What was holding him back? "I know you don't do this very often."

He didn't. Ross had a sudden, very unpleasant thought that maybe that was why Shaw had stopped.

"Is that why?" he asked, before he could stop himself.

"Why what?"

Ross took a step back. "Why you stopped kissing me. Because you think I don't have any experience."

"No, no, no," Shaw said, and to Ross' surprise he chased after him, following him just as Ross backed up. "No," he repeated again, insistently. He reached up and cupped Ross' neck with his hand, tugged him down, closer. "No," he said again. "I didn't want to stop. Truly I just don't want to move too fast for you."

Ross thought about this for a second.

There was definitely a part of him—okay, it was hands down his cock—that wanted to keep going.

But maybe Shaw was right. Now that thought and sanity had returned, he wasn't quite as sure.

He wanted to kiss Shaw again. He knew that. But he didn't know . . . it was a bigger step from kissing to letting Shaw touch him. To revealing how hard it was for him to come, sometimes.

Men didn't like that. In his experience, men liked it fast and quick and dirty, and sometimes Ross couldn't deliver on that.

Even if Ross was dying to.

He nodded.

"But," Shaw said wryly, "you'll tell me if things change, right?"

"I will."

Ross was tempted to tell him just his trust had been enough to make him want to throw caution to the wind, but that last little remnant of fear stopped him.

"Good," Shaw said, and took a step back and a deep breath. "Now, I'll . . . well, I guess I'll let you keep making those waffles." He grinned. "Long as I get the first one."

Shaw didn't feel like he could even take a deep breath until he was in his room, getting ready for bed.

He'd shared his sandwich and fries with Ross and then watched as he finished cooking the waffle. Then Shaw had eaten it, the brownie deep and complex and chocolatey, and the caramel rich and delicious, and then he'd eaten two more and would *definitely* be going for a run tomorrow because of it, but he found he couldn't regret it.

Just the way he couldn't regret the kiss.

Kissing Ross had been . . . well, the most amazing kiss he'd ever had.

And not only because he'd been dying for it, he wanted it so much, but because it had eclipsed all of his many fantasies.

Ross was intense and focused and dedicated and all of that turned on him . . .

Shaw's fingers tightened on the button of his jeans.

His cock was hardening again, with just the thought.

He'd never been so grateful that he had this room to himself, including a door that locked. Because he fully intended to spend the next ten minutes coming his brains out.

Shucking his jeans, he lay back on the bed and was just about to conjure up the feeling of Ross' mouth on his, the feel of his hands on his body, when he heard a sound from the bathroom.

He'd been pretty damn sure that after the episode of *Home Town* had finished playing and he'd turned off the TV, Ross was going to retreat into the bathroom and well . . . do the exact same thing that Shaw had planned on doing. The air had been too sexual, too charged. It was going to be impossible to resist, even if he'd tried.

Still, he hadn't expected to *hear* Ross in the bathroom.

Maybe in his wildest fantasies he might've imagined listening to Ross getting off, the rough, desperate sound of his breathing echoing in his head. But he'd never actually thought it was going to happen in real life.

Shaw listened carefully, quietly. There was that sound again.

It was just as rough. Just as desperate.

Oh God.

There it was again and Shaw's cock grew even harder, throbbing in his boxer briefs.

And then again.

And again.

And again.

Shit. What if something's wrong?

It kinda sounded like something was wrong. Not just like Ross was getting off, but that he was struggling, straining almost, and then, just when Shaw had resigned himself to listening but not doing anything about it, he heard a different sound.

Like someone was banging on the wall.

And not the fun kind of banging either, Shaw thought with resignation.

It sounded like frustration. It could also sound like panic.

He was going to have to go see what the fuck was going on.

He pulled his jeans up but didn't zip or button them, willed his cock to behave and went out into the living room, rapping quietly on the bathroom door just around the corner.

"Ross?" Shaw asked. "You okay in there?"

There was silence for a long moment.

Fraught silence, if Shaw had anything to say about it.

And then Ross said, "No. I mean. Yes. I mean . . ."

"Do you need help?" Shaw squeezed his eyes shut and tried to think of everything unsexy he could, to try to alleviate his arousal, but that didn't work.

He wanted to help Ross alright. Help him out of his pants, and help him to an unbelievable orgasm.

There was another long, almost painful pause.

"I think . . ." Shaw heard Ross take a deep breath. Unsteady. Nervous. Maybe even confused. "I think I do," he finally finished. "If that's okay with you."

Shaw cursed his natural instincts to help people who needed it.

"Okay," he said, "I'm coming in."

He pushed the door open, and all the thoughts in the world of Jackson and Alexis fucking couldn't have made him soft.

Ross was standing there, completely naked, his hand wrapped around his cock.

For a second, Shaw just stared.

You really couldn't blame him, because Ross was fucking gorgeous. A huge hunk of a man, with thick thighs and arms and *yeah,* Shaw thought with a hard swallow, *thick everywhere.*

But then he got up to Ross' face and the concern on his face, the utter terror, undid him and pushed him into the room.

"What's going on?" Shaw asked, trying to look anywhere but at Ross' naked body. Yes he'd looked before, but the guy was clearly not okay and he wasn't going to be that creeper roommate, even if they'd shared an epic kiss earlier.

The trust in Ross' eyes nearly undid him. "You wanted me to tell you," he said unsteadily. "This is me telling you."

Shaw barely kept his jaw from dropping open. Ross was already clearly so distressed, he didn't want to upset him more by showing his shock. But he *was* shocked.

"What do you mean?" he asked, needing to be sure.

Ross waved his hand—his *other* hand, Shaw thought—and said, "You know what I mean. You told me to tell you when I wanted to. And I want to."

He glanced down. "And you want to, too, I can tell."

Shaw cleared his throat. "You mean you want to have sex. Get each other off."

"Yes." Ross shot him a glance like he was crazy.

And maybe he was crazy! Why wasn't he jumping all over this? Why wasn't he throwing caution to the wind and replacing Ross' hand with his own and gluing their mouths together again, losing himself in the unexpected heat of their passion?

"I . . ." It was the look of distress that Ross had worn earlier. Only a minute earlier. That was what was stopping him.

He started again. "We don't have to do this, unless you want to. I can turn around and go back in my room and well . . ." Shaw hesitated. "We can both do what we were going to do."

"But I want it to be you. It . . ." Ross glanced down. "It wants it to be you."

"You don't want to jerk off, by yourself," Shaw clarified.

Ross shot him another look. Impatient. Frustrated. "I . . . it's hard for me sometimes," he admitted. "I don't always . . . I know you'll be patient. You'll be good. You'll treat me good."

Shaw was hardly the most selfless person in the world; or the best, either. He could barely *not* look at Ross' cock. But he was a listener, and he was listening now.

He took a step closer. Then another. Put his hand, not where he really wanted to put it, but on Ross' chest instead. Feeling his sharp intake of breath.

"Can you tell me why?" Shaw's fingers traced downward. Lower, and then lower still.

Ross shuddered at his touch. "It's too much sometimes. Feels too good. And I have to stop. And then start. And then stop." His gaze was beseeching. "You can't get mad."

"I'd never get mad," Shaw said gently.

"I know."

The trust in Ross' eyes blew Shaw away. He was asking him now, for this, not just because he liked Shaw, but because he trusted him. He believed in him. He knew, without a doubt, that Shaw wouldn't ever hurt him.

That he'd be with him every step of the way, no matter how long it took.

"Then . . . will you?" Ross asked again.

"Yeah, yeah, I will." Shaw's voice felt gravelly to his own ears, and his blood was thumping hard, he could feel it in his cock, twitching with it. But he ruthlessly pushed his own pleasure to the side, and focused on Ross.

"Okay." Ross sounded uncertain, and for the first time, loosened his grip on his own cock, like he was inviting Shaw to touch.

But instead of reaching out for it, instead Shaw lifted his head and kissed him.

Ross kissed back instantly, without even the slightest bit of hesitation, tilting his head so he could kiss him deeper.

Only when Ross was lost in the kiss, did Shaw, barely hanging on to his own control, reach out and wrap his fingers around Ross' straining, rock-hard length. Not hard, but *gently*, because he didn't want to scare Ross away or overwhelm him.

Ross gasped into his mouth and he reached up, his fingers sinking into Shaw's hair tugging his head so he could find an even deeper angle.

Shaw twisted his fingers and was rewarded with another deep, pleasured sound. He did it again, and then again, until Shaw could feel Ross trembling against him.

It killed him, but he was doing this for a reason—and then there was that deep trust shining in Ross' eyes—so he stopped. Just stood there for a minute, kissing Ross, feeling his cock twitch in his hand. Then he ran his thumb across the tip, gathering the precome there, and gave another sharp twist.

Between the kiss and the slow, deliberate pleasure he was giving Ross, Shaw felt like his own dick was going to explode—but he held back. Resisted the urge to press it harder against Ross' hip, even though he desperately wanted to.

He started and then stopped twice more, the last time Ross making a high, whining noise in the back of his throat, and Shaw hoped then that he was ready to come, because he needed it more than he needed his own orgasm.

Ross tore his mouth off Shaw's and groaned long and rough as Shaw began to work him again, this time in earnest, pushing Ross right up to the point of no return, and then right when Shaw thought he was going to shake apart in his arms, he kissed him again.

Moaning through the kiss, Ross began to tremble and that was when Shaw knew he had him. He gave one last rough stroke and Ross' cock twitched, his body quivering as he came and came, emptying into Shaw's hand.

"Oh God," Ross groaned, his head falling onto Shaw's shoulder. "Oh, God, you are really good at that."

"Better?" Shaw asked.

Ross was quaking harder now—more like *shaking*, Shaw realized. Release must not come for him very often, and Shaw promised himself that he would do whatever he could to make it easier.

Then it occurred to him that he wasn't crying or upset.

He was *laughing*. With relief?

"I can't believe . . ." Ross raised his head and wiped his eyes. "You knew exactly what I needed."

"It was a lucky guess," Shaw said, reaching back to flick the water on, washing his hand off.

Ross' eyes darkened even further. "Speaking of lucky . . ." He glanced down at Shaw's obviously hard cock.

"You don't have to do anything you don't want to do," Shaw said.

Ross shot him a look. "You think I don't want to?"

And then he shut Shaw right up by dropping to his knees, tugging Shaw's jeans down, and then his boxer briefs.

"Like I wouldn't . . ." Ross grumbled under his breath, Shaw barely catching the words right before his mouth slid all the way down, taking him in in a long, slick, mind-blowing slide.

Shaw had just a split second to think, *Oh my God, Ross Stanton is sucking my cock* before he was definitely sucking it in earnest, eagerly tonguing him, before taking him back into his mouth.

He stumbled back, the sudden blinding pleasure overwhelming him, his back hitting the sink vanity. Reaching back, he gripped the edges of it with his fingers, trying to hang on to the little bit of control that Ross hadn't eroded away.

He was passionate and committed, his fingertips digging into Shaw's hips, devouring him like he'd been wanting Shaw's taste on his tongue forever.

Shaw had a fleeting, disbelieving thought, *How long* has *he wanted to do this?*

The truth was, Ross' waters ran deep, and it was possible that this had been going on for him just as long as it had for Shaw.

And that blew his mind the rest of the way, one hand letting go of the counter to drift down to Ross' hair. Ross groaned around his dick, like that was the sexiest, hottest thing he could imagine, and any control left? Disappeared completely.

It was inevitable that this was going to be quick, especially since working Ross up to his orgasm had turned him on so much, but Shaw was shocked at *how* quick it was, feeling his orgasm overtake him.

Ross sucked him dry, sinking back onto his heels when Shaw finally stopped twitching through the orgasm of the fucking century.

It had been that amazing.

For a long moment, neither of them said anything. Ross was still looking at the floor. Shaw couldn't look anywhere else but at

Ross' bent head. Finally he reached down and wrapped his hand around Ross' upper arm, helping him to his feet.

"That was . . ." Shaw realized, halfway through his sentence, that he didn't know *what* it was.

Extraordinary?

Incredible?

Life-changing?

Just the kiss had blown his foundations apart, and what they'd just shared had been even hotter, blasting him with an incendiary heat.

Ross licked his lips, like he could still taste Shaw on them, and finally met his gaze. "You liked it?"

"I loved it," Shaw said, and then he was laughing too.

In a million years, he'd never imagined that he would be more than just passingly attracted to Ross Stanton. But it was more than just that. In a few weeks, he'd become vital to Shaw. He couldn't go a day without seeing him, without talking to him.

He didn't know if Ross felt the same way, but the way he'd trusted him? Opened up to him? Shaw wondered if maybe they were on exactly the same page.

He almost asked. The question was right on the tip of his tongue, when he remembered.

He'd made a promise that Ross could set the pace. He would have to let Ross decide when it was time to talk about more than just a few kisses and some mind-blowing orgasms.

But he could do this. He reached out and pulled Ross into a long, tight hug.

I really like you. I like you more than I ever thought I would.

I think this surprised you just as much, but I'm here with you, every step of the way.

Maybe he couldn't say the words, but he could communicate them through his touch.

Finally Ross pulled back, and there was a quiet satisfaction in his gaze.

"Thank you," he said.

Shaw couldn't help the laugh that escaped him. "Trust me, it wasn't a hardship."

Ross' expression turned pleased and bashful. "For me either."

"Well, if you want more, you know where to find me." Shaw gestured towards his bedroom. For a second, he almost invited him into it. Wouldn't sleeping together be so much nicer than sleeping by himself on the couch?

It might be, but it would need to be Ross' decision.

As hard as that might be.

"Okay." Ross nodded seriously. "I will." He turned to go, and Shaw had to physically hold his hands back from grabbing for him again.

Ross was beginning to be one of those serious kinds of addictions.

The kind where you couldn't get enough, no matter how much you had.

CHAPTER TEN

"You're in a good mood," Harmony said as they prepped for the day's orders.

Ross didn't think he'd done or said anything to indicate that, even though *yes*, he definitely was. At least for him.

"What? Why?" Ross kept dredging the chicken pieces that had been marinating in the buttermilk and spices overnight.

"You keep grinning into the breading station," Harmony said. "It's not like you, that's all. But it's nice to see."

"It is?" Ross hadn't even realized he'd been smiling. But maybe he had been.

The kiss and then more with Shaw had been so unexpected—though he supposed that wasn't entirely true, because if he was honest with himself, it had been on his mind since he'd moved in—and so wonderful that maybe he couldn't even help himself.

"Oh yeah," Harmony said with a grin. "You gonna tell me what's going on?"

Ross didn't think Harmony was a gossip, but he also didn't know if he should share.

"Uh," Ross hesitated. "I guess . . . I guess I met someone?"

Harmony's face broke into a huge smile. "You did, did you? That's great."

"Yeah, yeah, he kinda is," Ross admitted. *Kind and sweet and generous and patient and well . . . hot as the fucking sun.*

And his hands?

Ross was still thinking about them. He couldn't figure out how to stop.

"Aw," Harmony said. "You're in love."

Ross dropped a whole piece of chicken. "What?" he exclaimed. "What? *No.*"

"Yeah, well, you tell that to the smile you keep sporting," she teased.

"We're just . . ." Ross cleared his throat. *We're just having incredibly spontaneous, incredibly sexy orgasms in the bathroom.* "We're just figuring things out. It's . . . it's new."

"Oh?" Harmony raised an eyebrow.

"It's new but it's good," Ross said with finality. Hoping that the conversation was over, and they could get back to work.

"Good," Harmony said. "You deserve good things, Ross."

Ross wasn't sure if he'd ever really believed that; probably why he'd never considered that Shaw could be interested in him back. But maybe . . . just maybe he did deserve Shaw's attention and his affection.

Shaw seemed to think so—and just the thought of it made Ross' heart light and buoyant, like it could float.

There was a sharp rap on the back door and Ross wiped his hands on a towel and walked over, pushing it open.

The produce delivery guy was standing there, but there was a look in his eyes that told Ross that this wasn't like other deliveries. Something was up.

Something was *wrong*.

Ross felt his stomach drop to the floor.

What other unpleasant surprises was he going to find out about, months after Aaron had been arrested?

"You Ross Stanton?" the produce guy asked, pulling a sheaf of papers out of his back pocket.

Ross nodded uncertainly. He could think of more than one occasion in the last six months that he didn't want to be Ross Stanton.

Definitely not last night.

But today? He wasn't going to have a choice.

"Yeah," he said shortly.

"I've got your delivery," the guy said, "but I've got some back statements that they asked me to give you, too."

"Oh?" Ross tried to sound imperious and unconcerned, but there was a coil of dread in his heart.

How much money did he owe now? How long would it take him to dig his way out of *this* hole?

If he could visit Aaron in prison and wring his neck—and get away with it—he'd do it. It was only a minor reassurance that Aaron *was* in prison.

The produce guy handed over the *thick* set of papers. They crinkled in Ross' hand.

"You do have the delivery though?" Ross asked, hating himself for needing to ask.

Hating Aaron more.

"Yeah, I've got it," the guy said, "but you gotta deal with . . ."

"I'll deal with it," Ross cut him off abruptly.

"Okay, good." He turned away, ready to unload his van.

When Ross turned back to the breading station, the papers shoved into *his* back pocket, Harmony was staring at him intently.

"Everything okay?" He already knew the mild tone of her voice was an act.

She was interested. There was that gleam in her eye. He'd begun to recognize it.

Maybe she should be interested, he thought, because the continued existence of this truck was her employment. And if he kept discovering more and more unpaid bills, he didn't know how he'd manage to keep it afloat.

"Yeah," he said shortly.

His good mood had been pricked with a pin. Abruptly.

"Doesn't seem to be," she said, coming to lean against the counter next to the breading station. "Sounds like the produce guy thinks you owe some money."

"I might," Ross admitted. Truthfully, he had no fucking idea, and that was the most terrifying part of all.

He was too anxious to even pull the papers out of his back pocket and begin to examine them. And even if he did, would he even be able to make heads or tails out of them? He wasn't sure.

The poultry distributor had worked with him, explained the balance on his account, so he'd been able to figure it out.

But this?

Ross didn't even know where to start.

"You want some help?" Harmony's voice was still casual, but he could *feel* how much she wanted to help.

Maybe . . . maybe he should let her.

But then maybe she'd end up being another Aaron, another snake in the grass, seducing him in with her offers of assistance and how good she was at this—and how bad *he* was—and then she'd betray him, in the end.

Ross knew he couldn't live through another betrayal.

He needed to approach this carefully. Deliberately.

"Maybe," Ross said again, and she made a face at his words.

"Really? But I can *help* you," she repeated again. "I've got the background, you remember that, right? I can go through the accounts, figure out what you owe, figure out how to pay them back. Maybe negotiate a monthly payoff amount."

"I've got it," Ross said stiffly. Maybe it wasn't fair to Harmony, but all he heard was, *and I'll take over again and leave you clueless, and maybe, ultimately, back in the same hole you were in before.*

Maybe an even deeper one.

"You're being stubborn," she observed.

"Yeah, maybe," Ross said. "But I'll think about it."

"You sure about that?"

Ross wasn't sure about much, not anymore.

Well, no, that wasn't one hundred percent accurate, not anymore.

There was one person he was definitely sure of.

Maybe he'd talk to Shaw about this, see what he thought. Shaw would tell him the truth—the whole truth, the unvarnished truth, even if he didn't like it—and maybe they could even talk about it.

He turned to Harmony. "I'm sure the rest of the dressings need made," he said, "and then the veggies inspected and prepped."

She smiled with resignation. "Yeah, boss. I get it. You've got this handled."

But he didn't.

Not at all.

He might not be the best in the world at this—likely he was closest to the *worst* in the world at this—but he knew that much.

Ross had just finished beating the cream and the sweetened condensed milk together for his ice cream, when Shaw walked in the door.

He'd not been able to leave Harmony early tonight. It had been busy and it had taken them both an hour after their last customer to clean the truck to his satisfaction. It was later tonight; Ross had half expected that he'd be too tired to test the ice cream, but he'd reasoned with himself that it had to freeze. He might as well get it in the freezer, working its magic. Shaw had clearly not gotten off early either, and maybe, Ross had decided, that was better.

Better, because with enough time to settle, he didn't feel like the first thing he'd do was jump the guy.

"Hey," Shaw said, walking into the kitchen, "you're still testing?"

"No-churn ice cream," Ross said, pouring the first layer of the mixture into the loaf pan he'd ordered from Amazon yesterday. It had been waiting for him tonight when he'd come back to the apartment.

"You don't have to churn ice cream?" Shaw sounded fascinated.

"I mean you *can*," Ross said, sprinkling in toasted pecans on top of the first layer, and then swirling in the extra caramel he'd made the other day and then re-heated until it was pourable. "But it's just as good like this. Better, even, 'cause you don't have to work so hard."

But Shaw didn't look entirely convinced. "It's just as creamy as if you churned it?" he asked.

Ross shot him a look; didn't hold back. Yes, he was kinda enthralled by the guy. He wasn't only patient and kind, he kinda gave a shit about him, plus there were those hands . . . Ross almost got lost, thinking about Shaw's hands. But nobody got away with questioning his superior culinary skills.

"Haven't you ever watched *Chopped*?" Ross asked. "And seen the issues with the ice cream maker? It's not a foolproof method. It's so easy to over or under churn. Or not have precisely the right amount of butterfat. This? This method is not only easy, it's foolproof."

"Fine, fine." Shaw was laughing now. "You win. It's better. I guess you're going to have to prove it to me."

"You can try some when it's frozen," Ross said, drizzling more caramel sauce and more pecans over the top of the mounded cream in the loaf pan.

"Aw, I gotta wait?" Shaw questioned in a teasing voice, leaning over and brushing a quick kiss across Ross' cheek. "Sad. I'm gonna go take a shower, then. Watch an episode of *Home Town* when I'm done?"

"Sure, I'm almost done here."

He wrapped the loaf pan carefully in plastic wrap, making sure to insulate the contents from freezer burn, and then cleaned up his mess.

He'd just gotten an episode queued up when Shaw emerged from the bathroom, damp hair and tired eyes and looking far too edible for Ross' liking.

Normally, he'd have eaten him up with a spoon, but he was still thinking about what Harmony had said.

On a quick break later this afternoon, he'd read through the papers, trying to understand what they meant, but it was like they were written in a different language that he just didn't speak.

He didn't want to ask Harmony, because it was hard to admit that he couldn't do something. But maybe he should.

"You look more intense than normal," Shaw said, taking a seat next to him. Over the last few weeks, the space between them on the couch had grown smaller and smaller until it didn't exist anymore. Shaw cuddled right up next to him, and Ross was glad; he wouldn't want him to be any place else. "Everything okay?"

Ross hesitated. One of the reasons he'd always avoided relationships was he was fucking terrible at being vulnerable, at opening himself up. He'd done a little bit of it so far with Shaw—without, he realized, even meaning to; it had just *happened*—but this would be far more deliberate.

"Vendors keep coming out of the woodwork with more money I supposedly owe them," Ross said. He clenched his fist, and then forced himself to relax.

"Supposedly?" Shaw questioned.

"It's probably accurate," Ross admitted. "But I can't fucking figure out what it all means. How to fix it. How to prevent it."

Shaw looked sympathetic. A situation that normally would have annoyed Ross considerably. He didn't necessarily *like* it now, either, but he was willing to tolerate it because he needed Shaw's advice, and on top of that, Shaw had never held back with him. He deserved someone who was honest about what shit they were going through.

"I could ask Jackson to help you out, he's great at this kind of stuff," Shaw said.

Jackson? *Ugh*, Ross thought, *no, thank you.*

Maybe Jackson had been a bit friendlier the last few times they'd seen each other, but they weren't ever going to be friends. Ross was fairly certain that he wasn't happy that his brother was . . . well, whatever they were doing . . . with Ross.

If Shaw had even told him yet.

"Actually, I was thinking about Harmony," Ross said hesitantly. "I guess she's got a background in this kind of stuff. Accounting and business. She got a degree before she decided she'd die in an office."

"She offered?"

"Yeah." Ross looked at the hole forming in his flannel sleep pants. Picked at it further, the threads unwinding. "I didn't handle it well."

Shaw chuckled. "You weren't the most trusting guy in the world before Aaron fucked you over. Nobody can blame you for being nervous about trusting someone else after everything he did to you, even someone who seems as trustworthy as Harmony does. I'd offer, but I'm shit at this stuff, too. What you need is . . . well, how about this? What if she taught you?"

Ross frowned. "She taught me?"

"Not *taught* necessarily, but what if she went over with you everything that she was doing? Explained it? In detail? So you wouldn't ever be in the dark."

"That sounds awful," Ross grumbled. "Boring and difficult and awful."

"Yeah, well, you wanted to start a small business." The edge of Shaw's mouth quirked up. "This is the price. And hey, maybe in a few months, you'll feel more comfortable giving Harmony more responsibility. If she's good at this, she could be an asset. You wouldn't have to worry about it anymore."

Ross would give anything—except Basket, he refused to give that up—to not worry about money and bills and keeping everything afloat anymore.

He'd almost sacrificed his dream before, because he'd been too eager to trust the wrong person. "I think if . . . if she kept me in the loop, if I knew everything . . ." Ross took a deep breath. "If she *taught* me, okay, I could be okay with it."

Shaw smiled, and then leaned over, resting his head on Ross' shoulder. "See? That wasn't so hard."

"Easy for you to say," Ross retorted. "You've got your brother to manage things."

"And Jackson might be a lot of things but at least he's honorable?" Shaw laughed. "Yeah. I'm lucky. I know it. But seriously, I get you being hesitant to bring Harmony in, fully. But I think it could be good for both of you."

Ross shot him a look. "You think it's going to be good for me to study numbers?"

"Well, good for you in the long run," Shaw said, his smile lopsided. "Might even help you learn to trust again."

"I do . . ." Ross took a deep breath. "I trust *you*, more than I ever trusted anyone else. Even Aaron. Especially Aaron."

Shaw's expression grew serious. A pleased kind of serious. "I trust you, too."

"And I like you," Ross said in a rush, before he could think better of it. "I like you a lot."

Shaw reached out and took Ross' hand, still picking at that hole in his pajama pants. Gripped it tightly, reassuringly. "I like you too. A lot. Back when you moved in, I thought, if it's just me feeling this way, it won't be a big deal. I can control it. I can deal with it. But then . . . then it wasn't just me, and that was . . ." Shaw paused, the smile on his face blinding with happiness. "That was the best fucking thing ever."

"You liked me *before*?" Ross couldn't believe it. That felt . . . well, too good to be true.

Shaw flushed pink. "Yeah, yeah, I did. A little. That attraction thing, that wasn't new."

Reaching out, Ross tucked Shaw more solidly under his arm. Straight up *snuggling* with him. He'd never, not in a thousand years, imagined that he'd ever want to do this. And now not only did he want to, he didn't know how he'd ever live without it.

Shaw had changed him. Yeah, learning to be on his own, after Aaron and what Aaron had done, that had changed him too. Maybe not all in good, productive, positive ways. But Shaw? Shaw made him want to be *better*.

Shaw made him, for the first time in his life, wonder what it might feel like if he wasn't just happy with his work.

"I didn't know why you kept coming around my truck . . ."

"'Cause you make the best food ever," Shaw interrupted.

"But I wasn't going to stop you. My day? Always a little bit better when you smiled at me."

Ross remembered one of the last conversations he'd had with Aaron. *You're stunted and stuck and you're gonna be alone forever*, he'd said to him.

Sometimes Aaron's tough love had been a little too tough.

It had hit a nerve, and Ross had thought, at the time, that he was probably right.

Or, maybe, he wondered, he hadn't just met the right person yet.

"This isn't easy for me," Ross told Harmony as they sat at one of the picnic tables in front of the truck. It was mid-afternoon, and there'd be almost no customers til dinner, probably, and if anyone did show up, he could always see them approach the truck and hop over to help them.

Harmony shot him a look. "I didn't think it would be," she said.

Ross sighed. Long-sufferingly.

"Here's the deal. I can't do this. I tried. I fucked it up. Well," he added wryly, "it was fucked up to begin with, that wasn't me. But I'm not sure I made it any better."

Looking over the piles of papers that Ross had set on the table, Harmony tapped a finger on the wood top. "This is everything you've got?"

Ross turned his laptop to face her. "And there's some stuff on there," he said. "But it's not up to date. Aaron was using Quickbooks but I don't think he was very good at it, or else he was deliberately not entering what was right into the system."

"You said he stole money?"

Ross nodded.

"Well, he was probably putting false amounts into Quickbooks, claiming he'd paid bills, and then just pocketing the money."

The surge of anger felt familiar. Ross was used to tamping it back down after it roiled through him. But he was so fucking *tired* of it.

Maybe it would be good to have Harmony get to the bottom of everything, once and for all, and then he could stop being surprised. He'd know exactly where he stood.

"I want to know what's happening. You have to tell me every-thing."

Harmony's sympathetic look galled more than Shaw's had, last night.

"Of course," she said, "but it's going to take me some time to get to the bottom of all this. There's a . . . well, there's a lot of shit here."

"Okay," Ross agreed. "But I really want to deal with the pro-duce one first, since they're threatening to stop deliveries."

"Sure, we can do that. I can probably figure that one out today." Harmony pointed to a pile in front of Ross. "This is what they gave you, right?"

He nodded.

"Okay, let's go through this." Harmony pointed to the laptop. "Mind if I open a spreadsheet?"

"No, go right ahead."

Harmony clicked away at the keys, looking very much like she knew what she was doing.

She does, Ross reminded himself. *She was going to do this for a living.*

Before she came to her senses. That voice sounded like Shaw's, and it was amused.

Ross took the opportunity to text Shaw. He was probably just opening the bar, getting it ready for the evening. **You were right,** Ross sent to him, **but don't get all uppity about it.**

Shaw's response back was almost immediate. **About Harmony?**

And me. Ross hadn't really meant to type it, but once he did, he knew it was true. Shaw *had* been right. This was good for him, even if it was difficult.

Especially because it was difficult.

Well, I'm glad she's working out. You coming by the bar later?

Ross hadn't planned on it. But maybe he'd grab the ice cream from the freezer upstairs and surprise Shaw at the bar, later. Catch him on his break.

I might, Ross ended up texting back even though he already knew he would be.

Hope to see you, Shaw replied.

It warmed his heart, even though he'd already known that was why Shaw had asked—because he genuinely did want to see him.

"Hey," Harmony said, catching Ross' attention, pulling it away from his phone.

"What is it?"

"Some of these figures don't make sense," Harmony said, a crease appearing between her dark brows. "Would you be okay if I called the company and asked to talk to the accountant? I want to verify some of the numbers."

Ross' first inclination was to say no. This wasn't Harmony's job.

Except it was. He'd come to her and asked her to help. This was what the help looked like.

His next inclination was just to say yes and let her deal with it.

And then he remembered what Shaw had suggested.

"I don't have an issue with that," Ross said, "but I want to understand too, before we call. If that's okay?"

"So this doesn't make sense," Harmony said, pushing the laptop around. "See this line of figures?"

Ross nodded.

"They should add up. I pulled them from the statement they gave you yesterday. Each entry is a delivery they made to the truck, a charge for produce you ordered."

"Okay," Ross said. "This isn't that complicated."

"It's not," Harmony said. "The problem here is that the numbers don't add up to the same total they have at the bottom of the statement."

"Why not?"

Harmony shrugged. "I don't know. It doesn't make sense. That's why I want to talk to them. It looks like maybe payments were applied but not actually applied? It's possible that Aaron didn't screw you over here."

"You really think so?" Ross could barely believe it. He realized that every single time something like this came up, he was always bracing for the worst. Preparing for the scenario in which he might have to do something drastic to save the truck.

What if he didn't? And he didn't because he'd asked Harmony for help?

Shaw was never going to let him live this down.

And even worse, he'd be *right*.

"I know, it's shocking, right?" Harmony said wryly. "From everything I've heard, he was a rotten guy—and that's before I started working for you. You don't say much about him but it's clear he left you in a bad spot."

"Yeah." Ross rubbed his face with his hand. "Yeah, he really did."

"Well, let's see if we can get you out of it," Harmony said. "Is there anything else you know about this account that I should be aware of before we call?"

Ross had to give it to her; she learned *fast*. Had already figured out that he was way less on edge if it was *them*, and not *me*.

"Uh, well, sometimes I'd be unhappy with one of the deliveries. Not all of it, but some of it. Enough that they'd credit me back for what I didn't like."

Harmony nodded, her fingers tapping away on the keys.

"You have any records of those credits?"

Ross felt ashamed. "No," he said. "The few times I brought it up with Aaron, he'd just smile and nod, say it was all taken care of. I . . . I should've asked to see things. I should have not made it so goddamn easy for him to fool me."

"You guys were partners," she said, tucking a strand of hair behind an ear. "You'd known him for years. Why would you imagine that he'd cheat you?"

"I wouldn't." And that was the truth. Ross still woke up some mornings and found his equilibrium off because of it.

"Right. So, we know there should be some credits, but . . ." Harmony trailed off. "There's no record of them in these bills or this statement. And nothing adds up."

"Sounds about right," Ross said.

When he found the number and dialed, finally getting through to the person who claimed they were the accountant for the small local produce company, Ross was smart enough to essentially introduce Harmony and let her handle the direct questions.

He tried to pay attention, which didn't come naturally to him, because what he really wanted was to zone out and think about food, because numbers were boring, but he'd already leaned the hard way what the cost of doing that was, so he did his best to follow what Harmony and the other woman were discussing.

When Harmony got through explaining the initial situation, there was a long sigh at the other end of the phone.

"What is it?" she asked.

"Sometimes there's a bug in the system," the accountant said. "Not frequently, but sometimes. And it's hard to find, because no offense, Mr. Stanton, most of you guys don't really review your bills or your statements."

"No offense taken," Ross said. He *hadn't* reviewed any of them. And it was seeming like Aaron hadn't either.

"Let me do some digging, put together a better reporting," she said. "I'm seeing some of the credits as I'm looking at your file . . . but yeah, not reflected on your account, not on the statement anyway." She hesitated again. "And payments, too, actually."

Ross let out the breath he hadn't known he was holding.

"Payments?" He could barely believe it, even though Harmony had told him it was possible.

"Yeah," she said. "Like I said, let me do some digging here. Put together an actual accounting of where you're at, and I'll get back to you in a few days. This a good number?"

"Yeah," Ross said. "But let me know when you're going to call so I can make sure to have Harmony here."

"Sure thing," the woman said. "I'll text you ahead of time."

Harmony shot him a grateful and happy smile.

A *relieved* smile.

It boggled the imagination that she wanted to help as much as he needed the help . . . but that seemed to be how it was.

Shaw would no doubt tell him to stop looking for the worst in everyone.

Speaking of Shaw . . .

He was definitely going to bring him the ice cream tonight.

CHAPTER ELEVEN

I T   W A S   J U S T   P A S T ten when he and Harmony finished closing up the truck and he darted upstairs after his walk over to the bar, taking a quick shower and grabbing the ice cream from the freezer.

Shaw was behind the bar when Ross walked in, his back to the room, filling some pint glasses with beer, and when he turned he immediately spotted Ross and smiled. Big and wide, taking over his entire handsome face—somehow, impossibly, making him even *more* handsome.

That's for you, Ross realized, *that smile is* your *smile.*

"Hey," Shaw said. "You came after all."

"Can't be too predictable," Ross said. Even though he already knew he was painfully predictable. At least he'd been in the times Before Shaw.

"Right," Shaw teased. "Of course not. What you got there?"

"Ice cream for sampling," Ross said, waving the container. "You want to take a break and grab some spoons?"

"Yeah, I can do that," Shaw said. "Give me a few minutes. Meet me out on the back patio?"

Ross thought about this suggestion for a second, then shook his head.

"What about your storage room?" he asked.

Shaw gave him a blank look.

"You want to try the ice cream in our storage room?"

"This isn't regular ice cream," Ross said, "this is some serious high-powered ice cream. Does it have a door? That locks?"

"High-powered ice cream?" Shaw raised an eyebrow. "And yes it has a door, but it doesn't lock."

Ross considered this for a moment.

He'd come here with not just the ice cream in mind, and even though no lock wasn't optimal, he'd figure out a way to make it work.

"Okay," Ross said finally with a decisive nod. "The storage room, then."

Shaw shook his head, smiling again, like he was charmed in spite of himself. "You're not like other people, you know?"

Ross knew.

He'd known his entire life.

But usually when people told him that, they were frustrated and exasperated, and it was their way of telling him that they wished he were "normal." Whatever the fuck that actually meant.

Ross knew that wasn't what Shaw meant, though.

Ross also knew that Shaw didn't want him to be anything else but exactly who he was.

"It's why I like you," Shaw added wryly as he grabbed glasses, mixing drinks. "You know that, right?

Ross nodded. "I do know."

"Good. Let me make these drinks and check in with Bryan. Then we should be able to head to the . . ." He grinned. "The storage room, I guess."

Ross waited until Shaw had helped the other bartender catch up on the drink orders, and then Shaw beckoned him towards the narrow hallway next to the main bar area.

Ross knew this was the same direction as the bathrooms, and he thought he'd heard someone mention once that Jackson had his office down this hallway, too, but other than needing to pee a handful of times, he hadn't been down this way.

"Here, your highness, the storage room," Shaw teased, pushing the door at the end of the hallway. Ross followed him in, juggling the container of ice cream in one hand.

Shaw fumbled for the light switch, but before he could find it, Ross pushed him against the door, pressing him against it firmly.

"Wha . . ." Shaw said, but that was all he got out before Ross tipped his head down and kissed him insistently.

It only took an instant before Shaw stopped struggling and started kissing him back, Shaw not even hesitating to match his urgency. Like he'd been thinking about it, too, and once Ross had pushed them onto this path, he was helpless to avoid following wherever Ross led.

Their tongues slid together, and Ross felt his pulse begin to beat even faster.

They probably wouldn't have much time, but it was hard to stop kissing Shaw because it just felt too goddamn good.

But finally, he managed to pull back. It was too dark to see Shaw's face, but Ross could *feel* him.

"I thought we were gonna try some ice cream." Shaw sounded like he was both incredibly turned on and unbelievably amused.

"We are. But first . . ."

Ross had seen, right when Shaw opened the door, that there was a section of shelves to the right and he took advantage and deposited the ice cream container onto them.

"First what?" Shaw sounded fascinated.

"First, I wanted to do this," Ross said, and slid a palm down Shaw's chest, tugging open the button on his jeans.

"Oh . . . *oh*," Shaw said, wonder and amazement in his voice as Ross dropped to his knees. "What about . . . what about if anyone comes in?"

Ross glanced up. Could only make out the barest outline of Shaw's face. "Will someone come in?"

"Uh, well, *maybe*?"

"You sound unsure," Ross said. "Guess you should make sure you hold that door closed."

"What?" Shaw's voice sounded strangled as Ross pulled down his jeans, and then his boxer briefs.

"Hold the door shut," Ross said, licking his lips. "You do good, you get ice cream."

"What about a blowjob?" Shaw wondered. His voice went contemplative, like he was talking to himself. "You know, Jackson's always fucking on his couch."

"Jackson fucks in his office?" Ross leaned forward and licked up the underside of Shaw's cock, hearing the sharp intake of his breath.

"More than you'd imagine," Shaw muttered. "I guess I know why now."

Ross smiled, despite himself. He enjoyed giving blowjobs—had especially enjoyed giving Shaw one the other night—but there was something special, something he couldn't quite put his finger on, that drove him now.

He'd wanted to give Shaw something.

Not just words. Because God knew he was shitty at words.

But an action, an experience that he wouldn't ever forget, that he might remember long after they didn't know each other anymore.

Ross felt his heart beat a little harder at that thought, not sure he liked it. Pretty sure he hated it.

He leaned forward, letting Shaw's cock slide into his mouth, remembering every bit of how it felt, the taste, the girth, the scent of him. He was amazing, and he couldn't get enough.

Shaw was groaning above him, hands splayed out on the door, like he was holding it shut—or using it to hold himself up.

"You are way too fucking good at that," Shaw moaned. "I'm never . . . goddamn it, I'm never gonna be able to come in here again without getting hard."

Ross lifted his head, taking a quick, deep breath. "Good," he said, feeling the satisfaction spread deep within him. *He'd* done that. Shaw would remember this, long after he moved out.

Maybe even after they stopped . . . well, whatever it was that they were doing.

He wrapped his hand around the base of Shaw's cock, giving it an experimental stroke as he sucked on the head, and was rewarded with a whole string of dirty words.

One of Shaw's hands drifted downwards, cupping the back of his head, encouraging him, not exactly pushing him—he must have realized that Ross would hate that—but guiding him, and less than a minute later, Shaw was digging those fingertips into his skull, swearing as he came down Ross' throat.

He swallowed, panting a little with his own arousal as Shaw reached down and dragged him to his feet.

"What the fuck," Shaw said, clearly delighted, and then kissed him again. He'd been enthusiastic before, really enjoying their make-out session, but this time? It was like he wanted to devour Ross alive.

His own cock throbbed in his shorts, and he almost wanted to pull away, wanting some of his own satisfaction. But he didn't, because that hadn't been what this was about.

"Wait." Shaw sounded breathless when he finally pulled away. "Wait, wait, wait."

"What?" Ross didn't know what they were waiting for.

"I . . . why didn't we just go upstairs?"

"Did you hold the door closed or not?" Ross asked, answering Shaw's question with one of his own. Normally that would've driven him insane, but Shaw didn't have an issue with that. He was different. Honestly he was *better*, if Ross had anything to say about it.

"I did," Shaw said. "But we still could've gone upstairs."

"You wouldn't have liked it as much. And this way . . ." Ross hesitated, not sure how much he wanted to say. "This way you'll remember."

"Even if we'd gone up to the apartment, I would have," Shaw said, his voice sounding like a vow.

But Ross knew better.

People always thought they'd remember forever. But things faded. Events and friends were forgotten.

That was part of the inevitability of time.

"Here," Shaw continued, and Ross missed that he was reaching for him until his palm was against his cock, and he was twitching against the firm pressure.

"No," Ross said, moving away from his touch, even though it nearly killed him. "No, not this time."

"Why not?" Shaw sounded mystified.

"Because this wasn't about me," Ross said bluntly. "This was about you."

Ross almost wished that he'd let Shaw turn the light on, because he wanted to see his face. Wanted to *see* if he understood, not hear him say it.

"Like . . ." Shaw hesitated. "Like the other night."

"Exactly," Ross said with a sharp nod.

"And you got me off then, too, so it wasn't just about you," Shaw reminded him gently.

"It . . ." Ross shook his head decisively. "No, I wanted to do this for you. I . . . do you know what happened today, with Harmony? Because you suggested it? I asked her to help and she helped and well, things aren't as bad as I thought they might be. Because of *you.*"

"No, because of you, and because of Harmony."

Ross was pretty sure Shaw was smiling now.

"I don't . . ."

Shaw wouldn't let him finish. "I just gave you the extra push that you needed. Helped you see it from a different perspective. That's all."

"Well, thank you anyway. For whatever you did. For *everything* you did." Ross already knew it was way more than just a different perspective, or whatever. He knew because if it had been only that, he wouldn't have changed his mind. It was so much more than that.

Shaw was so much more than that.

"You're welcome." Shaw reached down and pulled his briefs and his pants up, buttoning and zipping them. Then he reached into his back pocket and Ross heard a metallic clatter before he realized what he'd taken. The spoons. "Now, if you're not going to let me return the favor, at least let me try the ice cream."

"That's what I came here for," Ross agreed, reaching out and grabbing the container from the shelf he'd stashed it on. He pulled the plastic wrap back. Saw out of the corner of his eye as Shaw reached for the light switch again, but Ross stopped him before he could turn them on.

"No," he explained gently, "it'll be better like this."

"In the dark?"

"You'll have a stronger sense of taste, if one of your other senses is dulled," Ross explained. "You want it to taste good, don't you?"

Shaw's voice was wry. "It's going to taste fucking amazing no matter what my senses are like," he said. "I know your food, Ross."

"Thank you," Ross said, holding out the container. "But this way you'll really get to focus on it."

Shaw held out the spoons, and Ross took one, and they both dipped them into the container.

Ross liked to taste potential recipes the way that sommeliers taste wine. The first taste was often overwhelming, so many flavors on his tongue, overwhelming his senses. The second taste and then the third, he could often really pick out the individual tastes: the saltiness, the sweet, the sour, and then the various different textures. In this case, the cold hit his tongue first.

Then he tasted the creaminess. It was just as smooth and creamy as any ice cream churned the traditional way—maybe even creamier—which made him proud.

Shaw moaned around the spoon in his mouth. Ross was distracted for half a moment, because the remnants of arousal were still simmering in his blood, and the sound of his enjoyment turned those up to a slightly higher boil. He normally never let himself get distracted during tasting, but he had today, and he *definitely* had the other night when he'd kissed Shaw.

That was unheard of.

"I was right; this is fucking delicious," Shaw said.

Ross took another spoonful and let it rest on his tongue. He needed less sugar, next time. More caramel, more pecans, maybe. He liked the saltiness. Maybe he'd toast the pecans even further. Make them deeper and darker and add more flavor.

"It could use a little work," Ross admitted. He was happy but he thought it could be better. Everything could always be better.

"Seriously?" Shaw asked and then ducked his head. "You know what, of course you'd say that. You're such a perfection-ist."

Ross couldn't count how many times he'd been called that in his life—but it had never sounded so matter of fact. Or non-judgmental.

Even Aaron had hated how many times Ross had changed their recipes, altering them slightly or significantly until he was finally happy, though that rarely happened. Most of the dishes he served at Basket were works in progress. He rarely was completely, totally satisfied with how something turned out.

"I am," Ross said. It was good that Shaw knew the worst of him; it might mean that whatever was happening between them might have a longer shelf life.

"I get it, I'm always tweaking things on the drink menu, too," Shaw continued.

"Yeah?"

Ross took another bite, rolled the flavors in and around his mouth.

It was definitely good. But it could be even better.

What was wrong with being the best?

Ross had never understood why people didn't want to do better. *Be* better. Why was settling for mediocrity okay?

"I was actually thinking about adding your Shirley Temple with a shot of vodka to the menu."

Ross was surprised. It wasn't the most original drink ever, but it *was* delicious.

"Really?"

"You enjoy it, right?" Shaw was at least five spoonfuls into the ice cream, eating it like he was a starving man. Or maybe he thought it was just that good.

"Well, yeah," Ross said. "I said I did, didn't I?"

Shaw grinned. "It's got Ross-approval. Means it's really fucking delicious and I'd be stupid and short-sighted not to take advantage of that."

"What are you going to call it?"

Shaw shot him a look. "A Grown-Up Shirley Temple, of course."

"Oh, that's good." Ross hesitated. Aaron had named all their dishes. He'd been much better at it. "Maybe you should name the brownie sundae."

"You'd want me to?" Shaw looked up from the ice cream container. "That would be so cool."

"Yeah, you should," Ross said.

"Aw." Shaw leaned in and kissed him on the cheek. "I'd be honored. I'll think about it. And I know you want to change it, make it better, but you gotta know it's fucking delicious."

"Uh, thanks?" He was never good at taking compliments. But something about the earnestness in Shaw's voice made him want to try.

"You're welcome." Shaw sounded firm and certain—certain enough that maybe he knew just how uncertain Ross was about compliments. "I gotta go back to work soon."

Ross knew he shouldn't feel disappointed, but he did, anyway.

It must've shown on his face because Shaw moved closer, crowding the cold pan of ice cream against his chest. "I don't want to, either," he said, his voice hushed. "I like this."

"I love this," Ross said, before he could stop himself.

Remembering, in spite of *not* wanting to, what Harmony had said. *Aw,* she'd crooned, *you're in love.*

Ross had never loved anyone, ever. He'd never had even the slightest inclination. But he could acknowledge that there was something fundamentally different about his relationship with Shaw.

Was it love? He didn't know yet. How did you even know it was love? He didn't think even Google would be able to tell him for sure.

All he knew was that the feelings buried deeply in his chest were feelings that he'd never experienced before.

But that didn't mean it was love.

Even if it was, it might be him, alone, who was feeling so serious about what was developing between them. Maybe for Shaw this was just a fun way to pass the time, a happy accident of that acknowledged attraction plus spending so much time together in a small space.

"I love it too," Shaw said and reached up, kissing him firmly. Fiercely. With conviction.

Like he knew it and he wasn't afraid of it.

But Ross knew if it was love—and that was still up in the air—then he didn't think he could be as calm as Shaw was about it.

And yet, it didn't matter, because when Shaw's mouth touched his, it was like all those unpleasant, difficult thoughts quieted and all he felt was the good. The decisive. The concrete.

The *real*.

"Have you thought any more about the bar?"

Shaw looked up from the drinks he was pouring to see his brother sliding onto the barstool directly in front of him. The barstool he liked to think of as "Ross' barstool" in his mind.

He opened his mouth, about to tell Jackson to move, that Ross had texted him about an hour ago that he'd be coming by with "another surprise."

He'd responded that as fun as the last time was, it had better not be another blowjob in the storage room, because they'd barely gotten away with it the first time.

The last thing he needed was to piss Jackson off, no matter how many times he and Alexis had undoubtedly fucked on that couch in his office.

"I think about the bar all the time," Shaw said.

Jackson shot him a look. "I meant the *new* bar," he amended.

"Oh. *That* bar. The bar that has yet to exist." Shaw deposited the drinks at the other end of the counter, so Chelle could pick them up easily and deliver them to the patio.

"You're being unusually stubborn," Jackson said thoughtfully.

"I told you, I don't know why we have to start fucking with something that's working."

"Because . . ."

But Shaw was annoyed that Jackson wouldn't leave it alone. And on top of that, refused to acknowledge why it really was that he wouldn't drop it. So he finished his brother's sentence. "Because you feel guilty that Dad left you fifty-one percent?"

Jackson frowned. "No, no, that's not why, I just . . ."

"You want me to have something that's *mine*, and not yours, first, right?" Shaw wiped up his work space even though it was already clean.

Jackson sighed, placing his elbows on the bar, his gaze concerned. "I never wanted it to be like that. You know that."

"But that's the way Dad wanted it," Shaw said firmly. "And you know what? He wasn't wrong. I don't have a problem with it. You're older. You're more responsible. You like the spreadsheets and the employment contracts and the dollars and cents. Well, you didn't at first, but you do now, and you're fucking good at it. You know what I'm good at? I'm good at tending bar."

"You're good at more than that," Jackson argued. His eyes got a sly glint to them. It was a look that never boded well for Shaw. "I bet you that Ross would say you're good at more than just slinging booze."

"Ugh, of course you have to bring him into it," Shaw complained, tossing down the towel. "Why you gotta do that?"

"Listen, I know what it looks like when a Finley falls in love," Jackson said. "You're crazy about the guy and I never thought I'd say this, because I didn't think Ross was interested in anything but his food truck, but the feeling appears to be mutual."

"I'm not . . ." Shaw trailed off, ready to argue, except that he didn't really want to, because he thought his brother had pretty much nailed it.

He was in love with Ross.

It wasn't so much a revelation as it was an inevitable conclusion that he'd already been most of the way to. He'd been drawn to Ross so much from the very beginning and he'd only been falling harder and faster the more he got to know him.

And Ross? Well, he wasn't always easy to read, even for Shaw, but he was pretty sure that he wasn't in this alone. Normally that would have felt really great and he'd have felt immensely reassured that his feelings were essentially returned, but with Ross there were always additional questions.

Did he realize it? Did he *want* to be in love with Shaw?

Shaw wasn't sure of the answer to either of those questions, and honestly, that was what kept him from fully embracing his own feelings.

Definitely what prevented him from saying anything to Ross.

"Yeah, well," Shaw corrected with a semi-embarrassed shrug. "Maybe I am."

"Hey," Jackson said, "I think it's great."

Shaw couldn't quite believe it. "Really?"

"Nobody is more surprised than me," Jackson said wryly, "but you're happy. And that's all I ever wanted for you."

"And," Shaw added with a grin, "for me to own fifty-one percent of another bar."

Jackson rolled his eyes. "Maybe, yes, that too. You said you'd think about it."

"I'm still thinking about it," Shaw said, even though that wasn't exactly true. Other than the handful of times that it had come up in his conversations with Ross, he *hadn't* thought about it.

He'd been too deep in with Ross to think about anything else. If he hadn't realized he was in love with him, that probably would've been a light bulb moment.

Ross was all he'd thought about for weeks, now.

"No, you're thinking about Ross," Jackson teased. "But I'm glad you haven't completely dismissed it, honestly. Because I want to go look at the space again next week, and I want you to come with me."

"That's not going to change my mind."

"Maybe. Maybe not. I won't do this if you're not on board, even if technically I *could,* I just want you to visualize it. See all the possibilities."

"Fine." Shaw sighed. "I'll go."

"Okay, I'll check the schedule and arrange it for when you've got some time off."

"You could always give me some *more* time off," Shaw joked.

Jackson's expression softened. "Want to spend some more time with your boy?"

Jackson *would* understand, because Shaw knew that one of the ways he and Alexis made their relationship work was because they carved out time for each other from their busy schedules and refused to let anyone else touch it.

"Yeah, I do," Shaw said with a grin.

Jackson shrugged. "I'll see what I can do, but you know, Ross is a workaholic. You might find it harder for him to make the time for you."

Shaw knew it, but he pushed the concern aside. "Ross makes enough time for me."

"Good." Jackson's smile was warm. "See that he does. I think you deserve the best you can get. If that's Ross, then that's Ross."

Shaw cashed out two bar tabs and then turned to his brother. "I have to admit, I'm surprised at how well you're taking this."

Jackson looked self-conscious. "Uh, he's not a bad guy?"

"Alexis yelled at you, didn't he?" Shaw chuckled.

"Alexis informed me that I was being very unfair, blaming Ross for Aaron's destruction," Jackson admitted. "And for the record, I *was* wrong, and I never really, truly disliked him. I don't really know him. He doesn't let people get close." He paused. "But then you know that, don't you?"

"He can be a bit prickly, but he's sweet underneath," Shaw agreed. "What he really just needs is some kindness. And patience. To know that people give a shit about him, because I think for a long time, people didn't. Aaron sure didn't give a crap."

"I'll keep that in mind." Jackson would, Shaw knew it. He wasn't as good with people as Shaw was, but he was, for all his pushiness over this bar thing, a really fucking good big brother.

If he had to work harder to befriend Shaw's new boyfriend, he'd do it without a single complaint.

"Thanks," Shaw said, hesitating, because for the first time in a long time he was speechless, unsure of how to express his gratitude to his brother.

But Jackson just smiled, leaned over the bar and patted him on the shoulder. Like he understood. "He's lucky to have you, and you're lucky to have him."

Shaw had been grateful for his older brother many times in his life, but this was pretty high up there on the list.

"I'll figure out the schedule for next week," Jackson continued, heading towards his office. "And let you know what I come up with."

Five minutes later, Ross walked in, carrying one of the biodegradable bowls in one hand.

"Hey," he said, approaching the bar and setting the bowl on the hardwood. "Told you I'd bring you a surprise."

"What is it?" Shaw said, pulling the bowl closer and pulling the corner of the lid up.

"For your sweet tooth's enjoyment, the final version of the brownie sundae. I just finished tweaking the recipe," Ross said, sliding onto the same barstool that Jackson had occupied only a few minutes earlier.

"For now," Shaw said, grinning as he reached down, grabbing a fork from the silverware tray stored underneath the bar top.

"Believe me, I'm gonna enjoy this. Maybe not as much as your last surprise, but still a whole fucking lot."

He pulled the rest of the cover off, and set it aside, digging into the ice cream drizzled with caramel sauce and pecans, right down to the crusty brownie waffle, oozing more caramel from its interior.

He lifted the fork to his mouth and let the sweet salty rich flavor overwhelm him.

"Ugggghhhh," Shaw moaned around it. "So fucking delicious."

The ice cream before had been delicious—of course, he'd been riding on an endorphin high when he'd tasted it, but despite that, it had been undeniable. The waffle before that, equally as tasty. But together? It was bliss. Plain and simple.

Ross had a gift, whether he felt comfortable acknowledging it to the world or not.

"Also, I wanted to tell you," Ross said, his eyes glued to where Shaw kept shoveling brownie sundae into his mouth, "Harmony and I had a phone call today with the produce supplier."

Shaw chewed and swallowed. Thought maybe he should do the basics of his job. "What happened?" He began to mix a Shirley Temple, non-Grown-Up Edition.

"You're not going to fucking believe this," Ross said, leaning closer. "But I didn't owe a dime."

"What?" Shaw couldn't quite believe it. Best scenario, he'd hoped that Ross might owe less than he thought, and with Harmony's help, he could work out a reasonable payment plan to catch up his account. He'd never anticipated that Ross didn't owe *anything*.

Clearly, from the shock in Ross' voice and on his face, he hadn't either.

"*Yeah*," Ross said, sounding like he didn't quite believe it yet. "The accountant lady went over the whole thing three times, and Harmony got it, and I did too in the end, but it's still hard to believe. Not only do I not owe them a dime, I've actually got a credit on my account."

"What was the explanation?" Shaw stabbed four cherries on the wood stem of a bright pink paper umbrella and set it across the top of the drink, right next to two lime slices.

Okay, that's a lot of garnish, Shaw thought as he set it in front of Ross. He usually garnished based on how much he liked someone.

That was definitely a love's worth of garnish.

Ross took a sip of his drink.

"I guess there was some kind of bug in their software, where it didn't apply payments. Turns out that I have an automatic payment on my credit card every month. Plus the credits they never properly applied from the rejected produce."

"How come they didn't realize this bug existed?"

"Oh, they did," Ross said, flushing, his voice growing hushed. "They thought they'd cleaned all the accounts up, but since Aaron was such a shit accountant and never bothered to actually check the statements to make sure we were good, and well, *I* never did either, nobody noticed it."

"But Harmony did?"

Ross nodded. "I'm . . . well, I'm fucking grateful, Shaw. If you hadn't encouraged me to talk to her, to let her help, I would've been paying them *double*, for God knows how long. When I couldn't really spare the money."

"That wasn't me, that was you."

"No, I wouldn't have done it. I . . ." Ross hesitated, reaching out towards where Shaw's hand sat on the bar top. Shaw realized he was holding his breath as Ross' fingers ghosted over the top of his own. Not quite holding his hand, but he swore he saw the yearning to do it in Ross' face.

That was enough. Shaw flipped his hand and captured Ross' hand for a split second, squeezing it tight. "You'd have done it," Shaw said, "*eventually*. But I'm glad you listened so you got this fixed right away. Is Harmony going to do more work on your accounts?"

"Yeah," Ross said with a nod. He'd already stolen his hand back, but Shaw could still feel the pressure of it, hard and strong and capable, and he couldn't wait for another few hours when he'd come home and those fingers would be on *him* again. "Yeah, we talked about it. She's going to go over everything with me, but I gave her my laptop." Ross was smiling now. Like he was so proud of himself for finally taking that step, for overcoming his fear, that he couldn't even help it.

"Good for you," Shaw said. "That couldn't have been easy."

Ross was still grinning away, and it was so bright and wonderful that Shaw could barely look away.

You are totally fucking in love, Shaw thought to himself. Wallowed in the feeling for a split second, because he knew that Ross wasn't even nearly ready to hear it yet.

"It actually wasn't that hard, in the end," Ross said.

"Because you knew it was right." Shaw understood. Wished that he had as much clarity as Ross did with Harmony, and that Jackson had over this new bar idea.

Instead, he knew he was head over heels over this guy, and that he didn't want to go anywhere. He wanted to stay right here, just like this. No matter what.

"Yeah," Ross agreed, nodding his head. "I knew it was right. I knew it was right before, but I was afraid. I didn't want it to be like Aaron, all over again."

"It's not gonna be."

"No, it won't, because I won't let it. Harmony's going to organize and deal with the accounts, and the business side of the truck, but I'm going to be aware. Of every fucking thing."

"Yeah?" Shaw dug his fork back into the brownie sundae, scooping up a heap of melting caramel ice cream.

"Yeah. And maybe over time, I can let some of that go." Ross took a sip of his drink. "But for now? Yeah, I'm good with this situation."

Shaw swallowed his mouthful of deliciousness, and grinned at the man he loved right back. "Hey, me too."

It wasn't quite the declaration of love that still felt like it was hovering on the tip of his tongue, but it was something. Even if Ross didn't quite get it the way he meant it.

It was enough.

CHAPTER TWELVE

The first indication something wasn't quite right was that Shaw didn't text him back right away.

Ross leaned against the back counter, taking a break from finishing cleaning up the truck, and stared at his phone. Shaw hadn't only not responded but he hadn't even read the text.

The Funky Cup was always busy, and since it was a Friday night, it was one of their busier nights, but they had enough bartenders and servers that they rarely got overwhelmed. Shaw could always take a moment to check his texts, Ross had learned, especially if the text was from him.

But tonight? There was nothing.

Ross was tired, it had been a long and busy day, so he hadn't really intended to stop by the bar on his way to the apartment, but as he shut up the truck, and said goodbye to Harmony, he knew he couldn't just go upstairs and not see what was going on.

As soon as he pushed the door open, he knew what the problem was.

The bar was *packed*. The overwhelming wall of noise hit Ross immediately, reminding him of why he didn't usually spend time at bars. The Funky Cup did a solid, steady business, but it was rarely full like this—which was why he liked hanging out here.

All the tables in the front room were occupied, there was a steady stream going out to the back patio, and there were at least three or four people deep at the bar. Since Ross was taller, he could see around them enough to see Shaw, as busy as he'd ever been, and Jackson was there too, behind the bar, even though Ross had never actually witnessed Jackson serve drinks before. Probably because, Ross thought, he'd never needed to before. And the other bartender, Bryan, who normally helped out in the evenings? Nowhere to be seen.

"Hey, you waiting for a drink?" a college-aged guy, with a bright pink streak in his blond hair and a flirtatious smile, asked.

Ross stared at him. "No?"

"You seem unsure. But trust me, this is a great place," the guy said, "I like to come here a lot, but it's packed tonight. One of the LGBT-friendly frats at USC is holding a rush event."

Ross felt like the guy was speaking a different language that he couldn't quite grasp. "Rush event?"

"You know, rushing for the frat?"

Ross must have had a bewildered expression on his face, because the guy finally stopped explaining and just shrugged. "Well, if you're not in line, I'll get in front of you, then."

"Okay," Ross said, skirting around pink-hair guy, giving him a wide berth. It felt weird to leave like this, when they were so clearly slammed.

If it was just Shaw and Jackson for this crazy crowd . . . Ross didn't even think.

No, that was not entirely true.

He *thought*, but what he thought about was the day when he'd been so busy and Shaw had come by for lunch at the truck, and then dropped all his day-off plans to help *him*.

How much that had meant to Ross, even though he knew he'd been an ass about it at first.

What he didn't do was hesitate.

He walked around the bar, opening the pass-through. Shaw gave him a sideways glance as he came over.

"Sorry, but I'm a little busy," Shaw said wryly. His hands never stopped moving. Ross knew he liked to make drinks slow—to make them perfect, just like Ross wanted every dish that left his own kitchen to be flawless—but right now, it seemed like he'd found a whole new gear that Ross hadn't even known he had.

"I noticed," Ross said. "I can help."

Shaw opened his mouth and then shut it again. "Okay sure," he said. "You any good at this?"

"I know my way around enough. I get something complicated, I'll let you handle it," Ross said.

It was definitely not his first choice; spending a Friday night after a very long week and a very long day of work, tending bar to a bunch of drunk, horny college kids, but he wasn't going to leave Shaw like this.

Not *his* Shaw.

Ross realized with a jolt as he approached the first guy at the bar, waiting with an impatient expression on his face, that he had been thinking of Shaw like that for awhile now.

"What can I get you?"

The guy gave him a dubious look. "You a bartender?"

"For all intents and purposes, I'm *your* bartender," Ross said in a clipped voice. He did not like people questioning his abilities, and while *no*, he was technically not a bartender, he could pour beers and mix drinks and hand out shots. None of these kids were going to order anything complicated anyway. They weren't looking for a craft cocktail experience; they wanted to get trashed as quickly and efficiently and *cheaply* as possible.

Ross had been there, a long time ago, and so he understood how it worked.

"Fine," the guy said with a long-suffering sigh, "I've been waiting forever, anyway. Two Coors in a bottle, a vodka cran and a rum and Coke."

Ross had spent enough evenings here, his eyes watching Shaw prepare hundreds of drinks. In theory, he knew where everything was kept: the glasses, the ice, the mixers, the different bottles of alcohol. He knew that Shaw and Jackson had a similar point of sale system to the one he'd used at Hook & Slope, Atkinson's restaurant where he used to work before he and Aaron had started Basket.

Of course when he finished grabbing the drinks, his hands surprisingly steady despite the newness of the activities, taking the guy's credit card, he didn't realize his problem until he turned to the computer console and he reached into his pocket. The action was automatic, but he realized only belatedly that he didn't have the card that granted him access to the system.

Not even a second later, before he could even turn to Shaw to ask him where he could get an access card, one was being pressed into his hand.

"Here," Shaw said in a clipped voice. "I've got others. You can use mine."

"Thanks," Ross said, sliding it through the reader, the computer unlocking.

It took him a minute or two to find the right screens, but he got there eventually, and next time, he'd be faster because now he knew how the system was organized.

The guy gave him a sour look when he got back with the credit card slip.

"Took you long enough," he grumbled as he filled out the receipt. "What are you, new?"

Ross pressed his lips together and didn't bother answering. Just moved on to the next customer, a girl with a much nicer smile.

He took her order, and the guy's next to her, and discovered after pouring their beers, and starting tabs for them both, that it seemed the wait at the bar was getting even crazier.

"Behind you," Jackson snapped out, his voice tense and his posture rigid as he maneuvered behind the bar, now actually pretty crowded with three people, and delivered food to someone sitting at the very end.

Ross was about to turn to the next group, waiting for their turn to order, when Shaw touched him on the shoulder. "Hey," he said, even though his hands never stopped unloading clean glasses from the dishwasher tray, "you're actually pretty good at this. Can you handle the majority of the walk-ups while I deal with the table orders?"

"Yeah," Ross said. Feeling proud that Shaw didn't think he was a total fuckup as a bartender. Of course accompanying that pride was a slight panic that he wouldn't be able to handle it.

But before the voices in his head started telling him things like *you can't* and *you shouldn't,* he nodded to Shaw.

He couldn't let him down. Not *his* Shaw.

"Great," Shaw said, and this time when he patted him on the shoulder, his fingers lingered for a fraction of a second longer. Just enough, Ross decided, to tell him just how much this meant.

And he got it. He'd been there, right where Shaw was.

That day that Shaw had stepped in? He'd saved him.

Ross usually liked to think he did his own saving, but sometimes? It didn't hurt to take a little help, especially when the hand giving it was so generous and caring.

Ross turned to the next group, and then the next, and then the next. He learned how to make his favorite grown-up Shirley Temple. Even made one with tequila, which he would *not* recommend, but the guy said he'd been getting them for a week and he loved them.

Ross barely held back the face he made.

He poured shots. He told Shaw when a keg ran out.

And for what felt like hours, the crowd barely died down at all.

At one point, he saw Jackson and Shaw in a huddled conversation, clearly upset about something, but he was too busy making sure that everyone got their drinks. And it was a *thirsty* crowd.

Ross took advantage of a moment's break, and instead of resting, helped Shaw load up the dishwasher trays with dirty glasses.

"You good?" Shaw asked, shooting him a quick sideways look.

Ross' feet hurt. His eyes hurt. His ears hurt, from all the interminable noise. He was feeling overwhelmed, and not in a good way, necessarily, but he'd learned to compartmentalize all of that long ago.

Working in a Michelin-starred kitchen for a notoriously sadist boss would force you to learn how real quick.

Ross had always been good at that. At focusing so hard and so tight, that he could push everything else away, even though occasionally even the anarchy of the kitchen occasionally defeated him.

Aaron had always been jealous of that particular talent, but then Ross had never had the heart to tell him that all the social skills—the easy conversations, the polite chitchat, the effortless way he charmed people—were the cost.

"I'm okay," Ross said. He wasn't going to lie, but he also knew if he told Shaw the truth, he'd force him to stop.

And he wasn't going to leave Shaw alone to deal with all of this.

That wasn't what you did for someone you cared so much about. The way Ross was pretty sure he cared about Shaw.

"You're . . ." Shaw hesitated, the warmth in his eyes making it clear just how meaningful Ross being here was. "You're just really great, okay? And a pretty decent bartender, all things considered, though we could work on your flash."

"Flash?"

Shaw smiled more brightly than he should've been capable of, not with the amount of work he'd done tonight. "You know, the way you pour the drinks. The way you engage with the customers."

"Yeah, I'm not ever going to be good with that," Ross mumbled as his fingers slipped on the condensation outside of a glass. "Sorry."

"Don't be," Shaw said. "I'm just glad you're here, honestly. Really fucking glad." His voice went soft and quiet, and when Ross looked over at him, the look in his eyes felt personal, private. Like it was just for him.

"Alright." Ross ducked his head, suddenly embarrassed. Like he'd been caught out, his feelings right there, in plain fucking sight, when he didn't even like to think he *had* feelings.

"So you're still good?"

Another group had just walked back in, and Ross straightened. "Yeah," he said. "I've got this."

"Thanks," Shaw said, and shot him another one of those gooey looks. Like Shaw was caramel, and he was melting—just for Ross.

It gave him the energy and the push to get through that group and then the next, and then the next.

It was after one in the morning when the crowd finally began to thin, and Ross finally began to catch up on washing all the glassware, carefully stacking it when it came out of the water, each glass almost unbearably hot to touch, but spotlessly clean.

That was definitely something Ross had *always,* even before he'd known Shaw personally, respected about the man and the way he ran the bar. Everything was always pristine.

"Hey," Jackson said, the exhaustion in his voice and on his face obvious to anyone who was paying even the slightest bit of attention. "I'm gonna do last call in five."

Ross watched as Shaw raised his eyebrow.

"They've all had plenty," Jackson said, by way of explanation, "and I'm fucking tired."

"Amen to that," Shaw said, and then glanced over at Ross. "You wanna finish up and then head upstairs?"

Oh, he did. More than he'd ever wanted to do anything.

He wanted to curl up with Shaw on the couch and just lie there.

Moving was a hundred percent overrated.

Except, he'd decided the moment he'd walked behind the bar that he was in this for the long haul. However long it was. However difficult it turned out to be.

"Nope," Ross said firmly. "What else do you need me to do?"

Shaw shot him a look. "Seriously?"

"We'll finish when we're both finished," Ross said stubbornly.

"You're a ridiculous, yet wonderful man." Shaw shook his head. "I'm kinda digging it."

Ross could practically hear the rest of his sentence, even though he didn't say it.

I'm kinda digging you.

"You're both crazy," Jackson said, slapping a cleaning rag on the bar and wiping it down. "Just so you know."

"Thanks," Shaw retorted fondly.

"But you, seriously, you saved our asses tonight," Jackson said, turning towards Ross. "Thank you."

"It's no problem," Ross said, feeling that wave of embarrassment swirl through him once again. "I didn't mind helping out."

"Well," Jackson said, patting him on the shoulder, "we sure fucking appreciate it, don't we, Shaw?"

Shaw nodded enthusiastically.

"I'm going to go let everyone know about last call," Jackson said, tossing the cleaning rag into the sanitizer bucket. "Considering this crowd, be prepared for anything."

"I don't think I've ever seen a Friday night like that," Shaw said as they climbed, slowly, and more than a little painfully, up the stairs to the apartment.

"What happened? Why was it so crazy? I mean, other than that 'rush thing.'" It was the first moment that Ross had really had a chance to ask.

Shaw typed in the code to the front door and pushed it open, collapsing onto the couch. Like he'd been thinking the exact same as Ross and didn't think he could make it another step.

Ross sat down heavily next to him, toeing his sneakers off, not even caring that his feet probably smelled. He'd been on them for almost twenty hours at this point. Shaw was going to have to take the bad with the good.

But Shaw didn't even blink; in fact, he took his own shoes off, groaning as he did.

"Well, the rush thing, *obviously*," he said, "but Bryan called in sick too. It was just a bad combo." Shaw sighed, his head flopping over until it was resting on Ross' shoulder. "A fucking insane combo."

"But you survived," Ross said, feeling awkward. He wasn't any good at pep talks.

Shaw put a hand on his knee, squeezing it gently. "With your help," he said. "You're not the villain that you keep seeing yourself as, you know?"

"The villain?" Ross wasn't sure he followed. Or maybe that was his tired-as-fuck brain.

"Yeah, you just assume you're always the villain in everyone's story. Even your own story. But you're not. You're good, not even very deep down," Shaw said, his voice a reassuringly deep rumble. "And you're good all the way through. Loyal and kind. But you let everyone believe you're an asshole."

Now Ross was following.

"I am an asshole sometimes," he admitted. This was a conversation he'd known would happen sometime. He'd been hoping for later rather than sooner, but life was full of tough breaks.

"No," Shaw said firmly. "No, you're not. What about the onion dip? Tony's onion dip?" He actually levered himself upright a little so he could look Ross right in the eye. And Ross could see, which had probably been Shaw's plan, that he meant every word he was saying.

"What about the onion dip?" he asked cautiously. He thought he might know where Shaw was going with this.

"I mean, Aaron stole it. You didn't steal it. But you let Tony blab about it forever. But it wasn't your fault, and you've never corrected him."

"It wasn't . . ." Ross hesitated, and then finally sighed. Maybe this story was inevitable too. "It wasn't really his recipe anymore. Yeah, Aaron gave it to me, said he'd found it somewhere, never told me he stole it, and I thought it had potential. So I tested it a bunch. Improved it. I doubt the end result had much in common with Tony's original."

Shaw was smiling now. Ross wasn't sure where he'd found the energy. "But Tony went around telling *everyone* that it was basically identical. That he'd tried yours and he knew it just had to be the same."

Ross couldn't do anything but shrug. "What was I supposed to say? Yours wasn't very good and so I made it better?"

Now Shaw was actually *laughing*. "God, I wish you had," he said, "even though Tony's head probably would've imploded. But that's what I'm saying right there. You kept taking the blame, even though you didn't have anything to do with it, and you hadn't even really copied him, in the end. You even gave in and took it off the menu when you joined the lot. You're *not* a villain, Ross. In your story or in anyone else's."

"I can be an asshole," Ross said again, but weaker this time.

Shaw just waved that off. "Were you an asshole tonight? Did you walk in and see us slammed and leave? After a hard day of work already, you could've said I'm done, and nobody would've blamed you."

"I would've blamed myself," Ross said quietly.

"And that," Shaw said, his voice exhausted but happy, as he poked him in the bicep, "is why you're the hero."

"I'm really not," Ross protested, even though he thought the words sounded wonderful coming out of Shaw's mouth.

But then it was Shaw's mouth. He fucking loved his mouth.

Even when it was just talking.

Shaw sighed, stretching again. He was quiet for a moment, and then he said, "Did you see who was there tonight?"

"The entire city of Los Angeles?" Ross thought he was too tired to make jokes, but with Shaw, it was surprisingly easy, even now.

"Ugh, yes, the entire city," Shaw said, chuckling, "but also . . . that LGBT frat."

"And?"

"They decided the bar was a safe space."

Ross didn't know where this was heading, or what Shaw was trying to say.

"Yeah," he said. "They clearly did. And they were all thirsty."

Shaw laughed again. Rubbed a hand across his jaw. "I don't know, I'm wondering if I'm being stupid about Jackson's idea."

"The other bar?"

Shaw nodded.

"Because you guys were busy tonight?"

"Yeah, that, and . . . well . . ." Shaw's voice trailed off, and then after a moment, he said, "Come on."

Ross didn't know where he'd found the energy to lift himself but he was rising off the couch, and he was holding out a hand to help Ross, too.

That was how beautiful Shaw was, inside and out.

He was kind and helpful and loyal—and he thought Ross was a fucking hero.

Ross didn't know whether he was brilliant or delusional.

But he took his hand anyway and stood, even though what he really needed to do was get ready for bed and close his eyes and fall asleep on this couch.

"It's late, we can talk about this later," Shaw said, tugging him towards the bedroom. "Let's go to bed."

"What?" Ross knew he was awkward. Couldn't help it. He was too goddamned tired to do any better.

"Heroes," Shaw said seriously, pressing a quick kiss to his lips, "don't sleep on the couch."

Ross woke up slowly.

In a bed that was definitely not the couch.

He rolled over, and the flash of disappointment at not seeing Shaw there surprised him. He'd never been the kind of guy who wanted to wake up in the morning and cuddle. He'd also never been the kind of guy who wanted to sleep next to anyone before. But Shaw made him want things he didn't quite understand.

Pressing a hand against the covers, he could still feel the warmth of Shaw's body. When he listened, he thought he could hear the shower going in the next room.

After glancing at his phone, he realized it was still early. He had an hour or so before he would normally head towards the truck, and even longer if he really wanted to take the time, as he and Harmony had gotten through much of the weekend's prep yesterday morning.

Ross groaned as he stood up, stretching out his sore, over-worked muscles. Maybe Shaw had the right idea and a hot shower was just what he needed.

He'd left the door open, which Ross concluded made sense. After all, they'd seen each other naked. They'd had sex. They'd even slept in the same bed together.

Still, Ross felt a tiny bit of trepidation as he walked into the bathroom, the steam already filling up the room.

Shaw was humming to himself, his figure mostly obscured by the fogged-up glass.

"Hey," Ross said quietly, so he wouldn't startle him.

"Oh, you're up," Shaw said, pushing the door open a fraction and sticking just his head out. "You know, I normally shower when I get home, all gross from the bar, but . . . well, you know what last night was like."

Ross nodded. He'd known. His head had barely hit the pillow and he'd been asleep.

For a second, Shaw just looked at him, dripping water all over the mat in front of the shower. Then he smiled, suddenly. "You should join me," he said.

Ross looked at the shower dubiously. "It's not very big," he said.

"We'll make it work." Shaw's grin went sly around the edges. "And then when we're all clean . . ."

Ross didn't need another invitation.

That itch? It was almost familiar now, like an old friend, but it still existed, and it still pestered him, like he couldn't quite get enough of Shaw.

You can't, he thought as he stripped down, leaving his boxer briefs in a pile on the floor of the bathroom.

Shaw pushed the door open further and Ross climbed in next to him.

It *was* small, the water already cascading down his head, but then Shaw's hands were on him, pulling him to the side, pressing him against his body, and suddenly the size of the shower didn't matter so much.

"Yeah?" Shaw asked, the light in his eyes making Ross feel alive and awake in a way he hadn't in a very long time.

Maybe ever.

Because, he realized as he washed his hair, Shaw's hands soaping him up, every inch he touched setting him alight, he'd never let someone in like this before. Not this close. Shaw knew more of his secrets than anyone else.

Shaw's fingers closed around his hardening cock and he gasped, the sound loud in the tiny space.

"Not yet," Shaw said, his voice near his ear, the low rumbling growl of it intensifying the itch inside him. "Just gotta get cleaned up first."

"First?" Ross wondered. The apprehension that slid through him was a mere shadow, the faintest echo of what he'd always used to feel when guys suggested they have sex. Shaw had already proved that he wasn't going to do something Ross didn't like.

But it was hard to silence all those demons. They'd been with him too long.

"I thought we could have sex in . . . you know . . . a *bed*," Shaw's voice was teasing as Ross finished washing the shampoo out of his hair.

"What kind of sex?" Ross could hear the uncertainty in his own voice. He knew he wanted it; his cock was undeniably hard, and it wanted more of Shaw's careful, deliberate touches.

"What kind do you like?" Shaw's tone on the other hand, was completely casual, like this was something he discussed all the time.

"The kind with you," Ross said.

It wasn't really an answer; he knew it wasn't. But he'd been waiting for the other shoe to drop and maybe this was the morning it did.

The day when Shaw realized that he wasn't ever going to be like the other guys he'd been with.

"I mean . . . if I wanted you to fuck me," Shaw said, "would you like that?"

It really wasn't too much to expect. There was a part of him that wanted it, that craved it, just the same as Shaw did, but then . . .

"If that's what you wanted, yeah, we could do that."

"No, don't do that," Shaw said firmly, and he was turning Ross around, staring at him right in the eyes. So he couldn't hide.

"That wasn't what I asked," Shaw continued. "I asked you, would you *like* that?"

"I don't want to . . . it's fine. Whatever we do, it's going to be great," he mumbled.

"Hey." Shaw lifted a hand to Ross' face, cupping his jaw with his fingers, gently raising it. He clearly wanted Ross to understand just how serious he was about this. "Hey, I don't want to do anything just for me, okay? That isn't what this is about."

"Okay." Ross believed that. Shaw had never given him a reason to believe anything else.

"What would you like instead?"

Ross shifted again. "I would . . . well, if I trusted someone, I . . . I would like it if you did it to me instead. It's . . ." He made a sound of frustration. "It's not as overwhelming as the other way around."

"When it's too much pleasure, you find it hard to come," Shaw said slowly, like he was putting the pieces together.

"It's not that it doesn't feel good, it's that when I do it to someone else . . . it's all that pressure and it's so tight and hot and slick . . ." Ross' cock twitched, despite the seriousness of the conversation. Despite all his worries that Shaw wouldn't understand. Wouldn't like it.

Wouldn't like *him*.

"It's too much for you," he guessed.

Ross nodded. "But we *can*," he said. "I just can't . . . I don't want you to have expectations . . ."

He knew he sounded humiliated and ashamed. Maybe he shouldn't have been any of those things, but it was hard to dismiss all that baggage.

"I would like to get my hands on the guys who made you feel like this," Shaw said quietly. "Like you're less than. Like you couldn't satisfy them because you couldn't come as easily if you stuck your dick into them."

Every time he thought he understood Shaw, he saw another side, another facet, another beautiful part of him.

"Really?"

"I'd like to hurt them. Slowly. The way they've hurt you."

"They didn't . . ." Ross took a deep breath. "I just . . . I want to be here with you now. We can make each other feel good, right?"

"Hey, look at me," Shaw said softly, and lifted his chin again. "I don't have *any* expectations, okay? Yes, we can make each other feel good, however that happens. It's felt good the last two times, right?"

Ross nodded.

"Well, that's all I expect," Shaw said. "For you to be honest with me about what you like, and for us to both feel good."

"I can do that." He'd been doing it, even though it was hard, because he knew, deep down, that it was right. That Shaw wouldn't judge.

"Good." Shaw pushed his hair back. "You done in here?"

He was definitely done in the shower, but he wasn't done with Shaw. Not by a long shot.

He nodded.

"Okay," Shaw said, and reached around him to flip the water off, grabbing their towels from the outside rack of the shower.

Ross had never thought in a million years that it would be sexy to watch as the man he desperately wanted dried off, his skin clean and damp, or that it would be so much like foreplay to stand side by side at the single sink, brushing their teeth.

But it was. By the time they were done, he was buzzing, he was burning, the itch a wildfire under his skin.

He knew what he wanted. He wanted to make Shaw feel just as good as Shaw made him feel. Every single moment of the day.

"Come on," he said, gruffly, tugging on Shaw's hand as soon as he returned his toothbrush to the cup.

Just the sight of their toothbrushes mingled together made him feel all warm and gooey inside, but he already knew what he was going to like even better.

Shaw naked and spread across his bed.

All his for the taking.

Shaw's own control was barely hanging by a thread, but when Ross grabbed his hand and tugged him into the bedroom, he clearly wasn't alone.

Shaw didn't know what he'd expected when Ross had taken control of the situation, but he'd deposited him at the edge of the bed and stood in front of him, naked and proud and *hungry*.

"Lube," Ross said succinctly, and Shaw opened his mouth and snapped it shut again, surprised at how confident Ross suddenly was.

Had he really believed that Shaw wouldn't understand? That he'd judge and then condemn him for his sexual preferences? For the reality of his life?

Ross was still staring at him, waiting, and stupidly, Shaw pointed to the drawer in the bedside table.

Shaw watched as he walked over, grabbed it and then, when he returned, Shaw reached up and tugged him down to his level, kissing him with every ounce of love and passion he felt. Ross groaned into his mouth, clearly just as into it as he was, his fingers scrabbling along Shaw's clothes, trying to get his t-shirt off without breaking the kiss.

He felt the smooth-yet-rough brush of Ross' tongue against his, his big, warm hands everywhere. He'd been the one to initially suggest coming in here, but he hadn't expected this. It was intoxicating. It was overwhelming.

Then Ross was pushing him up higher on the bed, caging him in as he climbed over him, their mouths barely taking a moment for a breath.

Shaw's skin felt like it was on fire as Ross' fingers traced their way down his bare chest, then lower, and then lower still.

"Wait," he managed to croak on a breath. "Wait, wait, what are you doing?"

Ross already had the lube open and was slicking his fingers up.

His gaze, when he glanced up at Shaw, was wild and intense. "I told you," he said, "I can make you feel good."

"But . . ." Shaw hesitated. This was what he'd done last time, overwhelmed him with pleasure and then declined to take his own.

He wondered if that was what Ross really, truly wanted, or if that was just how he'd been trained, by all those guys who hadn't been patient enough.

Their eyes met. "I want to make *you* feel good, too. That was the agreement," Shaw said, gasping when Ross slid a thumb against his hole, rubbing it in circles.

Had he fantasized about Ross fingering him with those big, calloused fingers?

Oh, just about a million times.

But in all those fantasies, they'd been sharing and trading pleasure. It hadn't been all one-sided.

"You can. After," Ross said, and slid his thumb inside.

Shaw bit his lip; it already felt good. It was going to feel even better. He was going to lose his mind with it, that much was obvious, because Ross was detail-oriented and focused. Like he'd studied Shaw and knew just how to unwind him.

"Wait," Shaw repeated, more forcefully this time.

Ross shot him a look. Disbelieving probably, that Shaw was this close to bliss and he was purposefully turning away from it.

It's crazy and you're crazy, but you're going to do this because it's not all about you. You fucking love this guy. Maybe he isn't ready to hear it but you gotta show him.

But Ross didn't end up protesting. Just stilled the movement of his thumb.

Shaw let his gaze drift down his body, enjoying every single bit of him.

Shaw still didn't know how he looked so strong and built, because he never went to the gym. He just worked really, really hard, day after day, week after week, never complaining, never asking for help, just shouldering all those burdens, physical and otherwise. Maybe other people wouldn't have found it sexy, but Shaw found his strength irresistible.

"Better?" Ross' voice was deep and rough, his cock hard as a rock as it jutted out from his body.

Shaw licked his lips. He really wanted to get his mouth around it. Wondered if that would be okay.

Ask, he reminded himself, *you told Ross to communicate. You've got to do the same.*

"Can we . . ." Shaw took a deep breath. "I'd like to blow you, while you finger me. Is that okay?"

Ross shot him another one of those looks. They shouldn't have been hot, but they lit Shaw up from the inside out.

Ross nodded, and slid onto the bed, lying down, and gesturing for Shaw to come over.

Shaw didn't need any further encouragement. He climbed onto the bed and then over Ross, the man gripping his hips with his fingers, as he lowered his own head closer to Ross' cock. For just a second, he hovered above it, admiring its length and its girth, the bright red flush of it, how it twitched when he wrapped his fingers gently around the base.

Then he leaned down, giving the head an experimental lick and Shaw could hear Ross' breath stutter, and the grip on his own hips tightened.

"You like that?" Shaw asked, even though it was clear and obvious that he did. Maybe he just wanted to hear Ross say it. Say he was going out of his mind, just like Shaw was.

But instead of vocalizing it, Ross answered by sliding his thumb right back where it had been before, gently corkscrewing it in and then withdrawing, the movement both intoxicating and inexorable.

Shaw remembered everything that Ross had liked about the way he'd touched him in the bathroom and tried, instead of overpowering him with pleasure, to dole it out in sweet, small increments. A lick here, a suck here, never being predictable or giving him too much. It was hard to focus, but he knew he was doing well because Ross' groans were becoming more commonplace, his muttered curses just what Shaw was dying to hear.

And why was it hard to focus? Oh, yeah, because Ross was taking him apart from the inside out, sliding his fingers in and finding just the right spot, barely glancing over it over and over, stretching him out, making him feel it, but also teasing him unbearably, until he felt like he was so far gone he might as well just scream with it.

His own cock was hard and leaking against Ross' chest and he gave an experimental thrust, and Ross' voice, deep and gravelly, gave his approval of that plan. He could tell Ross was close too, the precome leaking out of the tip as he licked it away, fingers loosely twisting as he jerked him off and licked the head, curling his tongue around it.

Pleasure shot through him like a bullet, blinding him for a split second as he tightened around his fingers and thrust helplessly against Ross' chest, the orgasm going on and on and wringing him out with the intensity of it.

Shaw had only a second to recover before Ross tumbled into his own, his cock jerking, come falling onto his thighs.

Shaw nuzzled there for a minute, working him through it as Ross moaned quietly as he came hard.

Maybe it wasn't traditional, Shaw thought as he came down from the endorphin rush, but it had felt goddamn incredible and who cared what was normal or right if it felt so good?

The only downside was the mess they'd made of each other.

Another quick cleanup and probably a change of sheets was definitely going to be in order as he carefully lifted himself off and then rolled onto his back.

"Ugh," Shaw said, "that was so great, but what a mess."

"And we just got clean?" Ross was smiling.

You made him look like that, all relaxed and happy. Completely unlike himself and yet, exactly, perfectly Ross.

"Yeah, we did, but it's okay. We can wipe up and then . . ." Shaw groaned, rolling over. "I gotta go to work."

"Me too," Ross said. "But it's gonna be a good day."

"After that, it's gonna be the *best* day, even taking last night into account," Shaw agreed. "Seriously, thank you again for jumping in like that. You didn't have to do it."

"Yeah, I did," Ross said. Much as he'd said the night before.

Shaw understood. He'd seen Ross in a somewhat similar position when this had all started, and he'd have done just about anything to help the guy.

But it still made his heart beat a little faster, anyway.

CHAPTER THIRTEEN

THE ORGASM HE'D EXPERIENCED this morning had been really fucking good.

And yet, Ross was still craving Shaw.

He was sitting here on the couch, freshly showered after a long day, trying to think of anything other than sex, and failing.

He'd put on an episode of *Chopped,* which he usually enjoyed because it was a good mental exercise, figuring out what he'd make with the basket ingredients. Then he'd settled on *Home Town,* even though that was usually what he and Shaw watched together, because he couldn't get his mind to fucking settle.

The problem was it didn't want to settle.

It wanted to fuck.

It wanted to *be* fucked.

Shaw had texted him earlier, saying Bryan was back and they'd brought in another temp bartender and Jackson had given him permission to leave early.

Ross wanted to think they were on the same goddamn page.

The Page: Shaw wanted to come home early, and he wanted to fuck.

This morning had been great, but he already knew it could be so much better.

The truth was, after a lifetime of mediocre sex, he was suddenly desperate to find out just how good it could be.

With Shaw. *Only with Shaw.*

The moment he heard telltale footsteps on the stairs, he turned the TV off, shifting his gaze to the door, his blood heating at just the thought that Shaw would be here in a second.

The door opened and there he was, staring at him, probably the same as he was staring back.

He hadn't bothered to put on clothes after his shower. Just a pair of boxer briefs, and Shaw was just standing there, speechless, staring.

Then suddenly, his arms were full of Shaw, and they were kissing and it was like they were inexplicably ravenous for each other.

Like they'd both thought about this all day, and couldn't wait a second longer.

"We gotta stop doing this on the couch," Shaw said, his mouth slick and hot against Ross' own.

He didn't know where to put his hands, so he put them everywhere, touching Shaw on his neck, cupping him there briefly, before sliding them down, across the firm planes of his back and then lower still, squeezing his ass as Shaw moaned into his mouth.

"What?" Ross knew that Shaw was speaking but something wasn't quite computing.

"The couch. We should . . ." Shaw gestured, but his words died as Ross leaned in and kissed him on the neck, right where he knew he liked it.

Shaw tilted his head for further access and for a minute, then two, there was nothing, just bliss and their mouths moving together and then apart, kissing every part they could reach, Shaw pressing his hard cock against Ross' equally hard one.

It was the hottest make-out session he'd ever participated in. He was burning with it, from the inside out.

When they finally pulled apart, they were both panting.

"I said . . . or I was *trying* to say," Shaw said, the corner of his reddened mouth tilting up into a knowing smile, "that we should go to the bedroom."

"Why didn't you?" Ross already knew the answer, but maybe he wanted Shaw to say it. To admit that he was as horny and distracted as Ross was.

"Because," Shaw said, leaning in further, his hand snaking down between them, cupping Ross' dick with his warm hand, making it strain and twitch, "then you'd stop and I really, really didn't want you to stop."

"What did you want, then?"

Shaw had made a point of saying this morning that they needed to lay everything out in the open, and Ross liked that. Knew he could, even though he still felt the slightest bit of tension when he asked the question.

"I think we talked about something this morning that we didn't get to do, that *I* didn't get to do, and I'm dying to." Shaw's expression was serious, but the look in his eyes was intense. "It was all I thought about the whole day. I think Jackson got really tired of me after I broke the third glass."

"You broke a glass?"

"I broke *three* glasses," Shaw said wryly. "Yeah, I know, unheard of."

"What you're saying, then, is that letting you fuck me is what . . . an act of sacrifice so you don't break every glass in the bar?"

Shaw laughed.

Ross had never known that you could laugh before or during sex. That he'd even want to.

But having sex with Shaw was like the polar opposite of every tense encounter he'd ever had.

"How about," Shaw said, leaning in even closer, his lips brushing Ross', "we call it an act of worship?"

"I like the sound of that," Ross said, hearing just how gravelly and rough his voice was. He was desperate for it and Shaw knew it, and somehow that was okay, because they were both right there together.

It wasn't so hard to lift Shaw, to let his legs wrap around him, though by the time they made it to the bedroom, he was distracted as hell.

The way Shaw kept kissing his neck and palming his dick might have something to do with it.

"God," Ross groaned, depositing him on the edge of the bed.

"Like that, huh?" Shaw said, toeing his shoes and socks off, and then yanking his shirt off, too. "I think you're gonna like this even more."

Ross couldn't stop looking at the beautiful man in front of him. Beautiful inside and out. How had he ever gotten so goddamned lucky?

Shaw was down to his own boxer briefs now, and the way he was looking at Ross?

Well, it was something fucking else, that was for sure.

"What are you gonna do?"

Placing a hand on Ross' chest, Shaw pushed him down onto the bed. "Make you feel so good," he said softly, reaching up to tug down Ross' underwear, his dick bobbing out hard and wet at the tip.

He'd done this a few times before, mostly when he'd realized that he didn't like being the one *doing* the fucking, and he'd learned this was easier to compartmentalize.

But he'd never done it with Shaw before, and it was clear, from the way Shaw climbed over onto him, caging him in, kissing him on the mouth, on the chest, on the stomach, and then at the crease of his thigh, that it was not going to be quite so easy with him.

Then Shaw gently parted his thighs, and Ross felt his thumb, wet with lube, circle his hole.

He tried to hold in the groan as Shaw pushed it in.

How had he not thought this was overwhelming? It was, in the best possible ways, in ways he'd never even dreamed of, before. He'd always imagined that it wouldn't matter to him who it was he was fucking or who was fucking him, but the fact that it was *Shaw*, tore him up.

He wanted more of his fingers, he wanted *all* the fingers. He wanted Shaw's cock.

Digging his fingers into the sheets, he tried to stay still, tried not to squirm as Shaw finger-fucked him, slowly, way too slowly, first his thumb, then another finger, and then finally two, barely brushing the spot inside him that lit him on fire.

"I think you *really* like this." Shaw's voice was dark, but not as dark as his gaze, fierce and erotic, on him.

Ross could barely stand it. But he was going to keep figuring out a way to make it work, because it felt too goddamn good to stop.

Then Shaw dipped his head down, his lips barely coasting over the overly sensitive head of his cock, and it twitched against his tongue, the pleasure intensifying tenfold.

Ross moaned then, the sound escaping out of him.

"Oh, yeah, you do really like this," Shaw said, sounding very happy about this fact. "Which is a relief, 'cause I do too."

"You gonna get on with it?" Ross needed more. He was dying for it. The want and the pleasure twisting him up, turning him inside out. He was straining and pushing and trembling, and then, worst of all, Shaw's fingers disappeared and he was empty again.

"Just a second," Shaw murmured. Ross heard him ripping open a condom and then he was back, caging him in again. "Like this?" he asked, after pressing a hot kiss to Ross' collarbone.

"Yes," Ross said. He wanted to see Shaw as it happened. For the first time in his life, he craved the intensity. Wanted to be devastated by it.

He lifted his head and kissed Shaw, catching him off guard right as he lined himself up to slide in.

Shaw gasped into his mouth, and the kiss turned wild as he slid in just a fraction, Ross breathing through the stretch and the bite of pain.

He could feel himself mumbling something against Shaw's lips, didn't even know what it was, but the more Shaw slid inside him, the storm inside him grew until he was consumed by it.

Reaching out, Shaw took his hand, twining their fingers together and pressing them together into the mattress. "You ready?" he asked, his voice as unsteady as Ross felt.

Ross nodded, and then felt himself be blown away by the tempest.

It was like, he realized in a dim, still thoughtful part of his mind, comparing his onion dip recipe to Tony's. Maybe it had been the same, at the very beginning, but everything else was new and different. Ingredients, method, taste.

Being fucked by Shaw was like that. It was the most astounding experience of his life, to feel him all around, deep inside him, as close as anyone had ever been. *Closer* in fact, because nobody else had ever understood him the way Shaw did.

If he'd thought Shaw was beautiful before, watching him fuck him was a whole different kind of beauty. If Ross was consumed by it, then Shaw was the architect, barely holding himself back so he could give more. Make Ross tremble with it.

Shaw crooked his knee up, and thrust harder, leaning into it, and Ross was dizzy with the need to come more than he'd ever experienced before. He reached down and Shaw, nodding once, encouraged him, and Ross grazed his fingertips over his cock, twitching and straining against the touch.

The last thing Ross saw before he shattered was Shaw's face—and the look on it thrust him the rest of the way into the storm and he was lost to it, coming as hard as he ever had in his life.

He felt rather than heard Shaw shout and felt him jerk against him, coming too, and then there was just the warm pressure of Shaw's body as he collapsed on top of him.

For a long moment, neither of them said anything. Ross could feel the hitch in his own breathing, and could hear it in Shaw's.

He'd never imagined, not in a million years, that sex could ever be that . . . *personal.*

The truth is, an uncomfortably honest voice inside Ross informed him, *you've never let it be personal.*

He hadn't.

He'd kept everyone away, at arm's length, because they'd never understood him.

And the feeling was usually mutual.

With Shaw, it was entirely, completely, utterly different, and as blown apart as Ross had felt by the sex, it felt more like something else had just shifted between them.

He'd been curious when Harmony had insisted a few days ago that he must be in love with Shaw.

Now, he wasn't just wondering if it were true.

He was afraid it *was* true.

As Shaw lay there, finally spent from the orgasm he'd been thinking about all fucking day, he thought the only downside was the mess they'd made of each other.

A shower was definitely going to be in order as he finally moved, rolling onto his back.

"I think I might be dead. From the greatest orgasm I've ever experienced," Shaw said.

Ross laughed, a deep rumbling chuckle. Shaw's heart filled with joy. He'd done that. He'd made Ross sound like that.

It was worth all the awkward moments they'd endured ahead of it.

Every single fucking one of them.

God, he loved this man. Every single bit of him. Even the awkward parts. *Especially* the awkward parts.

"Yeah," Ross said. "You wanna go get cleaned up?"

They needed it.

"Yeah, that's a good idea, I'm all sticky," Shaw said, groaning as he pushed himself to his feet. He was pleasantly surprised when Ross followed along to the bathroom, like he wasn't quite ready to let Shaw out of his sight just yet.

Shaw flipped the light on, dealt with the condom, and then turned the sink faucet on hot. Ross was using a tissue to clean up the worst of the come spattering his body, but Shaw wet a washcloth and handed it to him.

"Here, this is probably a lot better," Shaw said.

"Thanks," Ross said, shooting him a grateful look.

There'd been affection and warmth in his eyes before, when he'd looked at Shaw, but it was different now, and Shaw couldn't help but wonder . . .

Should he say something?

Should he step out onto a limb?

Make his feelings known?

He'd said that they would take this at Ross' speed, but he seemed *plenty* okay with the speed they'd just been going, which was akin to hurtling down the autobahn.

He would . . . he would start small.

Small, Shaw repeated to himself firmly, *you will start small, and you will not scare this man away.*

"I'm glad you were honest with me," Shaw said. "And that was exactly what I wanted. Just for us to be honest and enjoy each other."

Ross looked hopeful. "You enjoyed it?"

"I fucking loved it," Shaw said, and then they were both grinning at each other. "Let's do it again as soon as possible."

"Next time," Ross said, ducking his head shyly, "I would not be averse to doing that again."

"Noted," Shaw teased. "I'm definitely not gonna argue about that."

"Is this . . ." Ross hesitated. "You want to do this all the time, then?"

Shaw thought he knew what Ross was asking. "Yeah," he said. Might as well be honest.

Ross' expression was closing, which was frustrating, and his voice was full of trepidation. Maybe he should back off . . . but Shaw really didn't want to.

"With just me," Ross stated.

"Yeah. I guess, I guess we should talk about this." He didn't want to, he just wanted to live in this happy, amorphous place where they made each other laugh, and they gave each other great orgasms, and Shaw was completely head over heels for him.

But even Ross needed more than that, clearly, and so Shaw knew it was the right thing to do to suggest talking about it, even if he didn't want to.

But Ross didn't seem reassured. His tone was even more unsure when he said, "Talk?"

"Yeah, just have a conversation about this." Shaw was already kicking himself. He'd thought that this was what Ross wanted—what Ross *needed*, but instead, it sounded like he'd terrified him.

Maybe even scared him off.

"About what?" Ross asked.

Shaw wanted to beat his head against the tile bathroom wall.

"Just . . . we don't have to, I just thought you might want to talk about your . . ."

The sentence hadn't seemed so unbelievably stupid when it was in his head, but once it was mostly out of his mouth, Shaw realized just how dumb it was.

He was standing here, holding a wet washcloth, after cleaning the come off himself, and he felt more like an idiot than he'd ever felt before.

If Ross was like he thought he was, then *no*, he wouldn't want to talk about his feelings. He'd just wanted to understand the parameters, without going into everything else.

"Talk about what?" Ross repeated, sounding more nervous. More impatient.

"Talk about that this is what we're doing," Shaw said, trying to make up for Ross' uncertainty with a false sense of confidence. "Just that we're you know, having sex. Hanging out. No big deal."

"No big deal," Ross echoed. "Okay."

It was definitely not how Shaw had expected the conversation to go.

The way he'd *wanted* the conversation to go.

Clearly it wasn't what Ross had intended either, because suddenly he was walking out, leaving the bathroom.

Shaw found him in the kitchen, pulling a bottle of water out of the fridge. "Uh," he said, hesitating. Wondering if he should say anything else. Wondering if that might make it better—or worse.

Ross glanced up at him. He'd retreated back behind the wall, the one that Shaw could barely reach over.

That's okay, he told himself, *you've reached him before, you've gotten to him, it's just a minor setback. You can still fix this.*

They'd shared the bed last night, and that had been wonderful. Maybe even more wonderful than what they'd just done. The way Shaw had felt waking up this morning and seeing Ross lying next to him, expression peaceful in his slumber? He'd wanted it every single morning going forward. But his tongue felt stuck in his mouth, and he didn't know what to say.

How to convince him.

Maybe it was too soon. Maybe he'd rushed him.

All things that were very last on the list of what he wanted so desperately.

"Thanks," Ross said shortly, already turning towards the couch. "I'll see you tomorrow."

It was a clear dismissal if Shaw had ever heard one. But he wouldn't be dismissed.

Instead, he reached up and wrapped his arms around Ross' neck, hating how he froze for a second before he melted into the hug, pressing their bodies together.

"Goodnight," Shaw said before pressing a hot, promising kiss against Ross' mouth. "See you tomorrow."

CHAPTER FOURTEEN

ROSS KNEW HE SHOULDN'T be having a bad day.

Things with the truck were going better than they had in months.

Harmony was an irreplaceable addition. She was sorting out the accounts, she'd made sure that Ross hadn't ended up paying double to the produce vendor, and he was chipping away a lot quicker than he'd ever imagined at the rest of his debt.

He and Tony weren't ever going to be close, but they were more cordial than they'd ever been, and despite his annoyance at Tony attempting to throw the Waffle Day contest so he'd win, Ross was more touched than he wanted to admit by the gesture.

The only reason he was in such a bad mood?

Well, the only explanation Ross could come up with was the aborted conversation that he and Shaw had *almost* had last night.

Last night had been . . . well, it had been pretty fucking amazing if Ross had anything to say about it. Every single time he expected Shaw to let him down, he not only avoided being as shitty as every other guy had been, but he was more caring and more thoughtful than even Ross could hope for.

He'd been kind and he'd been hot and the sex they'd shared? The best of Ross' life.

And then, right when he'd been basking in the otherworldly amazingness of it all, Shaw had started making noise about wanting to "talk."

AKA he wasn't happy.

AKA Ross had done something wrong.

Except Ross couldn't figure out what it was.

No matter how he wracked his brain, nothing came to mind.

Shaw had been relaxed and happy, with a smile that had set every inch of Ross' insides alight with pleasure, and then he'd started talking, and it had all gone to shit.

Ross still didn't know how, and it was evidence of how much he fucking liked Shaw that he was actually tempted to ask.

If you do, you're gonna regret it, a voice inside reminded him. *You never want to know what people really think of you. And him? It would be goddamn agonizing.*

But then it wasn't like Ross didn't feel goddamn agonized right now.

Harmony shot him one last look as she grabbed her bag, ready to head out into the cool evening. "You going to be staying long, boss?" she asked.

She'd quickly—because she was undoubtedly intelligent—figured out that Ross was in a rotten mood and had, from the opening of the truck hours before, given him a wide berth.

It was smart. Ross knew it was.

Didn't mean it didn't hurt.

Didn't mean he didn't wish he were different.

Every fucking day of your whole fucking life, Ross thought.

"No," he said. Even though he didn't want to go home. And the bar?

That was definitely out of the question.

Except that, more than he had in a really long time, Ross wanted a drink. Wanted to silence all these annoying voices in his head, who wouldn't fucking shut up about how he'd ruined it all.

There weren't many places he felt comfortable drinking at, and unfortunately, the Funky Cup was at the very top of that list.

Maybe he could go and avoid Shaw. Hang out on the back patio. Order some dinner that he didn't have to cook for himself and get a drink. Try to decompress before the inevitable confrontation he'd have to deal with when both he and Shaw returned home.

It wasn't the best plan he'd ever had, but by the time he'd closed up and locked the truck, Ross had decided.

Not many people knew about the side door into the back patio, since it was mostly covered with the creeping greenery that spread across most of the outside walls of the brick-walled patio. But Ross had been coming here long enough that he knew about it, and he used it now, grabbing a small table separate from the rest of the growing crowd.

Chelle arrived at his table just as he'd sat down.

"Hey, Ross," she said, "not hanging out inside today?"

He hadn't expected the question, but he shrugged it off. "It's a nice night," he said noncommittally. He'd hung out here before. Admittedly he'd been with other people, never by himself. Whenever he'd come here alone, he'd always done it because he'd wanted to see Shaw.

It wasn't that he didn't want to see Shaw; it was actually the opposite.

He wasn't sure Shaw wanted to see him.

"It is a really nice night," Chelle agreed. "What can I get you? Your usual Shirley Temple?"

He wanted to, but if he ordered it, Shaw would know it was him.

"Nah," Ross said, "vodka soda, please, with lime."

"Can I recommend the Deep Eddy grapefruit vodka?" Chelle said. "It's Jackson and Alexis' favorite, for a reason."

"Sure," Ross said. He didn't like flavored vodka, typically, but then he knew Alexis didn't either. So if he could stomach it, then it couldn't be that bad.

"Anything to eat?" she asked.

"You guys still have that steak sandwich special?"

Chelle smiled. "It's on the regular menu now. That was a Shaw request. He said you loved it, and he told Jackson that if you liked it, then it must be good."

"Oh." Ross didn't know what to say to Chelle's statement or the knowing look in her eyes. Like she, and everyone else, had figured out that they weren't just sharing the apartment upstairs for convenience, but because of more.

He considered telling her the truth; that it had started out as *only* a roommate thing, but then he'd have to explain it.

He definitely did not want to explain it.

"I'll put the order in," Chelle said. "Sweet potato fries? Extra chipotle aioli?"

Ross nodded. How did she know his order? Was he spending that much time here?

He didn't want to think about it, because he already knew the answer.

"Great," she said, "I'll be right back with your drink."

She'd left, heading back into the bar when an unexpected visitor sat down at his table.

It was a tiny table, meant only for two. Ross wouldn't have picked it if they'd had tables for one available but this was a bar. Nobody came to a bar to be alone.

Well, nobody else did.

"I wasn't expecting to see you out here, alone." Ren sat down in the other chair before Ross could protest.

"What are you doing here?" Ross asked flatly.

He didn't want to share his misery with anyone else. Especially Lorenzo Moretti.

Ren just shrugged, clearly unconcerned with Ross' lack of welcome. "I could ask you the same thing," he said. "You don't come here that often—well, until a few weeks ago, you didn't—and when you do, you don't usually hide out here."

"I'm not hiding," Ross said, knowing how prickly he sounded and not caring.

"Yeah, okay," Ren said. "If you're not hiding, you won't mind if I sit with you."

Ross actually cared a lot about him staying and sitting with him—he and Ren had only shared a handful of conversations ever, and one of those had been when Ren had supposedly hit on him and he hadn't realized what he was asking for.

Now he saw Ren and mostly managed to head the opposite direction.

Was he back here to hit on him again?

Ross really hoped not, because it would be awkward to turn him down again, especially now that he knew what Ren was suggesting.

And he definitely would be turning him down. He and Shaw had not discussed whether they were sleeping with other people, but Ross already knew he didn't want anyone else.

"I wish you wouldn't," Ross said, just as Chelle walked back with his drink.

"Oh, Ren, I didn't realize you were here," Chelle said, smiling at him with a dimpled expression. "What can I get you?"

"He's not staying," Ross said.

And was promptly ignored.

"Is that the vodka with Deep Eddy grapefruit?" Ren asked, gesturing at the drink Chelle had placed in front of Ross. When she nodded, he added, "I'll have one of those. And the buffalo chicken salad, thanks."

Ross sighed loudly when Chelle took down the order and walked off. He took a long sip of his drink, and was pleasantly surprised by how good it was.

"So, you going to tell me why you're hiding out here, or not?" Ren said, tapping his fingers against the table.

"I'm not hiding." It was not easy to maintain his composure, but Ross was trying. Harder than he wanted to be trying.

"You absolutely are. What happened with you and Shaw?"

"How do you know anything was going on between me and Shaw?" Ross wanted to know not just because he didn't want to answer the question and because he wanted to change the subject, but also because he was genuinely curious. How did everyone know? Had Tony told everyone even though even *he* didn't know for sure?

"Everyone knows." Ren leaned forward, his dark eyes gleaming in the dim light of the patio. "Shaw's been crushing on you forever."

"Oh."

"Yeah, *oh*," Ren repeated with a grin. "Don't tell me you didn't realize."

"I'm not good at this. You know that." It wasn't easy for him to admit it, especially to someone like Ren, who was *really* good at it.

Ross took another long drink. These were dangerous; he could down several and not even notice until he was tipsy with the booze.

But that's what you want tonight.

He wanted to drink just enough that he didn't give a shit anymore.

He didn't know how much booze that was going to take.

Maybe it would be better, if he was going to drink a few, that he didn't drink them alone.

"You're not," Ren agreed. "But clearly Shaw wasn't alone if you're hooking up—and you definitely are. You two are all cute and shit together." He snorted, clearly not buying into their supposed cuteness like everyone else was.

If Aaron wasn't in jail . . . if Aaron wasn't a fucking piece of shit, Ross revised . . . then he might have asked him what he could've done to fuck things up.

Ren did this kind of thing all the time. He was famous on the food truck lot for his hookups and his many conquests and the nonchalant way he collected them, with no embarrassment or shame.

Maybe . . . maybe Ross could ask him.

If he could get over the humiliation first.

He downed the rest of his drink in several long gulps.

"Shit," Ren said, watching as Ross knocked the drink back, "you *did* fuck it up, and you *are* hiding."

"Yeah," Ross said.

"You want to talk about it?"

"Not if you're immediately going to go running to Gabe or Tony about it," Ross said. He knew just how Gabriel Moretti, Ren's cousin, was. If anyone was going to challenge Tony for the title of Gossip Queen of the lot, it was going to be him.

Ren just chuckled and shook his head. "Don't worry," he said. "I'm a vault."

That was something that Ross *had* heard about Lorenzo. He did not kiss and tell.

Maybe his secrets would be safe with him.

"Okay, well, we have been . . ." Ross cleared his throat. This was a terrible idea, because he didn't even know the right terminology. What *had* they been doing? He didn't fucking know. Because it wasn't just sex.

He was clueless about all of this, but he did know that much.

"You've been fucking?" Ren finished for him, grinning wide.

"I guess," Ross said. "But not just that. Like . . . hanging out and shit, you know? Being . . . friends?"

Ren rolled his eyes. "You're all up in each other's business. You've got *feelings*, dude."

"I don't . . ." Harmony had said the same thing though. She'd said he was in love with Shaw, and well, he did feel a certain way about the guy. A certain way he wasn't sure he'd ever felt before. Was that love? How did you know?

"You're in love with him, and he's in love with you," Ren stated flatly. "If it was just fucking, you wouldn't be twinkling at each other when you're just hanging out. I've seen you two. It's gross."

"Twinkling?"

"Yeah," Ren said, waving around his head. "You know, all that heart eyes nonsense."

"I don't have heart eyes. And I don't twinkle," Ross stated, still not sure what Ren was referring to.

"Oh you fucking twinkle like a star," Ren said, his voice teasing. "But that's okay, because Shaw's twinkling at you right back."

"Oh," Ross said. He wished Chelle would come back. He needed a refill if they were going to keep talking about this.

"So, you're fucking, you're twinkling, and everything's going great," Ren said, "so why are you hiding out here?"

Ross tried to gather up what was left of his dignity. "I'm not hiding. I'm . . . I don't *have* to go in there and order a drink."

"Listen," Ren said, leaning forward, "it's easier if we're just honest with each other. I think that works way better all around—frankly, if you'd been honest with Shaw before now, I bet there wouldn't be any bullshit hiding happening—and if I'm gonna help you, I want to know the whole truth."

"Fine." Ross sighed. "I'm hiding out here because something weird happened last night. We had . . . we had sex." It was embarrassing how hard it was for him to say it. He willed himself not to flush. Not just because of the humiliation factor, but also because talking about it reminded him of *experiencing* it, and well, that was a *lot*. "We had sex and then we were in the bathroom together . . ."

"Wait," Ren said, holding up a hand. "Why were you in the bathroom together? Something real kinky, right?"

Ross shot him a look. "We were cleaning up," he said, with as much dignity as he could muster.

"Right, you made each other all messy with all your sex," Ren teased, looking him up and down in a way that made Ross want to blush again.

"Anyway, we were in the bathroom, and he said something about wanting to talk. He was really awkward about it. And . . ." Ross sighed. "Every single fucking time someone wants to talk to me about what we're doing, it's not good."

Chelle arrived then, and thank God for her efficiency because she'd spied Ross' empty glass and she had a refill for him as well as Ren's first drink.

"Shaw asked me if Alexis was out here," Chelle said as she set the glasses down, "I said no. Changed the subject when he asked." She shot Ross a hard look, practically pinning him to the chair. "Don't fuck around with our boy, you hear?"

"Your boy?" Ross was pretty damn sure that Chelle was not Shaw's mother.

She put her hands on her hips. "Listen, he's a good guy."

"I know he is," Ross said, still baffled where this was all going.

"Chelle," Ren inserted into the conversation, "I'm dealing with it. Don't worry. I think the last thing Ross wants to do is fuck Shaw up. Well . . ." He grinned semi-evilly. "Maybe not the *last* thing."

Chelle laughed, and patted Ren on the head. "Good to hear," she said. "I'll go check on your food."

"Okay," Ren said, turning back to Ross, "you're going to need to define not good."

"Not good? Like, they tell me to fuck off," Ross said despondently. He sipped his drink. "They tell me I'm way too weird. Too neurotic. Too much fucking work."

"Is that what Shaw said?"

"Not *yet*," Ross said.

"No, no, no," Ren corrected, and he was smiling now. Which only annoyed Ross more. Why had he thought this guy could help? He was fucking great at these things. The opposite of Ross. "He didn't say that at all. He just said he wanted to talk. Did he say what about?"

Ross thought about it. "Not specifically, no, but he was really awkward about it. The only conclusion I could come to was that he wanted to tell me he was tired of me or didn't want to do this anymore, but I was staying there, in the apartment, and he didn't want to force me to leave."

"Now, I'm no expert," Ren said modestly, which was ridiculous, because if there was an expert on fucking, it was absolutely Lorenzo Moretti, "but if I had to guess, Shaw wasn't going to tell you to quit kissing him or hanging out with him. And he definitely wasn't going to tell you to move out."

"Then what did he want to say? Why did he have to get so nebulous?"

Ren smiled. "Because he's not good at this either, which . . . I'm going to give him crap about."

"No, please, God, don't do that." Ross found himself begging.

If he did, then Shaw would know that he'd gone running to Ren for advice. And that was more humiliating than anything else.

"We'll see," Ren said, "but what he was *trying* to do was tell you that he wanted to be twinkly with you for the foreseeable future. You get me?"

Ross knew he was staring blankly at the other man. "No?"

"He wanted to be exclusive and all lovey-dovey and shit," Ren said baldly. "Like boyfriends." He shuddered.

"He wanted to ask me to be his boyfriend." Ross couldn't believe it. Nobody had ever wanted him that way before. They always got tired of him. Tired of all his baggage and his neuroses and the way he needed patience and understanding in the bedroom.

"You'd just had sex, right?"

Ross nodded.

"And it was hot, right? It *would* be hot, you and Shaw." Ren got a faraway look in his eyes, like he was thinking about it.

And ew, gross.

"It was good," Ross agreed. Hesitated. Didn't want Ren to think it hadn't been as stupendous as it was. "Best sex I've ever had."

"Well, there you go. It probably was right up there for him too, and he wanted to lock it down, you know?" Ren gestured.

"Lock what down?"

"You, your dick, you know, the whole package," Ren said.

"You really think that's what all this was about?" Ross couldn't believe it. It was too good to be true; but then he'd thought that the produce vendor situation had been as bad as it could possibly be, and it had resolved to be nowhere near the disaster he'd imagined.

"I think it's highly, highly possible," Ren said, sipping his own drink.

"Huh." Ross thought back to the evening before, and re-watched it with this new information and interpretation, and it *did* fit.

Maybe Shaw was just as horrible at this stuff as he was.

He'd have to tell him, if they ever got this worked out, that in the future, he should just come out and say things. That Ross wouldn't get confused if he did that. Ross already had resolved to be more honest with Shaw, even if it was scary. Even if he was afraid that what Shaw really wanted to tell him was that he was done.

"You should talk to him," Ren said.

"I'm going to," Ross said, feeling the certainty of it swirl through him.

They were going to have to be a lot more straightforward with each other, that much was clear.

"This isn't something I have much experience with," Ren said, "but I'm going to also suggest that you tell Shaw the truth about your feelings."

"My feelings?"

"That you care about him. That you love him. It's a big step, but I think he feels the same way about you, so it shouldn't be too scary."

Ross took a deep breath. "But how do I know if I *do* love him?"

Ren leaned forward. "That's a little trickier to help you with, seeing as I've never been in love either."

"Ever?"

Ren shook his head. "But do you . . . is he the person you always want to talk to? Always want to see? Even if you can't? The person you trust more than anyone else? The person whose gaze makes your heart beat just a little bit faster? The person who makes you feel like you can do anything?"

That was easy enough, Ross nodded. "I've never felt that way about someone before. Like I can trust him to . . . get me? If that makes sense."

"It does," Ren said with a smile. "Obviously, you can do whatever you want, and you're never obligated to tell someone your feelings for them, but I think . . . I think Shaw would want to know. I think he'd be over the moon about it."

"Yeah?"

"Absolutely," Ren said. "And not only that, I'd bet you that he feels the exact same way."

Ross couldn't deny that he'd hoped but . . . he could also admit that feelings were not his strongest suit.

"Here you go, you two," Chelle said, approaching the table with two loaded plates. "The steak sandwich, with sweet potato fries, and the buffalo chicken salad."

She set them down, along with napkins and silverware, and then took a step back, hands on her hips. "Y'all need more to drink?"

"Two refills, please, Chelle," Ren said, giving her one of his charming smiles.

"Sure thing."

The moment she was gone, Ren picked up his fork and then pointed it, very directly, at Ross. "So," he said, "while we eat you should give me the other scoop."

Ross stared at him warily. "The 'other' scoop?"

"You know, not you and Shaw, but what went down between you and Aaron."

Normally, this was the kind of question that Ross dreaded. He didn't want to talk about Aaron. He definitely never wanted to talk about the situation that had happened a few months back, the situation that had resulted in Aaron being arrested and Ash's truck burning up.

"Why can't you just ask Lennox? Or Ash?"

Ren leaned forward. "I have. They aren't talking. Have you ever met Lennox? He's closed up tighter than Fort Knox. And if Lennox isn't talking, then Ash isn't talking."

Ross' sandwich, which had tasted so good only a few moments before, felt like ash in his mouth. "Why does it even matter? Why do you even care?"

"I'm just curious. Not gonna blab if that's what you're worried about. Call it *quid pro quo*, for the advice I gave you on Shaw."

Ren *had* helped him. It would be rude to tell him to fuck off.

Of course, a month ago, Ross would've done just that.

You're the hero, remember, not the villain. Shaw's voice echoed in his head.

Ross sighed. "Fine. Fine, okay, I'll tell you. But you promised."

"Who am I gonna tell?" Ren's charming smiles, that he gave to everyone in such abundance, seemed bottomless.

For a second, Ross was almost tempted to ask him how he did it. But even if he knew, the chance of him being able to replicate Ren's talent and skill? It wasn't happening.

Besides, as long as he had Shaw in his bed—and in his heart—why did he need to charm the world?

"I should've known something was wrong," Ross said. "I'd known Aaron forever. From when I first came to LA, young and hungry and stupid."

Ren nodded sagely. "We've all been there."

Somehow Ross doubted it. Ren looked like he'd been knowing and worldly even as a child.

"I let him deal with all the business parts of the truck, you know, the money and the bills. We were always busy, right? But there never seemed to be any cash, especially at the end." Ross hesitated. "That's why Aaron wanted to join the lot. He said if we had it cushier, like Tony and y'all, that we could pay more stuff off. Have more of a savings."

"You guys were always booked though. You were everywhere."

"We were," Ross agreed, nodding. Feeling the sense of shame and guilt that he always did when he thought about how stupid and how gullible he'd been.

"So you believed him," Ren said thoughtfully.

"He was my friend." *My only friend.* "We'd started the truck together, because he wanted to get out of Atkinson's kitchen. When I told him that I only wanted to do it if we could use my grandmother's recipes, he just smiled and agreed. Working with him was easy . . . until it wasn't."

"You could've asked to see the books," Ren pointed out.

"Yeah, but it's gibberish to me. Always has been. I . . . I'm not good at that kind of thing."

"Bet you won't let anyone else take them over now," Ren said softly.

"Harmony's helping. She's teaching me," Ross said.

"So, what, you feel ashamed that he took advantage of you. You feel guilty that you didn't realize what he was doing, that he was using drugs again, that he was obsessed with Ash?"

Ross frowned. "Is it that obvious?"

"No," Ren said, and for the first time, there was a very human empathy in his eyes. For the first time, Ross wondered if they were all selling Lorenzo Moretti short.

If Lorenzo Moretti was selling *himself* short.

"No," Ren continued after a long moment. "It's what I would feel if I was in your shoes."

"But you aren't. It didn't happen to you."

"But it could." Ren's voice was thoughtful now. Considering.

"Gabe loves you like a brother. He'd never betray you."

"No, he wouldn't," Ren said. "But sometimes it's not about that. You trusted the right person. The person you wanted Aaron to be. He let you down, because he wasn't ever that person."

"You're saying . . . blame him. Not me."

"I'm saying, you don't have to take responsibility for everything that happens. Even if you were involved. You're a good guy, Ross." It sounded so much like what Shaw had said the other night that Ross had to wonder if they were secretly working together, on some kind of Make Ross Feel More Heroic plan.

Ross, who'd carried all of this guilt for months, realized that whether their efforts had worked, or time had done its job, he *was* beginning to feel better. Like he might emerge from the other side of this, when a few weeks ago, he'd wondered if he'd stay in this rut forever.

"Thanks," Ross said, and he nearly said something else—though God only knew what, because he was utter shit at this—but then Chelle appeared with their drinks.

"Shaw's a real thundercloud behind the bar tonight," she said as she set the drinks down in front of them. "Just warning you now."

"It's alright," Ren said, "Ross has got this. Don't you, Ross?"

Ross sure hoped he did.

CHAPTER FIFTEEN

SHAW DREADED WALKING BACK into the apartment. He'd wondered more than once, over the long-as-hell shift that never seemed to end, if Ross would already be asleep, hiding in plain sight and avoiding him again, when he came home.

But when he opened the door, the light was on, and there Ross was, sitting on the couch, with shorts on and no t-shirt.

Shaw swallowed hard. "Hey," he said.

Sounding utterly and completely stupid.

Stupid in love, he told himself. *That's what you are.*

Ross looked up. He was watching an episode of *Chopped,* Ted Allen and Scott Conant looking aghast at whatever one of the contestants was doing.

"You cut your hair," Ross said, and he sounded distraught by it.

Shaw had woken up this morning, walked out into the living room, and seen Ross was already gone, clearly leaving for work early, and had felt the urge to throw something.

Mostly at himself.

He'd settled for doing what the pop songs always suggested, and doing something rather less drastic. He'd stopped by the barber after grabbing coffee and had chopped his hair off.

It still felt weirdly lighter.

"Yeah," Shaw said.

Ross frowned. "I liked it long," he said.

"It's only hair," Shaw said lightly, because it was easier to talk about hair than anything else going on between them. "It'll grow back."

"You're gonna have to watch this," Ross said, changing the subject, and there was something off about him. Was it his surprisingly easy smile?

Oh shit.

"Are you . . ." Shaw flopped down on the couch next to him, all his anxieties forgotten because . . . "Are you drunk?"

Ross' eyes grew wide. "No," he said. "Well, a little bit, maybe. I had a few. Ren can really pound them, you know?"

"You were at the bar. With Ren." Shaw told himself that he wasn't pissed.

And he definitely wasn't jealous.

Nope. Not at all. Not even a little bit.

Ross shot him another smile, silly at the edges. "I hid outside," he admitted.

"Shit," Shaw said, rubbing a hand over his face. Over his weirdly short hair. "I didn't want to. I didn't mean . . ."

But Ross interrupted him. So much for Shaw being convinced that he was going to have to pull this out of him one uncomfortable bit at a time.

"It's okay, I know you didn't. You just wanted to tell me that you love me. Like I love you."

Ross looked the opposite of distressed. He looked relaxed and happy. Okay, maybe a little happier than Shaw had expected.

Truthfully, he hadn't anticipated any of this but . . . *yeah*, he loved Ross. And he'd suspected that Ross felt the same, but he hadn't expected to hear it so quickly—or with so little drama.

"Uh," Shaw said.

Ross reached over and patted him on the head. "It's okay," he said. "Ren explained it all to me. What you were trying to talk about. You weren't trying to get me to leave."

Shaw's tongue started to unstick itself. "Uh, yeah, no, that wasn't what I was trying to do at all."

"I know," Ross said knowingly.

"You do?" Shaw thought he was a lot brighter than sitting here, parroting Ross' words back at him, but right now? His mind felt blank, his carefully prepared speech blown to a million little pieces by Ross' confession.

"I told you, Ren explained it. You were trying to be exclusive." Ross leaned over, resting his head on Shaw's shoulder. "You wanted to be my *boyfriend*. You know I've never had a boyfriend before."

Shaw laughed before he could stop himself. "No?"

Ross shook his head in an exaggerated movement. "You'd be the very first. Is that what you want?"

"It is what I want," Shaw said. "Though I said from the beginning that I only wanted what *you* wanted. That we would go at your speed."

Ross frowned. "You think I don't want it?"

"You kinda made it clear when you . . . when you . . ." Shaw cleared his throat. He kinda understood why Ross had ended up getting a "little bit drunk," because he sure could use a drink right now. Except that one of them in this state was probably enough. "When you said . . ."

"When I said you loved me, and I loved you back?" Ross' smile was brilliant. "I know, I did, didn't I?"

Shaw laughed, because he couldn't help himself. Ross really did love him. And he sure as hell loved Ross.

"You did a hell of a lot better than I did," Shaw said.

Ross scooted even closer. "That might be the booze."

"You felt this way before it?" Shaw didn't want to ask—but he *had* to know.

Ross shot him a look. "Well, *yeah*. I guess I didn't know what it was, but . . ." And suddenly Shaw's lap was full of a big, *little bit drunk*, very affectionate man. "I want to see you every morning and every night, and I want to make you feel good and I want to feed you and I want to make you smile and you know what else?"

Shaw felt lit from the inside out. Like someone had just shone a very bright light and it was illuminating him. And that someone? It was definitely Ross.

"What else?" he asked, hearing just how affectionate and charmed he sounded. He was completely, crazy in love. He rested his cheek against Ross' warm chest, feeling his heartbeat echo under his skin.

"I want to watch *Home Town* with you. Like *always*. Never with anyone else. Just you."

Wrapping his arms around him, Shaw pulled Ross in even closer. "Yeah? You know what? Me too."

Ross' eyes were dark as he pulled back. "But not tonight."

"Oh, what are we doing tonight?"

The movement Ross made with his hips made it clear what he wanted to be doing instead. Shaw probably should've been turned on—*okay, you still are, you always are when Ross is around 'cause your man is big and hot and . . .*—but he knew that Ross didn't drink much and he was more worried than he wanted to be about how he was doing.

That was how he knew it wasn't just lust.

He'd been there before.

If all he wanted was a good orgasm, he could've taken plenty of people to bed. Ren, for example. *Which is why you shouldn't be jealous that he got drunk with Ross,* Shaw reminded himself. But he'd wanted more than that, and he wanted Ross to be happy and cared for and not about to vomit his brains out if they fucked.

"Yeah, about that," Shaw said, "how you feelin'?"

Ross pouting was way cuter than it should've been. "I'm fine," he proclaimed.

"You sure are," Shaw said. "I'd love to be able to pull a Ross Stanton and cart you to bed, but you've got me by about seventy-five pounds."

"It's okay," Ross said, his voice very serious, "I still think you're hot. And I love you."

"You gonna tell me that all the time?" Shaw thought this sounded like a fucking wonderful plan.

"Oh, yeah," Ross said, nodding enthusiastically. "I think I should."

"I'm down with that," Shaw said as Ross slid off his lap, and back onto the couch. Shaw felt the loss almost immediately and nearly reached over and pulled him back.

But something about the way Ross was looking at him stopped him.

Was it the undeniable love in his eyes?

Shaw thought that maybe the Ross he was seeing right now was him stripped down, without any of his walls, and it was the most beautiful thing he'd ever witnessed.

He understood why Ross had the walls; he'd had a tough life and he needed to protect himself. Shaw wouldn't ever deny him that. But this? This was special and it was a fucking privilege.

"I really do, you know," Shaw said, leaning over and pressing his palm to Ross' bare chest, right above his heart. "Love you."

Ross smiled. "Ren thought so."

"And what about you? What did you think?"

The look in Ross' eyes was soft. "I hoped you did."

Shaw curled his fingertips into the other man's skin. Felt like he couldn't get close enough. Why were they not cuddled up naked together in his bed? It felt like a miss that they weren't.

"I hoped, too."

Shaw's hand slid down and he intertwined their fingers together. "Come on," he continued, getting to his feet and pulling Ross up behind him. "Let's go to bed."

"But," Ross said, looking adorably confused, "this is my bed."

"Not anymore," Shaw said firmly. Then caught himself. "Unless you want it to be."

The frown on Ross' face deepened even more. "Why would I want it to be, when I could be with you? You really want me in your bed?"

"If you want to be there."

Ross elbowed him in the side, his confused expression melting into a sunny smile. "Where else would I want to be?"

"Okay, then," Shaw said as they entered his bedroom. "My bed is your bed."

"It's a good bed," Ross said, collapsing on it, all starfished across the covers. "Though I think I kinda like the person in it, more."

"I'm gonna take a shower, I'll be back in a few." He felt sweaty and gross and he hated to go to bed without a shower first. "You get all comfy," he added patting the bed. "I'll be back in a minute."

"I'm gonna time you," Ross teased, scooting over to one side of the bed. "Just so you know."

"I'll be quick," Shaw promised.

He was too, washing himself and his hair in record time, thinking as he rubbed his hands over his shorn locks that he hoped Ross wouldn't be too angry about the haircut when he woke up sober.

He knew Ross didn't like change. He probably should have checked with him first.

He loves you, not your hair, Shaw reminded himself, and found himself smiling again at just the thought.

For all his talk of being bad at relationships—and never having had one before—he'd actually very neatly solved the problem.

The Talk? Hadn't been much of a Talk after all, and Shaw was totally okay with that.

He was ready, arousal simmering just under his skin, to do something that didn't involve any talking at all.

But when he got back into the bedroom, skin still damp, Ross' quiet snores greeted him.

Shaw reached over and flipped the light off, plugging his phone in, and climbing into the other side of the bed.

As soon as he got positioned, Ross rolled over, and even though his snores didn't change, he wrapped a big hand around Shaw's waist, tugging him closer.

Yeah, sex was great, but this, Shaw thought, was even fucking better.

When he fell asleep, his cheeks were hurting from smiling so hard.

Ross woke up abruptly, his very least favorite way to wake up, with an ice pick to his eyes as the light streamed in, bright and unrelenting.

"Ugh," he groaned, rolling over. Realizing at the very last second that he was totally going to fall off the couch. Except that whatever he was lying on currently felt a hell of lot more comfortable than the couch, and his ass didn't immediately hit the ground.

He opened one eye a fraction, remembering in fits and starts what had happened the night before.

He'd ended up sharing way too many drinks with Ren, who was actually a pretty cool guy, all things considered, and then he'd stumbled home to wait for Shaw so he could have the Talk, Ross-style.

He remembered just enough of the Talk they'd had to both be excruciatingly humiliated and totally fucking thrilled.

He'd informed Shaw that he knew he loved him.

Not your finest moment.

And that he loved him back.

A little better.

Then he'd fallen asleep when Shaw had been showering.

Completely missing *I love you* sex.

Yeah, you suck. And not in the good way.

Groaning again, Ross rolled back over and realized that he was alone in the bed.

Where was Shaw?

He hadn't seemed mad last night; in fact he'd seemed just as happy as Ross.

Okay, not quite as happy as you were.

Embarrassment washed over him in another sickening wave.

Or maybe that was his roiling stomach, aided by the blinding headache.

This was why he didn't drink anymore. He didn't like the way he lost control. He didn't like the way he felt the next morning, full of regret and sick as hell.

He didn't know where Shaw was.

He didn't know where his phone was.

Ross put a hand over his eyes and just wanted to curl up and die. But first, he really needed to find his phone. Figure out what time it was. Take a shower. Drag his sorry, miserable ass to work.

He cracked his eye open wider and started feeling around on the side table for it, and finally he found it, nearly dropping it again when the light blinded him, and also when he realized what time it was.

It was ten thirty in the morning.

The truck was opening in half an hour.

He hadn't been there to help Harmony prep for the day.

And that totally explained why Shaw wasn't around either. He usually went into work about eleven, earlier if he stopped by his favorite coffee place first.

That sequence of thoughts had just finished cycling through his fucking dim brain when he heard the front door open and the sound of steps walking across the floor towards the bedroom.

A second later, Shaw was standing there, smiling way too widely, and he was giving him a coffee. From his favorite coffee shop.

"I texted Harmony when I woke up about seven," Shaw said conversationally, like he hadn't confessed *Shaw's* love last night, followed by his own, followed by falling asleep in his bed like a freaking chump. Followed by sleeping in until *ten thirty*. "I told her you might need the sleep and she said she'd be fine to prep on her own this morning. But . . ." Shaw hesitated, and glanced down at his watch. "You might want to get in the shower 'cause the lot's about to open, and I guaranteed you'd be there by eleven."

"You cut your hair." He'd probably noticed last night—he *hoped* he'd noticed last night—but God only knew how ridiculous he could've been.

"Yeah." Shaw ran his hand over it, ruffling the short strands. "You don't hate it?"

Ross grinned at him, despite the pounding behind his eyes. "I liked it long. I like it like this. Probably, I just like *you*."

Shaw smiled at him, and the relief in his eyes made Ross want to do a little dance in bed. Despite the hangover. He'd done that *right.* He could do this. He could make Shaw happy. He could make *himself* happy.

"I guess I should get up and get ready for work," Ross said.

But there was more he should say. More he should've said to Shaw some time ago.

Don't you think you've said plenty?

He had, but he forged on anyway, ignoring the way his head was pounding. "I should apologize," he said quietly. "For the way I . . . I didn't mean for it to happen like that. To clarify," he added, aware of the growing disappointment on Shaw's face, "I am *not* sorry for how I feel about you, or how you feel about me, but you shouldn't have found out like that."

Ross scrubbed a hand across his face. Took a long drink of coffee. It was perfect. Just the way he liked it.

"What I'm trying to say is that I don't drink for a reason. I . . . I've got all these sharp edges," he said. "I used to drink to make them duller. I thought maybe, well, maybe it would be good to take a bit of the edge off last night, and I went too far. Which is exactly why I stopped doing it. I wasn't good at stopping. It was usually," he added wryly, "a way for me to feel normal, and I'm not normal so . . ." He shrugged. "Seemed pointless after a time."

Shaw sat down on the bed next to him. "First, you don't have to apologize. Truly, it was cute as hell. And second, I like your sharp edges."

Ross felt the surprise filter through his uncooperative brain. He drank more coffee. Wondered if he'd misheard. "You do?"

Shaw nodded. "I love them, in fact."

"Oh."

"I love *you*," Shaw said. Reached out and tangled their fingers together, squeezing his hand firmly. "I hope you're okay with me saying it, because well, I can't seem to stop."

"I won't make you," Ross said seriously. He'd never imagined anyone loving him like this before.

His grandmother had loved him—had accepted him, in a somewhat similar way to Shaw, which he should have realized before this moment. He'd always escaped to her house, basking in the warmth of her complete acceptance. His parents had always loved him, of course, but they'd wanted to *understand* him more, and that had been impossible.

A fool's errand.

But his grandmother? She'd been the one person in his life who gave her love selflessly.

It was why when Aaron had suggested they start the food truck, Ross had said yes at all. He'd still been hurting from her death, wanting to do something with all this *feeling*, this overwhelming emotion, and keeping her recipes alive was something he could *do*.

"Did I ever tell you about my grandmother?" he asked Shaw.

"No," Shaw said. "But you should."

"While I shower, because Harmony is already going to kill me," Ross said, gulping the rest of his coffee down.

Shaw just followed him into the bathroom and then listened, leaning on the wall right outside the shower as Ross told him all about his grandmother, and the way they'd cook together in her little yellow house on the leafy side street in the small North Carolina town he'd grown up in.

"I felt like she really didn't care if I was fucked up or weird," Ross said as he washed the shampoo out of his hair. "She just wanted to spend time with me. And it was so refreshing."

"Because your parents didn't want to do that?"

Ross stared at the shower wall. Remembering that time. Remembering when he hadn't thought that things would ever change. That he'd ever be accepted by anyone except her.

"Nobody wanted to," Ross finally said. "When she died, my junior year of high school, I knew I couldn't stick around there. So I left as soon as I turned eighteen. Headed west, and met Aaron in culinary school and he actually, at least I *thought* he did, accepted me. It helped for a time."

"I don't think he *didn't* accept you," Shaw said, his voice full of love and empathy. Ross wished he could see his face. But the voice . . . it was almost enough.

He finished washing up and gave himself a final rinse.

"I think he was just an asshole. The *actual* villain," Shaw teased. "Unlike you."

Maybe it was crazy to think this way . . . but crazier things had happened. Maybe he wasn't the villain, after all.

Shaw had known who Ross was before this moment, he couldn't *not* know him, but in the last few minutes it felt like Ross had just opened up another little window into his soul and let him in.

Let him see the real him.

Shaw felt blessed. He felt privileged. And he felt loved.

"Hey," he said, after Ross had finished speaking.

"What is it?" The shower shut off and the door opened a crack. Shaw handed him a towel.

"I . . . I think I might have been wrong. I've actually been thinking I've been wrong for awhile now."

"About?"

Ross sounded concerned. Like Shaw was going to say, *after I heard all this about how much your grandmother loved you and all the recipes you make to honor her, I've decided I don't love you after all.*

Sometimes Ross could be a little stupid. But then Shaw was wild about him anyway, so what did that say about him?

"About the bar. I think Jackson might have been right about the bar," Shaw said with a heavy sigh. "There was the other night, and I've been thinking about it, but well, nothing makes me cringe more than admitting that I was totally, completely wrong."

"Well, might make you cringe more when you admit it to your brother," Ross said knowingly, emerging out of the shower, the towel wrapped around his waist.

"Yeah," Shaw said regretfully. "Yeah. But he's right. And I should tell him that."

"So why the change of heart?"

"It was the other night, actually, and you talking just now," Shaw admitted. "We're busier than we've ever been. You saw us the other night, and frankly it feels more like that most nights than not. Weekends are crazy. Don't even get me started with when there's a game at the Coliseum. I know you guys are packed before, but man, we're packed *after*."

Ross nodded.

"I've always been crazy busy on game days. Too busy to stop by but I've heard stories."

"From Tony?" Shaw asked, laughing. "He's seriously low-key jealous, I think. Probably wishes he could lure more kids away from the Funky Cup and over to the lot. But you guys don't serve booze. And we do."

"Yeah," Ross said, walking out into the living room, Shaw trailing after him.

"Gotta love him," Shaw said.

"Here's the thing," Ross said, "you're filling a niche. And you're doing it really fucking well."

Shaw watched as Ross grabbed some clothes and then dropped his towel, Shaw's heartbeat accelerating at just the look of him, fresh and clean and *naked*.

Shaw jerked his attention back to their conversation because sex was important but so was this.

"Exactly," Shaw said. "Maybe we should be filling it more. Is it selfish of me to stay where I'm at, when I could help create more safe havens? And you talking just now, you have so much passion for what you're doing, and so do I, but I'm not really utilizing it, am I?"

Ross pulled his t-shirt on and gave Shaw one of those intense stares.

"Do you think you are?"

Shaw sighed. "I'm not. You know I'm not. I know I'm not. Jackson knows I'm not. It's annoying."

"Well, you should talk to him," Ross said.

Unspoken, Shaw heard, *he's your brother, he's not allowed to give you* too *much shit.*

And Jackson wouldn't. He was a good guy, all the way down, though he would, undeniably, give him *some* shit. After all, he was his brother, and if Shaw had been in his spot, he absolutely would.

"I think I will."

"This morning," Ross said, with a hint of a smile. "Before you chicken out."

"What?" Shaw squawked. "Chicken out?"

Ross nodded his head firmly. Then reached out and tugged Shaw closer to him.

This, Shaw realized, was never going to get old.

Not the talking.

Not the sharing the things they didn't tell other people.

Not the touching.

Ross kissed him lightly on the lips.

Definitely not the kissing, either.

"I just want you to be happy. And satisfied. I'm realizing how important that is," Ross said seriously.

"How did you become such a font of wisdom?" Shaw wondered.

"Ren Moretti, believe it or not," Ross said, sounding like he didn't quite understand it either.

"Huh, well, I guess stranger things have happened." Shaw grinned. "Like you falling head over heels for the local bartender."

Ross' face broke out into a huge grin. "Guess so. Now, go get 'em, tiger."

"I'm sorry," Jackson said, glancing up from his laptop. "I'm not sure I heard you properly the first time." There was a glimmer of a smile on his face, but Shaw just shot him an annoyed look.

"You heard," he said. "I told you that you might've been right about the bar."

Jackson set his elbows on the desk and leaned forward. "Glad you finally got on board, baby brother. Do I have Ross to thank for your revelation?"

"No," Shaw said. *But actually yes, he's changed everything.*

"I don't know," Jackson pointed out in a soft drawl, "love changes a lot of things. Even things you wouldn't think. When Alexis and I fell in love . . ."

"Yes, yes, I know," Shaw said, teasing him. "You became miraculously, wondrously happy, you stopped being a workaholic, you found peace and acceptance, *blah, blah, blah*."

Jackson glared at him. "You're obnoxious, you know?"

"But I did just tell you that you were right."

"You did." Jackson leaned back in his desk chair. "I told you I'd find some time for us to go look at the space, but I think we should go take a look today. You should get a feel for it before you decide for sure."

"I should?"

"Well, you're going to be owning it, aren't you?"

"You think I should take the new bar?" It felt like a risk, scary and terrifying, a bit like hanging off a cliff.

But it was also a good kind of thrill. The endless possibilities of a blank canvas he could paint however he wanted.

He thought of all the things he wanted to do: host trivia nights, and a bunch of clubs, maybe even do an occasional drag revue. Live music. Poetry readings.

He'd always wanted to not just have a *bar*, but a community gathering place.

"Yeah," Jackson said, a smile emerging on his face. Like he could see all the possibilities emerging in Shaw's mind. "Yeah, I really think you should."

"Okay, then, can you get us in today?" Now that he'd made the decision, he felt exhilarated. Frightened. But also like the world had just opened up in front of him.

"Let me make a quick call," Jackson said, "but I'm thinking it's good. They know we're this close to signing."

"Oh?" Shaw raised an eyebrow. "And how did they know about that?"

Jackson looked a tiny bit ashamed. "Well, I might've given them that idea." He held up his hands in mock surrender. "I knew you'd change your mind and get on the same page. Just didn't know how long it would take."

He pulled his phone out of his pocket and dialed a number.

Shaw pulled his out too and shot Ross a text. **Going to look at the new bar today. Thanks for listening**. He hesitated. This was all still new, but it felt solid. Unshakeable. All at the same time. So he added, **I love you**.

Ross' answer came back almost immediately. **You're welcome**, the text said, **and I love you too.**

"Good news," Jackson said as he hung up. "They're going to meet us over there in thirty. Want to grab breakfast on the way?"

"Yeah, we can do that," Shaw said with a nod.

They stopped by a McDonald's drive-through on the way there, grabbing some more coffee and a few breakfast sandwiches, chowing down in Jackson's car in the parking lot of the restaurant.

"I'd ask if you've told Ross about your change of heart," Jackson said, "but since I think we can lay most of the credit at his door, I won't."

"He knows, but really, it's not about him. It's about me." Shaw hesitated, taking a bite of his sandwich and chewing. "It's about us."

"Me and you?" Jackson seemed surprised.

"Yeah," Shaw nodded.

"Huh." Jackson looked over at him.

"You've wanted me to have something of my own, I know you have, but you've also tried to protect me. I'm your little brother. I get why. And for awhile, I let you, because it was easy and because I enjoyed the work. But I can do more than just tend bar."

"Of course you can. Whose ass do I have to kick for making you think that's all you could do?" Jackson sounded amused and also kind of annoyed.

"Mine?" Shaw said sheepishly.

"Ah, well, you're wrong." Jackson grinned. "Hey, getting to say that twice in one day? Not too shabby."

Shaw punched him in the arm. Jackson laughed.

They finished their sandwiches and then drove over to the space that Jackson had described to him so many times.

It was a great neighborhood, a nice mix of residential and shopping, with a great small-business feel. Lots of shops had signs out, people were milling on sidewalks, walking their dogs, and grabbing coffee from the shop down the street.

Shaw looked up and down the block. A cafe— "They only serve breakfast and lunch," Jackson pointed out under his breath—looked busy, but there weren't any bars.

"There's also a wine shop with a tasting room a few streets away," Jackson said, "but what this place really needs is a great neighborhood bar."

Shaw found that he didn't disagree.

He also loved the exposed brick edifice, already imagining the things he could do.

"No back patio," Shaw pointed out.

"There's a catch there," Jackson said. "Wait til Rob gets here, and then I'll show you."

Rob arrived five minutes later, smiling and shaking both of their hands.

Normally, developers put Shaw on edge, but Rob had a genuine look and feel to him and he shook hands firmly, meeting both of the brothers' gazes directly.

Would he get his money and eke out everything he could from the deal? Oh, it was likely, but Shaw didn't think the guy would cheat them.

"Let's take a look inside," Rob said. He led them to the front door, and opened it using the code on the lock.

It was a big wide-open space, with huge towering ceilings, and a cool twisting metal staircase in the middle of it, leading to a big loft that took up about a third of the room.

Shaw was already thinking of where he'd put the bar. The stage. The tables. How he'd wall a bit of that left side off, to make an office. There was a rudimentary kitchen but it would be easy enough to expand it.

"That's the catch," Jackson said, pointing to that staircase, and Shaw realized then that he'd been so busy envisioning what he'd do to the ground floor that he hadn't really thought about *up*.

"Yeah, let's head upstairs," Rob said. They followed him up the stairs, which were, Shaw had to admit, pretty freaking cool. And then he realized they were even cooler than he realized, because they kept going up, through the loft, to a set of double doors that opened up onto the rooftop terrace.

"This," Jackson said with a shit-eating grin, "is your catch."

"Not a patio," Shaw said, rotating around, already seeing plants lining the brick walls and firepits scattered through the space, and lights, crisscrossing the open air, "but a terrace. A rooftop bar."

"Yep," Jackson said. "I saw it too, immediately."

Shaw could see it too, all in his mind's eye, and he felt himself getting more excited by the moment.

This could be amazing.

This could be his place.

Change, he realized, wasn't always easy, but sometimes it surprised you with all the new possibilities.

This time Shaw was going to grab on to them with both hands and hold on.

Just the way he'd done with Ross.

"I think," he said, turning to where his brother and Rob were chatting, "it's time to talk specifics. This is the perfect spot for the Fickle Cup."

Rob smiled, but Shaw barely saw it. He only saw his brother's proud expression.

"It really is," Jackson said, moving over and pulling him into a quick hug. "The Fickle Cup it is."

CHAPTER SIXTEEN

Waffle Day dawned bright and hot, sunshine already soaking everything as Ross and Shaw walked towards the food truck lot.

"You really didn't have to come," Ross said, for the fifth time in the last week.

Shaw waved around him. "You feel how hot it's gonna be today? You're going to sell an extra twenty percent just because of the heat. And I had the day off."

Ross knew that Shaw had actually switched his day off so he could help Ross and Harmony out on the big Waffle Day.

But no matter how much Ross argued that they'd be fine, Shaw had stuck to his initial prediction, which was that they were going to be slammed.

"Maybe." Ross didn't know how much he was going to sell, hot weather or not. Tony *had* gone all out for the event, doing a huge amount of promotion and even a few interviews, and they'd all been posting on social media this week. Even Jackson had included a mention of it in the bar's Stories on Instagram.

"I'm glad I convinced you to make a couple of extra pans of ice cream," Shaw said. He and Harmony had been putting their heads together on supply and demand equations all week, trying to make sure that the truck would be fully stocked for the big day.

Ross might quibble, and he might complain about it, but deep down, he was relieved that they'd taken over the problem and figured out what they thought was a reasonable solution.

"You and Harmony probably saved my ass," Ross agreed begrudgingly. "And Jackson, when he agreed to let us use the bar's freezers for the extra ice cream."

"You're welcome." Shaw grinned at him, and Ross didn't think that would ever get old. He'd see that smile in his dreams years and years from now.

He was hoping it wouldn't only be in his dreams, because he already didn't know what he'd do without him.

"Hopefully that raise I gave Harmony keeps her around after today," Ross said. Harmony had also become rather indispensable, and though he still struggled with trusting her—or trusting *anyone*—he was trying to take a step back whenever he felt overcome by the fear that she'd eventually betray him, too.

Everyone isn't Aaron, Shaw had said one night, when they'd been sitting together, hip to hip, on the couch. Ross had taken to repeating it to himself like a mantra, whenever he felt those feelings begin to overtake the rational, reasonable part of him. The part that knew he needed Harmony, and that knew she was really freaking great at things that he'd never be more than passable at.

"Who're you kidding? She's invested at this point," Shaw said as they turned into the lot. It was both earlier than he usually arrived, and definitely busier.

He saw Rachel and Tate setting out a sandwich board sign, proclaiming their special dish for the day.

As they walked by, he saw that they'd settled for a waffled macaroni and cheese with an Asian twist, topped with short ribs, a cilantro lime slaw, and a sweet chili drizzle.

It sounded incredible, and Ross knew that Shaw loved him, so naturally believed he was going to win the prize, but he wasn't so sure.

He was a really good chef. But the other guys that worked here were hardly slouches either.

They hadn't taken Tony's assignment and lain back and put in the barest amount of effort so that Ross could automatically win.

They'd worked hard, too.

Ross had to admit that he respected that—respected *them*—more than he'd thought he would.

"You think Tate and Gabe are gonna cancel each other out?" Harmony asked as soon as they walked into the truck.

"You two are ridiculous," Ross muttered. Shaw and Harmony had been watching and gathering info for the last week, as the other food truck owners had finalized their dishes. Discussing the merits and drawbacks of the various dishes.

"What did Gabe end up with again?"

"He and Ren were testing that waffle cannoli, trying to divide from our dessert stronghold," Harmony said confidently, "but I'm not sure it worked out, because they're back to the waffled garlic mozzarella with the spicy marinara dipping sauce."

"Huh," Shaw said. He turned to Ross, who was tying on his apron. "What do you think?"

"I think we should be worrying a lot less about everyone else, and more about our own shit," Ross said firmly. "Harmony, you got the first batch of ice cream from the bar?"

She nodded, patting the freezer next to her. "It's stowed away. Jackson said to just let him know when we need more, and he'll bring over the next batch."

"Good. And the batter?"

"I'm melting the chocolate next," she said.

"Okay, I'm going to get the pecans ready." Ross took a deep breath. "And we've got some other stuff to prep. Because I'm hoping we don't just sell brownie sundaes today."

"You won't," Shaw said confidently, grabbing his own apron. "You got chicken prepped? And those deep-fried tomatoes?"

"No, but you're going to start that now," Ross said. "Harmony, if you can deal with the brownie batter, I'll do the pecans, and Shaw can do the other prep work. He's capable."

Shaw batted his eyelashes in a purposefully exaggerated movement. "Aw, you talk so sweet to me," he teased. "I'm capable!"

Harmony laughed. "That's better than he said to me for a few days. But . . ." She shot Ross a quick approving look. "But I guess

I wouldn't have gotten a raise if he didn't think I was capable either."

"You're welcome," Ross said shortly. He hadn't wanted to talk about it—wasn't sure that he even could, because talking about how much he appreciated Harmony bailing out his ass, over and over again, made him uncomfortable. But the money? He could do that. He'd been hoping that she'd understand what he couldn't quite bring himself to say.

"Thanks, boss," Harmony said, patting him on the back as she passed him. "I know, you'd be lost without me."

"I would," Ross said stiffly. "I'm letting you make the brownie batter, aren't I?"

Harmony just smiled at him knowingly. She understood, then, and Ross let out the breath he hadn't realized he was holding.

Appreciation was not his strong suit. Especially *verbal* appreciation. But nobody could get by forever on just grunts of approval and barked orders. Even Harmony, who was delightfully no-nonsense and logical.

And truthfully, he *would* be lost without her.

She, just like Shaw, had come into his life, just when he'd been teetering on destruction and failure, and they'd given him not just the boost he'd needed to trust—and to love—again, but they'd made him laugh, and they'd supported him without once making him feel like he was incapable of handling things on his own.

They'd assisted, without ever taking over, being there when he needed them to be, and he was everlastingly grateful.

Whatever happened today, he'd gotten what he needed. What he hadn't even realized he wanted.

He knew both Shaw and Harmony wanted him to win, because he'd earned it and because he hadn't taken the easy way out—everyone was still incredulous that he wasn't serving chicken and waffles, though he had every intention of putting that on the menu post-Waffle Day. That had been the dish that Shaw named, eventually, calling it the Loving Brunch.

But to Ross, he already felt like a winner.

He had a great job. He'd shed the ugly weight in his life. He'd found a wonderful employee—and partner, honestly. And he was in a relationship and in love for the first time in his life and he hadn't ever been happier.

A kind of happy that he'd been so sure wouldn't ever be something he could *have*. With Shaw, love wasn't effortless, but he had no issue making the effort, because he was the best thing that had ever happened to him.

Ross had just finished pulling rack after rack of toasted, caramel-crusted pecans out of the oven for topping when Tony stuck his head in the open back door.

"Hey, guys," he said, then turned to Ross. "You all set? I've got your sign here, if you want to set it out."

"Yeah, you can set it out," Ross said. He was busy poking at the nuts, testing them. He'd added a touch—the very barest touch—of cayenne to the mix, and he thought it added this mysterious bite of spice at the end of every bite.

"You don't want to see it?"

Ross shot Tony a look. Okay, they were never going to be friends, maybe, but he could respect the guy, even if he was kinda a pain in the ass. "Is me looking at it going to change anything?"

"No." Tony grinned. "But I just thought you'd want to see the winning sign?"

Ross rolled his eyes. "Okay, fine." He set the pan of nuts down. "Just because these are actually done."

"You're a perfectionist," Tony said with a shake of his head.

"Yeah, I am," Ross said. And it occurred to him that maybe he *should* clear the air about that stupid onion dip recipe.

Maybe he really should've done it ages ago.

Shaw shot him a look right as he followed Tony out of the truck, and Ross was pretty sure he was thinking so, too.

It was probably the right thing to do. But it was especially the right thing to do considering that Tony had arranged this whole contest to help him get back on his feet, literally tailoring it to his strengths.

It wasn't Tony's fault he was stubborn and difficult, and he wouldn't just *take* it.

"The sign looks good," Ross said, taking it in from all the angles. The pictures of the sundae looked good. The hashtag was done in a bright orange font, clear and easy to read.

"I'm glad," Tony said, rubbing his hands together. "I think this is going to be a really successful event. I'm getting great feedback already from people. No matter what happens, it should be a really profitable day for all of us."

Ross sighed. "You know, I'm doing better," he said, even though he didn't want to. He wanted to say what he *should've* said to Tony ages ago and then leave and get back to work.

But Tony always insisted on making everything harder than it needed to be.

"I'm glad," Tony said, giving him a slap on the back. "We're all glad. You make us all want to work harder."

"About that . . ." Ross hesitated. Why was this so freaking difficult? Probably because he should've done it when he first joined the lot. He should've done it two years ago, when Tony had complained to everyone who'd been willing—and even a few who hadn't been willing—to listen, that Aaron and Ross had stolen his onion dip recipe.

But it had only been Aaron.

Ross squirmed in place. Hating how hard this was.

"About what?"

"I appreciate this a lot," Ross said. The words felt foreign and tricky on his tongue. "I . . . I know we haven't always gotten along. And that's my fault, because I should have told you before, told you years ago, that I didn't know Aaron had taken that recipe from you."

"You didn't know?" Tony sounded incredulous.

"I didn't," Ross confirmed. "And . . ." This was going to be cringeworthy, no matter how he put it. "I changed that recipe. A lot. I do that, you know. Always testing, trying to make the best version of everything."

Tony goggled at him. "You're telling me that you didn't *actually* copy my recipe?"

"It . . ." Ross hesitated. "It started as your recipe, yes."

"The version I tried?"

"Pretty different, in the end," Ross acknowledged.

For a long moment, Tony just stared at him.

Tony had an ego, like any other chef did. That had been a hard and fast realization when Ross had started working in the restaurant industry at eighteen; everyone had a fucking ego, and you had to walk on eggshells around them if they were above you.

And at the beginning, everyone had been above him.

Despite his *aw shucks* manner, Tony wasn't any different. He definitely had his share of pride.

And Ross had just pricked it with a pin.

In a particularly sensitive spot.

"Well, shit," Tony said, suddenly laughing. "I'm going to have to apologize to *you*, aren't I?"

"Are you?" There were moments when Ross didn't think he'd ever get used to people. Sometimes they surprised the hell out of him.

The silver lining was that sometimes the surprise was a good one. Like Harmony. Like Shaw. Like . . . to his own shock, *Tony fucking Blake.*

"I probably should." Tony leaned against the side of the truck. "I've given you shit for that forever."

"Yeah, well, Aaron *did* steal it. That was crappy of him, though in retrospect, not the crappiest thing he's done." *Understatement of the century.*

Tony patted him on the back again. Tony touched everyone, but he didn't usually touch Ross. So Ross decided this meant something. Like maybe all was forgiven, and they could finally move past it. "Listen, the worst thing he did was to you," Tony said, "so if anyone has a reason to be pissed, it's you."

"I don't know, Ash has a pretty good reason," Ross observed.

Tony laughed. "But he got a brand-new truck and a boyfriend out of the deal. So, I think he came out ahead, in the end."

"I did, too," Ross said before he could think better of it. "Not a new truck but . . ."

Tony raised an eyebrow. "A boyfriend, huh?"

"Don't spread it around," Ross said. Even though he knew by noon, it would have spread like wildfire. But Shaw would like it, and he'd discovered that he'd do just about anything Shaw liked.

That was love.

It changed everything.

Often, in the very best of ways.

Tony nodded. "I'm happy for you two. You're cute together."

Ross raised an eyebrow.

"Okay," Tony amended, "you're not *cute*, you're . . . I don't know, man, I just cook food people like to eat. You're cute, end of story. You're gonna have to be okay with that."

Ross thought about it for a second, and decided that *cute* was better than *heart eyes* or *twinkling,* which were the terms Ren had used.

"I think I can live with that," Ross said.

"Good." Tony, to his complete shock, actually pulled him into a quick hug. "Now, go kick all our asses, okay?"

Ross was so surprised that instead of arguing, he just nodded his agreement.

It was hard work.

Ross had known it would be, and he was hardly afraid of it by now, because he'd worked various kinds of hard his entire life.

But somehow the endless line, the constant orders, the itchy panicked feeling at the back of his neck that they'd fall behind and not catch up? It was better because Shaw was next to him, working just as hard as he was.

Harmony and Shaw were taking turns at the front, grabbing orders, but Ross had spent all day, now edging into dusk, working hard at the flat-top grill, dunking baskets of breaded chicken and discs of heirloom tomatoes into the fryer, and endlessly making one brownie after another on Tony's stupid, cheap, horrible little waffle maker.

One thing was for sure, he could not wait to buy something a little more commercial grade. Because this dish was probably going to need to stay on the menu, if the number of rave reviews that Shaw and Harmony had passed on was accurate. Plus, he'd promised Shaw he would add the Loving Brunch, AKA chicken and waffles, to the menu, too.

No way he could keep up with this normally on this crappy little appliance.

He was going to get a bigger, better one.

Harmony called out another two brownie sundaes and a basket of fried heirloom tomatoes and Ross dropped another order into the fryer and then turned to the device that was giving him all kinds of headaches.

Scratch buying one, he decided.

He was going to buy *two*.

All with the profits from this sundae.

The one that was currently ruining his life.

He scooped out batter, stuck in the caramel filling, set the timer and went to pull the herb dipping sauce for the tomatoes, and construct two more salads that he hadn't had time to make before yet another order had come in.

But Shaw was already on the salads, building them a bit more painstakingly than Ross would have. But he wasn't going to complain. It was one less thing to do.

"This is crazy," Shaw muttered as he passed the salads up to Harmony. "Are they ever going to stop eating?"

The entire lot was packed.

Rach had come begging Harmony for some extra buttermilk. "I know you have it," she'd said. "I need it. We're slammed."

Harmony had deferred to Ross, who had been glad that his boyfriend and his best (only) employee had spent so much time deciding how much stock they needed that they actually might be able to give some away.

He'd worried a little at the time that they were spending too much on supplies, that they'd never make it back, but he could already tell, without ever having checked the point-of-sale app on his phone, that they were going to be massively in the black today.

Even counting the fact that he was already planning on giving Shaw *something*. Not money, because he wouldn't take it, but something meaningful as a way to thank him for being there for him.

Today, and for all those days before.

But he'd given up the buttermilk to Rach, and now he was glad he had, because he was probably going to need more red onions tonight, and he knew Tate had gotten a big shipment in since he also pickled onions for his short rib mac and cheese.

"I don't know if they will," Ross muttered. "I've never seen so many people here. Not on opening day, not on the anniversary celebrations, not even when the band everyone likes is playing."

"No way you don't win this," Shaw said with a sharp nod. "You've got it in the bag. Our line has *never* let up."

"But neither has anyone else's," Harmony said as she grabbed the fried tomatoes from Ross. He'd pulled out the first brownie waffle and was spooning more batter in. "Did you see the line at Alexis' truck? At Gabe's? And don't even get me started on Ash, who made a freaking chicken curry empanada *waffle* that's apparently to die for."

Shaw grabbed the paper plate with the waffle and opened the freezer, scooping out two big scoops of their pecan brittle ice cream. Topping the entire thing with a swirl of fresh caramel sauce and another sprinkling of the spiced sugared nuts that Ross had perfected.

"All I know," Shaw said, "is that I've never seen people eat so many brownies in my life."

"Amen to that," Harmony said, taking the finished plate from his hand. "And, Ross, two more fried tomatoes, a chicken dinner, and an order of deviled eggs."

Ross considered groaning.

But then considered all the extra energy that was going to take, and instead, got to work.

"I've got the deviled eggs and the rest of the dinner," Shaw said gamely, already heading to the cooler with the eggs.

"Thanks," Ross said gratefully. More than once, when he'd had a spare second to think today, he'd imagined what it would've been like if Shaw hadn't given up his day off to be here.

It wouldn't have been pretty.

At first he'd been worried they wouldn't mesh well together when they worked. But the truth was, they meshed well all the time.

Cuddling on the couch.

In bed.

Just talking.

And even, to his surprise, working.

It shouldn't have surprised him, he realized, because that was how this whole thing had started, wasn't it? With Shaw giving up his day off and helping.

Shaw had made an offhand suggestion that Ross should consult on the new bar's menu, which he was considering revamping and starting fresh for the Fickle Cup's grand opening, but he'd shied away from giving an answer one way or the other.

Now, it was clear. This might not be what they did best together, because everything else they did together was so goddamned spectacular, but now he knew that he couldn't say no.

And maybe, it would even be a mighty fine thank-you present, for all his hard work today.

By the time Ross scooped the very last of the ice cream out of the last hotel pan, he did not give a single shit who won the contest.

As far as he was concerned, they'd all won.

All the trucks were closing for the night. Everyone had been forced to put makeshift signs on their boards, apologizing for running out of their waffle special, and though some sales had continued, they were sluggish in comparison, and Harmony and Shaw had reported as each truck had closed their doors.

"As soon as we're out of ice cream," Ross had said, hating his own workaholic drive a little by this point, "we'll close."

It had taken half an hour longer, which was both a good and a bad thing.

Good, because they'd probably sold another couple hundred bucks of food.

Bad, because his back was freaking aching and his feet were killing him, and if he ever saw another waffle again, he might be tempted to commit murder.

Maybe good, because both Shaw and Harmony were convinced they'd won.

At this point?

Ross wasn't sure he cared.

He drizzled on the caramel sauce, gave this last hurrah sundae a hearty helping of pecans and then passed it to Harmony, who handed it with extra special fanfare to their last customer.

"Quick," Shaw said, "before Ross changes his mind, shut the window, turn the sign."

Harmony laughed. It was more of a hysterical giggle. Probably a result of acute exhaustion.

Ross leaned back against the counter.

He wanted to sit down more than he'd wanted anything in his life. For half a second, he nearly went and sat down on the floor. But after a crazy day of food preparation, the floor was . . . well, not a place he was going to willingly spend his time.

"Come on," Shaw said, wrapping an arm around his shoulders, "let's go sit down outside for awhile."

"But the cleaning . . ." Even his own words didn't carry a ring of confidence.

Yes, the truck *definitely* needed to be cleaned.

Extensively.

But fuck it, he could do it later.

Or even tomorrow morning.

It must have been *that* insane of a day because that was a thought he'd never, ever allowed himself before.

"I'll come in before work and help you do it tomorrow," Shaw said, coaxing him slowly but surely out the back door of the truck. "It's time to take a victory lap."

"I don't know that I won yet," Ross argued, as they stepped down the stairs.

The crowd, despite having eaten all day, was still present, most of them towards the front of the lot, grouping together by the stage, where one of Tony's favorite bands was playing.

"Here," Shaw said, steering Ross towards where all the other owners sat, looking just about as shell-shocked as he felt, "sit down. Relax. Try not to make any food for five minutes."

Ash laughed tiredly as Ross plopped down next to him. "He's funny," he said, "is that why you keep him around?"

"One of many reasons," Ross said, yawning.

Gabe's head was resting on the table. Like he'd run out of energy to hold it up. "I've never . . ." he mumbled . . . "*never* made so many meatballs in one day before."

"Do you *know* how many pans of mac and cheese we went through?" Tate demanded. He was resting his own head on his hand. Like he couldn't keep it up either. "And don't get me started on the short ribs. I made twice as much as I thought we'd need, and we ran out at seven."

"Ross here prepped better than y'all," Shaw said. "We *just* ran out of our waffle dish."

"Actually," Ross argued, "that was all you." He tilted his head towards his boyfriend. "Thank you for that, by the way."

Shaw grinned. "It was absolutely my pleasure."

"It's bad enough that Ross here is a shoo-in for the win, does he need a fan section, too?" Gabe grumbled.

"It's okay," Sean said, reaching out and squeezing one of Gabe's hands. "I'll be your fan section, babe."

"Ew," Ren said, from the other end of the table. "Do you have to, *right* now? You know, when we're all exhausted as fuck?"

"Yep," Sean said decisively, and Ren rolled his eyes.

Ross realized, a single thought filtering through his exhausted brain, that he recognized some of Ren's defensive mannerisms.

Because that's what they were.

A defense.

He was afraid, of what Ross didn't know, but he recognized it because he'd lived it. He'd pushed everyone away forever, and he'd been even worse post-Aaron and his betrayal, until the best person in the world, the most beautiful, inside and out, had held up his hand and said, *you've gotta stop this right now.*

Thank God he had.

Thank God for Shaw.

Ross, losing the rest of his fucks, actually tilted his head to rest it on Shaw's shoulder. "I love you," he murmured so only his boyfriend could hear. "I'm grateful for you. I'm blessed to have you."

Shaw's smile was warm and sweet and tender. Meant just for him. "I love you too."

"That consultation?" Ross said. "I'll do it."

"Oh, good," Shaw said, "I'll ask Jackson to . . ."

"For free. As my gift to you. For . . . well, for everything."

Shaw's eyes shined. "You're the best."

"I think . . . well, I think that's actually *you*," Ross said, and couldn't believe that he was saying it. Or he was meaning it.

So many things had changed.

For once, not for the worst.

"Hello all," Tony shouted happily as he walked over to the table. "You guys ready to find out who won the big contest?"

There was a collective groan around the table.

"Just let it go, Tony," Gabe said. "We all know who won."

"Maybe," Tony said with a glimmer in his eye, "or maybe not. But whoever won, the results were *very* close. Closer than you might think. Y'all gave the winner a run for his money."

Ross considered saying he'd already won, because he had Harmony and a more stable business in his truck than he'd had in forever, and because he'd met Shaw, who'd ended up being the perfect key to his particular lock.

But he didn't, because even though these guys were becoming friends, it was still hard for him to say those things.

To acknowledge that good—even great—things happened to him. That he *deserved* those things.

The band played a final chord and waved themselves off, taking a break.

"That's my cue," Tony said excitedly. Way more excitedly than anyone had a right to be after a day like today. "Get ready for the announcement!"

Ross watched as Tony walked up to the stage, grabbing a microphone from the stand.

"Hello, everyone!" he called out over the crowd, who cheered and applauded at seeing their mastermind in person. "I hope you guys had a great day today, and ate some delicious waffles!"

There was another wave of sound, and Ross was relieved that at least he was in the back, that mostly it just washed right over him.

Though, frankly, maybe he was too tired to even care at this point.

"Great, great," Tony said. "I want everyone to know that this contest was the first of many we'll be hosting here at Food Truck Warriors, so make sure to check our social media for upcoming events. But now, finally, to what everyone wants to know. Who won Waffle Day? Well, it's no big surprise, but maybe more astonishing than you'd expect, because instead of going the expected route and putting together a dish that would've inevitably been a home run, our winning chef did the opposite. Stretched his muscles and did *dessert*."

Ross flushed. He had won. Maybe, *hopefully*, fair and square. Shaw brushed a kiss across his scruffy cheek and gave him an extra hard squeeze.

"Knew you could do it," he said quietly, his voice full of loving confidence.

He had known. Before Ross did. Before Ross had even cared.

Tony was still talking. Not surprising. He loved the sound of his own voice.

"This same chef's been through some struggles in the last few months, but I'm happy to say he's the winner today, not only because of that, but because he's a standup guy and frankly, more talented than I feel entirely comfortable admitting. A huge round of applause please for our big Waffle Day winner, Ross Stanton from Basket."

The roar of the crowd did overwhelm him then.

Or maybe it was the fact that, like they were all on cue, the rest of the owners shed their exhaustion temporarily and stood too, applauding and cheering for him.

And Ross?

It suddenly occurred to him, as he sat there, and people he hadn't ever counted as friends but *were*, congratulated him, the man he loved at his side, that maybe Shaw was right after all.

He wasn't the villain in his own story.

He *was* the hero, after all.

To continue the Food Truck Warriors series with *Ride or Die*, Ren and Seth's story, click here.

INTERESTED IN READING MORE OF
BETH'S BOOKS?

CHECK OUT A FULL LIST OF TILES
BY SCANNING THE QR CODE
OR VISITING HER WEBSITE

WWW.BETHBOLDEN.COM/BOOKLIST

WANT TO FOLLOW BETH?

MAKE SURE YOU NEVER
MISS A RELEASE?

SCAN THE QR CODE BELOW
OR VISIT HER WEBSITE
FOR A SOCIAL MEDIA LIST,
NEWSLETTER SIGNUP,
AND SO MUCH MORE!

WWW.BETHBOLDEN.COM/ABOUT

www.ingramcontent.com/pod-product-compliance
Lightning Source LLC
Chambersburg PA
CBHW051506050726
47594CB00010B/3989